S0-EIJ-161

Miss Sedgewick
and the Spy

Miss Sedgewick and the Spy

Geraldine Burrows

64461 – Feb. 2001

Five Star
Unity, Maine

This book is a work of fiction. Names, characters, places and incidents are either products of the author's imagination or, if real, used fictitiously.

Five Star First Edition Romance Series.

Published in 2000 in conjunction with Spectrum Literary Agency.

The text of this edition is unabridged.

Set in 11 pt. Plantin by Elena Picard.

Printed in the United States on permanent paper.

Library of Congress Cataloging-in-Publication Data

Burrows, Geraldine.
    Miss Sedgewick and the spy / by Geraldine Burrows.
      p.cm.—(Five Star first edition romance series)
      ISBN 0-7862-2215-8 (hc : alk. paper)
      I. Title. II. Series.
    PS3552.U7642 M55 2000
     813'.54—dc21   00-046650

This one is for my little sisters-in-law,

Barbara Longo Lanigan
and
Joyce Longo Berlinski

Chapter One

Introducing Our Heroine, Miss Drusilla Sedgewick, Who Is About to Be Abducted by French Brigands

In the autumn of 1814, it seemed that all the Fashionable World was intent on traveling abroad now that England's great enemy, Napoleon Bonaparte, had been defeated and exiled to the island of Elba. The European continent, reopened to Britons after nearly two decades of war, beckoned alluringly to the travel-minded; and so, with July bringing an end to the London Season, August and September saw a steady stream of moneyed English tourists crossing the channel and setting out for the great capitals of Europe.

Among the English excursionists making their way toward Paris were the Misses Faith, Hope, and Charity Thornrose, three wealthy maiden ladies of estimable character, high principles, and reformist convictions. No light-minded desire to sightsee motivated their trip to Paris. They were on a mission—dispatched by no less a personage than that sainted reformer, William Wilberforce, founder of the British Society for the Abolition of the Slave Trade. Once the Thornrose ladies arrived in Paris, they were to join forces with that formidable woman of letters, Germaine de Staël, to campaign, crusade, agitate, pamphleteer, and generally hector the newly restored Bourbon monarchy into outlawing slavery in the French colonies.

Although the Thornrose ladies were well practiced at campaigning, crusading, agitating, pamphleteering, and hectoring in the English language, they were less certain of their ability to do so in French. They were, therefore, fortunate that their eminently sensible secretary, Miss Drusilla Sedgewick, in addition to writing in an elegant hand, also spoke perfect colloquial French.

Miss Sedgewick, a willowy young thing with chestnut hair and a fine pair of hazel eyes, was even now straining those fine eyes to translate for the ladies a French-language guidebook that extolled the rural beauties of the Picardy countryside through which they were passing. The fifth female of their company, Lady Christabel Toddington, had no patience for this, however. She was in mourning—for the loss of her corded wardrobe trunk, which had disappeared from the Calais docks as she and her traveling companions were disembarking.

"Are you quite sure," her ladyship inquired of Drusilla, peremptorily interrupting her translation of an elegiac passage about the beauty of the Picardy mustard fields, "are you quite sure, Dru, that you made that shipping-clerk fellow understand about my trunk?"

Drusilla sighed inwardly, wondering if she would ever be free of the fluttery toils of Lady Christabel Toddington. She had already endured an entire Season—a very long Season—as Christabel's protégé on the London Marriage Mart. The matchmaking attempt had not prospered; hence, her current employment as secretary to the Thornrose ladies, an occupation that suited her natural inclinations far better than did that of social butterfly. Even so, Christabel continued to take a proprietary interest in her, shamelessly throwing eligible young men at her head, as well as burdening her with secretarial tasks even though it was the Thornrose sisters who paid her salary.

"Well?" Christabel tapped an expensively shod foot on the floor of the coach. "Did you make the fellow understand that they must send a messenger when the trunk is discovered?"

"Yes. But are you sure, Christa, that you have not miscounted your trunks? You do have rather a lot of them."

This was certainly true, for clattering along behind the Thornrose traveling carriage was the Toddington baggage train, consisting of three coaches filled with Christabel's clothing, along with the several downtrodden minions whose job it was to maintain the wardrobe of Lord Toddington's young and beautiful wife.

"And," Drusilla further reminded her ladyship, "you've always owned you have no head for figures."

"That may well be," retorted Christabel, "but I know my wardrobe down to the last stitch, and when I say I am missing a trunk—"

There was a sudden lurching of the traveling coach as it ground to an abrupt halt, tossing the Thornrose ladies into a heap and propelling Drusilla against Christabel's knees.

Regaining her seat, Drusilla pulled aside the window curtain and saw an ominous sight. A large tree had fallen across the country road on which they were traveling, and coming out of concealment from amongst the rural beauties of Picardy were a dozen rough-looking men attired in a manner that caused Drusilla to feel an increasing sense of danger.

The men closing about the carriage like a pack of wolves all wore shirts and breeches of tattered canvas, their shirts emblazoned front and back with a broad black arrow. Dru instantly recognized their garb as the type issued to French prisoners of war by their British captors.

Crowds of similarly clad men were to be seen disembarking every day at Calais as the French prisoners of war returned home by the thousands from the prison hulks and gaols of Edinburgh and Dartmoor. They were coming home bitter, defeated, and unpaid, and it appeared chillingly obvious to Dru that a gang of them had turned brigand and were now preparing to fall upon this unguarded cavalcade of English ladies and their luggage.

One of the men strode up to the carriage door—*her* door—and wrenched it open. He had shaggy, dun-colored hair, a lean, unshaven face, and eyes that shone with a green light, like the eyes of a wolf.

In comic-farce English he inquired, "Wheech one of you ees zee Ladeee Toddeengton?"

"Have you found my corded trunk, then?" chirped Christabel.

The wolf-like eyes quickly scanned the carriage interior, flickering from the serenely stupid Christabel to the stunned Thornrose ladies. Then those eyes fixed penetratingly on Drusilla. *"C'est la femme!"* he shouted to the other men. And in the next instant, Dru found herself seized by the arm and jerked from the carriage, Christabel's clear, carrying, oh, so upper crust voice calling after, "You there, fellow, what are doing with my secretary?"

Keeping an iron grip on Drusilla, the brigand whipped a pistol out of his tattered canvas shirt, rested the gun barrel on Dru's redingote-clad shoulder, and aimed the weapon directly into the carriage at Christa. "You! Serving maid who ees squealing. Quiet! Or I blow your head off!"

Being mistaken for a member of the serving classes on top of having her life threatened was altogether too much for Christabel, who subsided onto her seat in a decorative swoon.

Having successfully rendered Christabel *hors de combat*, the Frenchman shoved Dru into the midst of the brigandage gathered about the carriage. "This is the one!" he again

10

shouted to them in French. "This is the English milady we seek."

An answering shout of triumph went up from his men, a shout such as might have been heard during the Revolution when the mob dragged an *aristo* out of hiding.

As the granddaughter of Lord Sedgewick of Sedgewick Downs, Drusilla, though penniless, might reasonably qualify as an *aristo,* but it was patently obvious that her captors had gotten the wrong "milady," that the wealthy Christabel was their real quarry. But she, Drusilla Sedgewick, was not Judas enough to betray her hapless friend, who was also the mother of a young child, to these ruthless men. And so she said nothing when the brigand chief jerked her about to face him. She did her best to face him down as a flower of patriotic British womanhood ought to face down a French brigand: with firm chin, courageous mien, and good posture.

Her defiance seemed to amuse him. He swept her a mocking bow. "One hears zee Engleesh miladies are great walkers, *non?* Let us hope so, for your sake, milady. For now you walk."

And with his gun barrel pressed between her shoulder blades, he forced her off the road and into the tangled woodlands of deepest, darkest Picardy.

Chapter Two

In Which Drusilla
Is Determined to Be Clever

The trail was not hard going—at first—and Dru had never lacked for stamina when it came to long country rambles. She had the further good fortune to be wearing sensible walking shoes, since sensible walking shoes were all she could afford on a secretary's salary.

The shock of what had happened to her gradually ebbed as she trudged along an ever-narrowing track in the midst of the company of brigands. As the woodlands closed over her head in a canopy of dark branches, she felt the welling up within her breast of a strange sort of courage, a courage she had never known she possessed, having had no need of it before. But she had need of it now—that was certain. She must put her wits to work on her own behalf. She must keep her bearings as best she could, and she must learn all she could about her abductors.

It helped that her captors—except for their pistol-wielding leader—were all possessed of the garrulousness typical of the French. They conversed freely and volubly in front of her in the apparent belief that she hadn't the language, and she listened carefully to every word they spoke, to every name they called each other.

They were an oddly named lot, to be sure. There was not a Jean, an Antoine, or a Philippe among them. Instead, they had nicknames, some of them almost comical, like Sergeant Red Legs, Old Moustaches, or the Grumbler. But the one name among them that struck fear into her heart was the name of their leader. He was *le Loup de l'Empereur*—the Emperor's Wolf—who had just snatched the wrong English lamb, thanks to her.

And what, she wondered with a cold shudder, *would the Emperor's Wolf do to her if he ever discovered how she had deceived him?*

That the Emperor's Wolf was wary of pursuit was certain. He often ordered the band to stop while he surveyed their surroundings with a collapsible telescope or loped down a side trail to scout the terrain.

During these stops, Dru would sink to the ground as if exhausted and listen intently. The things she heard made her suspect that her captors were not ordinary brigands, although exactly what these kidnapping Frenchmen might be up to, she could not imagine. As for their leader, she learned that he had been dispatched by someone named Excelsior for the express purpose of carrying out this ambuscade. She learned also that in the late war the Emperor's Wolf had been an "escape agent," a man who volunteered to be captured by the British in order to engineer the escape of French soldiers from the British prisoner-of-war camps.

A brave and dangerous man, this Emperor's Wolf. The enemy of her country—and of her.

In an effort to stoke her courage, she told herself over and over again that surely her captors wouldn't harm her as long as they thought she was Christabel . . . and surely the kind and wealthy Thornrose ladies would ransom her . . . and certainly Christabel's husband, a high-ranking diplomatist, would insist that the French police launch an immediate search for her.

13

Had she been privileged, however, to see the dispatch that Lord Toddington had penned upon learning of her capture, she might have been considerably less sanguine.

From the Rt. Hon. Lord Toddington to the Foreign Office
Private & Secret
Item: I believe this abduction to be a Bonapartist plot aimed at myself, and I fear we can put no dependence on the French authorities in this matter. . . .

The trail turned difficult now, winding sharply upward over rocky terrain, and Dru soon realized why the brigands were not mounted. They expected pursuers, and this steep, uncertain trail was fit only for goats. If a chase ensued, it would have to be on foot, and that would make rescue all the more difficult. It was a dispiriting thought, and the next time they paused to rest, she sank to the ground with unfeigned fatigue, for the going was getting strenuous indeed.

This time, the brigands paused to eat. Apparently they had missed their midday meal while waiting for the Thornrose carriage, and now, with no sign of pursuit, they felt safe enough to take out packets of bread, cheese, and sausage and to pass around several bottles of wine.

Dru got the end of a bread loaf and a *cantine* of water, delivered to her silently by Old Moustaches. This was a heartening development, she surmised, since they would hardly feed her if they meant to kill her.

When it was time to move on, the Emperor's Wolf himself came to retrieve the *cantine*. He hunkered down beside her, and Dru saw, inside his tattered shirt, the gleam of a pistol against the bronze of his chest. She wondered if somehow she could contrive to snatch that pistol from him. . . .

He caught her look and, seeing what she would be about,

14

said softly, "You would shoot me, milady? Or do you merely admire my manly form?" Dru flushed and drew back as he went on, "I warn you, milady, my ribs bear the scar from a British bayonet, and I do not think the sight would charm."

"On the contrary"—she spoke each English word with precision, to make sure he understood—"the sight would charm me utterly, for my father was shot in the back by a French marksman on the retreat from Corunna in the late war in Spain."

Instantly his voice snapped back at her like a whip. "You are fool to say such things, milady! Perhaps you plot to escape, *non?* But you have no chance. The nearest village is too far even for such a great walker as yourself." He gestured through a gap in the trees, to where several thin columns of smoke rose against the distant sky. The buildings were not visible among the rolling hills, but the smoke was a helpful guide, letting Dru know in which direction the closest hamlet lay.

I thank you for that information, Monsieur Wolf, she told him silently even as he grasped her arm and dragged her roughly to her feet.

Soon—too soon for her flagging strength—the brigands resumed their formation around her, and she was forced to once more set her sensibly shod feet on the upward-winding trail. The going was very hard now, requiring much scrabbling up sharp inclines and inching around huge boulders that forced her to teeter on the edge of sheer hillside drops. Christabel, who was afraid of heights, would surely have expired at this point, assuming she hadn't already driven the brigands to strangle her out of sheer aggravation.

Drusilla was near to expiring herself, and with every exhausted step she felt the green eyes of the Emperor's Wolf on her back like a goad. Pride forced her to go on without complaint, however, and once or twice in the steepest spots, when the Emperor's Wolf offered her his assistance, she spurned it with her best English milady's icy look, for it would not do to take the helping hand of an enemy.

Evening shadows were crowding out the daylight by the time the trail ended in a high meadow. Dru's earlier belief that the path was fit only for goats proved perspicacious. The meadow was grazed down to a green carpet, and at the edge of it stood the goatherd's lodgment, a small stone-and-timber cot, unoccupied for the moment.

"Milady's mansion awaits," mocked the Emperor's Wolf as he swung open the heavy wooden door, which was fastened to the doorpost by leather hinges.

It was dark inside the cot, and the ceiling was low, as Dru discovered when she bumped her head on a roof timber. Her foot soon encountered a clump of straw and sacking piled on the dirt floor for bedding. Collapsing wearily upon the goatherd's pallet, she was not surprised to find that it smelled strongly of goat.

Though the cottage was cold, she would have no fire, of course. That was for her captors outside, and the aroma of roasting rabbit soon wafted tantalizingly into her prison. Never had she been so desirous of sampling authentic French cuisine, but all she got was another ration of bread and a re-filled *cantine*. There were no windows in her makeshift gaol, but she did not immediately feel the lack, since the crack between the door and doorpost as well as several large gaps between the roof timbers let in a more than sufficient amount of frigid night air.

Shivering in her redingote, she pulled the sacking around her, reflecting miserably on the amazing disaster that had turned her life upside down in the course of a single day. Last night, she had slept in a commodious chamber in the best inn in Calais. Tonight, she slept in a stone hut at the mercy of the Emperor's Wolf. Suddenly she felt very young and alone, and very afraid of what would happen to her on the morrow.

She thought of her father, killed with Sir John Moore at Corunna, and of her mother, dead these past six months of a wasting disease, her dying words, *Don't grieve, darling. I am going to join your dear papa in heaven.*

As the night deepened, Dru gazed up into the starry heavens that showed through her prison roof and hoped desperately that her parents were watching over her.

The brigands woke early and proceeded to make preparations for the expected onslaught of *gendarmes* who would be searching for Lady Christabel Toddington.

Watching her captors through the crack between door and doorpost, Dru saw the Emperor's Wolf take a knife from his belt and carve a map on the bare ground, marking certain strategic points where the men would keep watch for the rest of the day. As for himself, he would rendezvous with Excelsior to plan further strategy.

"But what of the English milady?" protested one of the brigands. "This plan will leave her unguarded until we return."

"Do not concern yourself, *mes amis*," said the Emperor's Wolf. "I will attend to the English milady most particularly before we go."

Dru felt her heart sink into her sensible shoes, but the hut had no hiding place, and now the Emperor's Wolf was at her door, coming in with coils of rope slithering meaningfully through his sinewy hands.

"So, my preetty Engleesh peagoose, for the trussing, you will please to sit," he ordered, flicking the rope in the direction of a crude chair, upon which she had so far declined to seat herself, as it had looked too rickety.

She sat now, for she could think of no way out of her predicament, not with a dozen men just beyond the door. The Emperor's Wolf was very close to her, looping the rope round her, not tightly and cruelly as she would have expected, but almost teasingly, as if the two of them played some secret game in which it would amuse him to let the pretty peagoose win. His shaggy hair fell across his forehead like a boy's cowlick, and even as he wound the rope around her wrists, she experienced a wayward desire to reach up to smooth the brown locks back from his lean face. She found herself hoping that he possessed a warm cloak, for the muscular exertions involved in tying her up seemed on the verge of reducing his tattered prison shirt to mere threads across his shoulders.

He looked up abruptly, pinioning her eyes with his own. A shiver ran down the length of her body, whilst at the same time a blush more burning than any she had ever felt before rose up in her face.

"How you are in a fury, milady," said her captor softly. "You would strike me down if you could."

Yes, agreed Dru as the rope went about her in a final twist, *but before I did, I would give anything to tell you that you have been outwitted, and that I have done it.* She suppressed the urge, however, for she knew it would be beyond foolish to say such a thing.

Her captor stood back to admire his handiwork and then smiled down into his prisoner's indignant gaze. "*Au revoir, mon ange.* Do not miss me too much." Then he was gone, and through the walls of the cot she heard the sounds of the brigands breaking camp as they prepared to be off about their brigandly business.

Silence soon fell about the goatherd's hut. Still Dru made herself sit and wait patiently. It would be so like the Emperor's Wolf to let her think she had a chance to escape and then to pounce on her the instant she stuck her nose out of her gaol. She made herself deliberate carefully, searching for some flaw in her plan. Finding none, she finally decided that it was now or never—now or never for Drusilla Sedgewick to become her own "escape agent."

She rocked forward until she was on her feet, albeit in a most inelegant posture, with a chair tied to her posterior like an old-fashioned bustle. By dint of several vigorous waggles, she bashed the chair against the stone wall, smashing the crude piece of furniture back to the kindling from which it had been constructed. The rope that bound her slackened, and she was free.

Once she was out of her prison and into the bright fall sunshine, she surveyed the brigands' campsite, hoping that they had left some provender behind. They had not, but they had left their map, incised into the earth before their campfire. She spared a few moments to study it, and though she did not comprehend all the landmarks, it seemed to her that no men would be stationed on the goat path itself, although several had been posted along the main road to watch for mounted patrols. She would watch for those patrols as well, once she got down the path.

She soon discovered the happy fact that it is much easier to go down a goat path than up one. Her descent was not without adventure, however, in the form of several slips and near falls. She was also in constant fear that she might encounter a returning brigand or, worse yet, the Emperor's Wolf and his master, Excelsior. Her luck held, though, and she came out of the Picardy woods exactly where she had been marched into them the day before.

Further luck was hers, for there she saw a crew of laborers

working to clear away the tree that blocked the road—a tree that she now realized had been deliberately chopped down and dragged across the thoroughfare to stop the Thornrose carriage. A squad of uniformed *gendarmes* was also upon the road, waiting for the laborers to finish. Waiting also was a *diligence,* one of those wonderfully roomy, albeit slow-moving, public stagecoaches that crisscrossed the French countryside.

There was not a brigand in sight as far as she could tell. She was saved.

She approached the *gendarmes* and presented herself. Her French was so good that the constables did not at first believe her to be the young English lady who had been abducted by brigands. Dru assured them that she was indeed the very same, then further informed them where they would find a map showing the current location of said brigands. This intelligence was of such startling and timely usefulness that it served only to engender further doubts amongst the police as to her identity.

After much voluble discussion amongst themselves, they finally dispatched a man to investigate. By the time this course of action was decided upon, Drusilla had formed no high opinion of the local constabulary. She knew assuredly that this troop of bumbling French Dogberrys would never catch a man like the Emperor's Wolf.

In the meantime, a ticket was procured for her on the *diligence,* which was bound for Amiens. Upon her arrival she was taken in at the residence of the British consul and shown every kindness while arrangements were made for her transport to Paris.

Once again her world was turned right side up, and that night she fell asleep upon feathery pillows, a cozy fire on her bedroom hearth. Her last thoughts as drowsiness overtook her were of the Emperor's Wolf, of the impotent rage on his handsome face when he returned to the hut to find her gone, of the fury in his green eyes when he discovered how she, Drusilla Sedgewick, in her cleverness had outwitted him.

She fell asleep smiling.

Chapter Three

The Scorpions of Paris

Restoration Paris: the city of the ascendant Bourbons and the fallen Emperor—fallen but not forgotten. The Bourbons may have regained the throne in the corpulent person of Louis XVIII, but Napoleon Bonaparte still retained a magnetic hold on the imagination of the French people, even as the Quadruple Alliance that had defeated him prepared to convene in Vienna for the purpose of carving up his empire.

Paris seethed with intrigue in the fall of 1814. The member countries of the Quadruple Alliance—Austria, Russia, England, and Prussia—trusted each other not at all and schemed constantly to insinuate confidential agents into each other's embassies. There ensued, as a consequence, much melting and forging of wax seals on secret dispatches, much sifting through office scrap baskets, much eavesdropping and transom-lurking. "Four scorpions trapped in a bottle" was how one Parisian wit described the internecine intrigues of the Allies.

In one matter, however, the Allies were united, and that was in the belief that King Louis and the Bourbons were corrupt, inept, not to be trusted, and therefore to be spied upon as well. The French king and his brother and heir, the Comte d'Artois, had meanwhile set up rival secret police forces, for the royal Bourbon siblings trusted neither the Quadruple Alliance, nor the French people, nor each other.

22

The French body politic was in turmoil as hordes of aristocratic *émigrés* returned from penurious exile, determined to reclaim their lands, their fortunes, their feudal prerogatives, and their social ascendancy. The thoroughly revolutionized French populace was not inclined to oblige them, however, and secret anti-royalist societies were sprouting like truffles in the dark back rooms of the cafés and coffeehouses.

All up and down the social ladder the conflict raged.

In the soldiers' taverns, the veterans of Napoleon's wars brawled with King Louis's newly commissioned musketeers.

In the gilded salons, the poor but haughty *émigrée* ladies snubbed the ladies of the Napoleonic nobility, who retaliated by flaunting their silks and their jewels. The *émigrée* ladies were equally determined that the *parvenu* countesses and duchesses would not flaunt their wealth with impunity. There was, as a consequence, much dealing out of stinging slights and severe setdowns, much casting of slurs and bandying about of barbed tittle-tattle, and much giving of cuts, from the direct to the sublime.

Scorpions, indeed, in the drawing rooms of Paris in 1814.

Drusilla knew nothing of this—yet—as she looked out of her carriage to behold Paris in all its autumnal glory, the wide avenues lined with tall chestnut trees, their turning leaves glowing in bursts of color against the white marble of the great buildings. Though she no longer had the benefit of her guidebook, Dru was conversant enough with Parisian landmarks to recognize the magnificent expanse of the Place de la Concorde. Crossing that famous square where the guillotine had done its bloody work on king and commoner alike, her carriage proceeded onto the rue St. Florentin, one of the city's most fashionable addresses.

Here were to be found the *hôtels privés* of the wealthy, each mansion rising four or five stories high, backed by exquisite formal gardens and fronted by walled courtyards with wrought-iron entry gates manned by liveried servingmen. Amongst these grand mansions was situated the Hôtel Toddington, identifiable as a diplomatic residence by the presence of a pair of red-uniformed guardsmen who snapped smartly to attention as Dru's carriage rolled through the gates.

She was greeted by an English butler named Grimthwaite, who looked exactly as one would expect an English butler named Grimthwaite to look. He bowed her though the front door and led her to the office chambers of her host, Lord Charles Toddington, a distinguished, frank-looking man verging on his middle years.

But Lord Toddington's frank-looking features hid many a secret, as Drusilla was soon to learn.

Also awaiting her arrival was another titled diplomat, Lord Fitzroy Somerset, the up-and-coming young secretary to the British Ambassador to France, His Grace the Duke of Wellington.

His Grace, it turned out, was acquainted with one of her Sedgewick uncles (this did not surprise Dru, as she had nine of them), and Lord Somerset had been dispatched to convey Wellington's ducal solicitations regarding the distressing incident that had befallen her. It soon became obvious, however, that what Lords Somerset and Toddington were really after was a detailed account of said distressing incident. She willingly told all—except for her strange fire-and-ice reaction to her captor, the Emperor's Wolf. That she kept to herself.

The significant looks her two auditors exchanged during her narrative convinced her that deep doings were afoot among the diplomats. But then Christabel came knocking, thereby ending any chance for a discussion of deep doings. Dressed in a new gown of beryl green, Christabel stood on the threshold, poised for compliments, which she duly received from her adoring husband. In the presence of his beautiful young wife, Lord Toddington's distinguished features were wont to take on a slightly dazed expression, as if he were still unable to comprehend how he had managed to acquire anyone as dazzling as Christabel. In point of fact, it was Christabel who had acquired him, having set her cap for him in her first Season, since a wealthy, adoring husband whose diplomatic career required constant socializing suited her taste exactly.

At the moment, however, her ladyship was in a mood to chide her life's companion. "Charles! You've monopolized Drusilla long enough. Here I am, fairly eaten up with curiosity to hear of her adventures, and what do I find but the pair of you being secret with her so you may hear all the news first."

"Madam," protested Fitzroy Somerset with a laugh, "I promise you, we've done so merely in the line of duty."

"Then you are forgiven," said Christabel with an arch smile, "but only if you tell me that you and Lady Fitzroy are to accompany His Grace to my *soirée* next week." Christabel's close brush with abduction had not prevented her from launching into party-making plans the minute her dainty feet hit the parquet floor of her Paris establishment.

"We will be delighted to come," Lord Fitzroy assured her. "Emily is positively agog to see how the famous Belle Toddington will entertain in Paris."

"Belle" was the tonnish sobriquet that London Society had hung on Christabel, and from the martial light that came into her china blue eyes, it was obvious that she intended to score similarly with the Paris *beau monde*. "You may tell Emily

25

that I believe the evening will come off well. I'm determined to show the Parisians that we British are not the nation of dowdies they think us," she declared, cavalierly misquoting the exiled Emperor.

"Christabel intends to plant the Union Jack in all the best salons," Lord Toddington observed with an indulgent smile.

"And so I will," averred Christabel. "But in the meantime, I must make away with Drusilla. The poor Thornrose ladies are prostrate with worry."

Not so Christabel. Her corded trunk had been found, His Grace the Ambassador was to attend her *soirée,* and now her secretary had been reclaimed from the motley brigands. She was in high gig as she led Dru into her private sitting room, where the Thornrose ladies hastened to enfold her in lavender-scented embraces. The three sisters were far more somber in mood than Christabel, for they knew full well what motley brigands might be expected to do to young ladies who fell into their clutches.

"We're been so hoping that you weren't . . . harmed," ventured Miss Faith.

"We feared that you might have been . . . compromised," elaborated Miss Hope.

"That your innocence had been stolen," concluded Miss Charity.

Before Drusilla could open her mouth to deny it, Christabel dismissed the idea as entirely silly. "I've told you time and again, ladies, that Dru isn't the type of woman that men desire to ravish."

Christabel made this pronouncement with the airy confidence of one who knew that she inspired men with thoughts of ravishment wherever she went. "Of course," she continued in a more thoughtful vein, "people being what they are, ev-

26

eryone will secretly believe poor Dru has been ravished anyway, no matter what we say. So you had better wear your white muslin to my *soirée,* Dru, and do your best to look as pure as snow.''

Christabel's advice on wardrobe was not to be ignored, for whatever her mental failings in other areas of endeavor, there was no denying that she possessed clothes sense in the same way a professional gamester possessed card sense. She knew when to dress flamboyantly and when to underdress and thus rout her fashion rivals by sheer classic simplicity. She also had a superb sense of setting and occasion when it came to planning her entertainments. After sounding the social waters, Christabel had decided that tonight's occasion should be a very royalist one indeed. . . .

Bronze *flambeaux* in the shape of *fleurs-de-lis* were lit in the courtyard, and the entry hall had been carpeted in royal blue for the occasion. White bunting was affixed to the walls in such a way as to resemble a series of giant Orleanist cockades. (All the best hostesses would be aping this innovation within a fortnight, Christabel predicted confidently.) Gilded pots of white lilies lined each step of the curving stairway, the summit of which was graced by Christabel in celestial blue silk, the famous Toddington sapphires round her neck, the current Toddington lord upon her arm.

Drusilla appeared in ivory muslin, topped off by her grandmother's pearls, her sole family heirloom. To her considerable annoyance, Christabel insisted the ivory muslin should be rechristened Vestal Virgin white, and as the first guests made their way into the vestibule, Christabel's final words to her were a hissed admonition to "Look *virginal,* for heaven's sake!"

Christabel's guest list for the evening was a judicious

grouping of homing *émigrés* intermixed with diplomatist and military attachés from the Quadruple Alliance countries, plus a few Spanish and Italian *élégants* thrown in to leaven the Teutonic stiffness of the Austrians and Prussians.

As the guests paraded up the lily-lined staircase, Drusilla saw that many of the *émigrée* ladies had tied red ribbons round their necks without apparent regard to whether or not the ribbons harmonized with their gowns. Some of the ladies' necks were as enwreathed as Maypoles, whilst other ladies had chosen to entwine nosegays of red roses amongst their ribbons.

She and Christabel discussed this French fashion peccadillo behind mutually unfurled fans. "Charles explained it to me," whispered Christabel, looking wise. "The ribbons symbolize the number of one's relations beheaded in the Revolution, and the roses recall to mind how the *aristo* ladies went to the guillotine holding red roses to fend off the smell of the mob."

At that precise instant, the strangest shiver went though Drusilla, as if someone were treading on her grave, and her hand went involuntarily to her throat. How awful to face certain death from a terrible, descending blade. Thankfully, she would never know what it must be like.

There was a stir amongst the guests in the vestibule, and a steward announced in ringing tones, "The British Ambassador to the Court of the Tuileries, His Grace the Duke of Wellington, and suite!"

As the Great Man mounted her staircase, Christabel beamed pridefully, and well she might, for Wellington was the supreme ornament of this season's guest lists. Beak-nosed and pragmatic, he could, when he chose, be remarkably charming to the ladies and remarkably diplomatic for a soldier. Upon his arrival in Paris, he had put away his bemedaled field marshal's uniform so as not to play the red-coated conqueror. Even so, many in France still hated him as an enemy and an occupier.

In this gathering, however, Wellington was the man of the hour, and lovely ladies fluttered invitingly at him as he passed. Alas, they fluttered in vain, for, after greeting his hostess, the Duke conned the salon with a soldierly gaze and then moved purposefully to seek out the company of those well-known champions of abolition, the Misses Faith, Hope, and Charity Thornrose.

Since the British government attached the highest importance to ending the slave trade, Wellington could not but be gratified by the arrival of three such potent allies. He and the trio of lavender-clad sisters were soon deep in talk of abolitionist tactics whilst the fluttering ladies watched enviously and wondered what in the world His Grace could find to interest him in the company of three such dowdy spinster specimens.

"You must understand," Wellington was meanwhile telling the Thornrose ladies, "that many prominent persons have financial interests in plantations dependent on slave labor, and so they are eager to support the *colons* who own the plantations—and the slaves."

"It was the same in England," remarked Aunt Hope, "but in the end, humanitarian principles overcame the commercial arguments of the slaveholders."

"True enough," acknowledged the Duke, "but in France we labor under an additional difficulty. The French don't believe we seek to abolish slavery for humanitarian reasons, but rather because we wish to throttle their commerce and eliminate France as a trading rival in the West Indies. Furthermore—and you will scarcely credit this—the *colons* have put it about that once the slaves are freed, we mean to impress them into the British army and ship them to America to fight against the Continentals."

"Preposterous!"

"Ridiculous!"

"Utter eyewash!"

"It is indeed, dear ladies, but, unfortunately, such arguments, and others equally specious, are being bruited about by the *colons* and their adherents. I fear that our great and just cause is gravely endangered at the moment by falsehoods, distortions, and deceptions."

The Thornrose ladies responded to this declaration like war-horses to a trumpet call.

"The truth must be got out!"

"The public must be educated!"

"The claptrap of the *colons* must be exposed!"

The Duke nodded crisply. "My thoughts precisely. You ladies must do in France what you accomplished so successfully in England—create a favorable climate of public opinion amongst the populace by the use of pamphlets and tracts. The French people must be convinced in our favor. Madame de Staël informs me that she stands ready to help you in this endeavor, and I do not believe you will find anyone with a superior understanding of the Gallic mind."

The Thornrose ladies nodded eagerly. "We are engaged to visit her salon tomorrow evening and renew our acquaintanceship."

"Mr. Wilberforce has been in correspondence with her about how best to counter the arguments of the *colons*."

"Our secretary, Miss Sedgewick, has already begun translating several of our tracts."

The Duke nodded approvingly. "Excellent! I've every confidence that you ladies together, with your sharp wits and your sharpened pens, shall make a formidable collaboration against the *colons*."

He bowed himself off, leaving the Thornrose sisters fairly champing at the bit to start their new crusade in France.

The foregoing conversation was one that Drusilla would have given much to be a part of, but—alas—she was on the far side of the chandelier-lit salon, on duty as the interpreter of Christabel's fractured French. Though Christabel in her girl-hood had been sent to a fashionable boarding school to be "finished," her French remained woefully underdone. As a result, she had an unfortunate propensity to puzzle her French-speaking auditors with mangled copybook phrases such as "Great round cabbages are falling amongst the pretty lambs in springtime," and "I am hastening to the attic to clock my stockings upon a sconce."

It fell to Drusilla to tactfully elucidate her ladyship's remarks; to wit:

"No, Madame la Comtesse, Lady Toddington did not mean that she desires fashionable ladies to dine upon fur muffs for entertainment in the wintertime. She is saying that she desires to know whether fur muffs are much worn by Parisiennes to dinner entertainments in the winter."

"You misunderstand, Monsieur le Marquis. Lady Toddington is, in fact, enraptured by your cane and wishes to know where you procured it. She does not wish you to send it back whence it came."

Conversation with the English-speaking guests was only slightly less excruciating, since Christabel insisted on introducing Drusilla as the favorite granddaughter of Lord Sedgewick of Sedgewick Downs to every single male they encountered. This was a mendacity of mammoth proportions, for Dru's curmudgeonly grandfather had sired nineteen children on three wives and had so many grandchildren that he had long ago lost count of them, and when her existence was pointed out to him, he refused to acknowledge her because she had had the misfortune to have a governess for a mama. That Lord Sedgewick would cut up well to her benefit was an impossibility, though this did not prevent Christabel from coyly suggesting the same.

Taken to task for this sophistry, Christabel airily dismissed Drusilla's objections. "Who is to know, after all, what the wretched man has written in his will? And if you are not his favorite granddaughter, you certainly ought to be, and you would be if he would ever but receive you. Now stop being tedious, and smile for that handsome chevalier fellow who is coming over here."

The chevalier fellow, Guy de Saint-Armand by name, was indeed a handsome paragon, with ebony hair, fiery dark eyes, flashing white teeth, and a lithe, sportsman's build. He also (thank heaven!) spoke excellent English, having been raised in exile in England. To add to his perfections, he apparently did not care in the least that Drusilla was Lord Sedgewick's favorite granddaughter. The chevalier had eyes only for Lord Toddington's magnificent wife.

"My heart is languishing at your feet, madame."

"Well, of course it is," said Christabel complacently. "But for tonight only. Tomorrow, your heart will be at some other hostess's feet."

"You wrong me, madame. I would cheerfully attend you every night of the week if you would permit it."

"You would soon grow tired of my company, I fear," said Christabel quite insincerely.

The chevalier took leave to doubt her words as well. "How could a man grow tired of communing with such a divinity as yourself? It would not be possible."

"Oh, fie, Chevalier!" remonstrated Christabel, rapping her perfumed fan against his manly chest. "I apprehend, sir, that you are a shameless trifler."

Further badinage ensued, in which the chevalier asserted his earnest desire to be her *cavalier servente,* her *cicisbeo,* her gallant knight. Christabel, used to paeans to her perfection, accepted his blandishments without a blush before finally dismissing the ardent chevalier.

Whether the ardent chevalier intended to stay dismissed was another question. It seemed to Drusilla that the French nobleman's gallantries went beyond mere courtly flattery. As the evening progressed, she watched the chevalier watching Christabel, saw him tracking her with avid eyes as he contrived to encounter her again and again as she made her hostess's rounds, circling about her like a dark falcon circling a celestial blue canary.

For the second time that evening, Drusilla felt overtaken by a deep sense of foreboding.

Several hours later the *soirée* was beginning to wind down. As the guests bestirred themselves to decamp, Drusilla took the opportunity to flee the heated glare of the salon for the sanctuary of the library.

She found the Hôtel Toddington library both unoccupied and unlit, for Christabel frowned upon guests who absconded from her entertainments to take refuge in bookish surroundings, and anyone who did such a thing could jolly well sit in the dark, as far as Christabel was concerned. Darkness and solitude suited Dru at the moment, for she had been stung tonight by some of the drawing-room scorpions.

She had seen unwholesome speculation in the eyes of some of the gentlemen, heard whispers amongst some of the ladies. Gossip was putting the worst face on her abduction, and no dress of Vestal Virgin white could scotch such talk, she realized miserably as she rested her flushed cheek against the cool windowpane.

And yet, despite the sidelong glances that had followed her throughout the evening, despite the pitying whispers, she could still find it within herself to wonder about the Emperor's Wolf, to wish to know his fate.

Her mother had warned her, of course, to be careful what she wished for, for the devil might make that wish come true. . . .

As she looked out over the autumn-bare garden of the Hôtel Toddington, she saw a man vault the garden wall, his figure caught for an instant in the bright light of a full harvest moon. There was no mistaking that man. She knew him by the set of his shoulders, by the way he held his head. It was the Emperor's Wolf.

He no longer wore his distinctive prison garb but was dressed in dark, unexceptional clothing, garments that would blend in with those of the crowds on the street or with the shadows in the garden, clothes that would allow him to pass unnoticed through changes of place and scenery.

Workman's clothing. *Huntsman's clothing,* for the moment, Drusilla realized with a shiver.

The Emperor's Wolf had come hunting, but who was the quarry? Christabel? Lord Toddington? Or perhaps—she gave a gasp as the idea occurred to her—Wellington himself, for the Duke was still here, reminiscing about the late war with several of the military attachés.

Even as these thoughts flew through her mind, the Emperor's Wolf made his quick and stealthy way across the garden, a shadow moving through shadows. When he was directly below her, he gave the house a searching look, as if he sensed he was being watched. Drusilla froze into stillness, her heart pounding, but she was lucky in her concealment, her white dress and her rapidly paling face undoubtedly lost amongst the folds of the white voile under curtains.

He meant to get into the house, she apprehended, and she soon saw how he would manage it. One of the famously tall Parisian chestnut trees grew next to the Hôtel Toddington, its outstretched limbs embracing a corner of the mansion. The leaves were down, and she watched the dark-clad intruder climb up through the bare branches, his obvious goal the balcony outside Lord Toddington's study.

She knew she should sound an alarum, but she was also afraid that the wily Emperor's Wolf would contrive to vanish while she did so. Then, another possibility occurred to her, and once again, a courage she never knew she possessed took hold of her.

The study adjoined her library lurking-place, but, unlike the library, it had been left lit. A faint bar of light shining through the slightly ajar door gleamed upon the library writing desk. She knew that in the drawer of that desk was a pistol, placed there by Lord Toddington for his personal defense. If ever there was a time to make use of the pistol, that time was now, for she was very certain that the walls of the Hôtel Toddington would not long keep out the Emperor's Wolf. And if he got in and got past her, the great mansion held innumerable hiding places where he could conceal himself and lie in wait for his victim—whoever it might be.

Flitting noiselessly across the library in her satin slippers, she slid open the desk drawer and, after an instant's hesitation, took a pistol into her hand for the first time in her life. Moving like a white shadow along the book-lined wall to the study door, she cautiously peered through the opening.

What she half expected to see, she saw. The Emperor's Wolf. It was still shocking, nonetheless, to behold the unmitigated gall of the man sitting on the edge of Lord Toddington's desk, swinging a booted foot back and forth like a careless boy as he read Lord Toddington's newspaper.

Something about her former captor's arrogant self-assurance made Drusilla utterly bound and determined to be the one to turn the tables on him, to capture him as he had captured her. She raised the pistol, pushed open the door, and stepped into the study.

The Emperor's Wolf froze, his eyes turning to green ice at the sight of the pistol barrel pointed at his heart. Drusilla sensed instantly that this was a man who was not often taken unawares, and that he was not pleased to be ambushed by a slip of a girl in white muslin and dancing slippers.

She smiled her most charming milady's smile and addressed him in flawless French. "So we meet again, Monsieur Wolf. But this time I have the pistol, and you are my prisoner."

"Only if the pistol is primed and loaded and you are a dead shot," countered the Emperor's Wolf in perfect upper-class King's English. "None of which is the case, is it, my angel?" And he was off the desk and on his feet and a step closer to her.

Dru stared at him for a stunned instant, uncertain now whether the pistol actually was primed and loaded. And how did the le Loup de l'Empereur come to speak such perfect English all of sudden?

A fatal blunder, that stunned instant of uncertainty.

Her erstwhile prisoner, who had been gliding toward her, abruptly pounced, grabbing her wrist in a crushing grip and thrusting it upward, the better to safely wrench the loaded pistol—oh, yes, it was loaded, after all—out of her hand and toss it down on the desk.

And now she was disarmed and his captive all over again,

held against him, despite her struggles, by an iron arm across her back. His eyes glittered down into her face as he told in his perplexingly perfect English, "Lesson number one, my angel: Never point a pistol unless you know it to be loaded. Lesson number two: Never heed the blandishments of the enemy you are pointing the pistol at. And lesson number three: Never, but never, point a pistol at MacRory Holt."

She found herself unceremoniously released, but only so he could spin her round and deal her backside a stinging slap.

Furious, she whirled about, looking for something to throw at him. But even as she did so, the name he had called himself struck a chord of memory, and she knew she had heard that name before, spoken this very evening by Lord Toddington and the Duke of the Wellington . . .

As if on cue, Lord Toddington appeared in the doorway to exclaim, "Colonel Holt! Drusilla Sedgewick! What in God's name is going on here?"

Drusilla only wished she knew.

Of course, her erstwhile captor knew exactly what was happening and so informed his lordship, "The young lady believed she had discovered the Emperor's Wolf trespassing and so came bravely—if somewhat foolishly—to the defense of your household." He picked up the pistol and handed it to Lord Toddington, who instantly recognized it as one of his own.

"Drusilla, what were you thinking of?" he demanded. "You might have done Colonel Holt or yourself injury."

Holt nodded in cool agreement. "I was just pointing out to Miss Sedgewick the error of her ways when you came on the scene."

Despite the blandness of his voice, Dru was certain that a wicked, masculine smirk glinted behind those green eyes of his and that he had very much enjoyed punishing her for having the temerity to take him unawares. At that moment, she formed a resolution that someday, one way or the other, she would see that smirk wiped off his face and replaced by a look of respect—although how she would accomplish such a goal, she could not begin to imagine.

Still baffled by the seeming acquaintanceship between Lord Toddington and the mysterious Colonel Holt, Drusilla was on the verge of demanding an explanation when she apprehended that Lord Toddington was regarding her and Colonel Holt with a troubled expression. "Never was anything more unfortunate than this encounter. It would have been far better for everyone if you two had never crossed paths again."

"Perhaps," acknowledged Holt, "but now that we have met again, you must allow me to felicitate Miss Sedgewick on her escape from the Emperor's Wolf."

"You are too generous in your praises, sir," replied Drusilla, who had been thinking furiously despite her shock and ire, "particularly since I now realize that the Emperor's Wolf facilitated my escape, even to leaving me a map. I might have guessed the truth sooner had your French been less authentic. You speak it to perfection."

"My birthright, Miss Sedgewick," said MacRory Holt. "I'm from an old Franco-Scot family. Whoever coined the saying 'All good Scots go to Paris when they die' certainly had the Holts in mind."

"But you're one Scotsman," Drusilla deduced shrewdly, "who has come to Paris to spy. Am I right, Colonel Holt? Though why that pursuit should involve abducting and imprisoning me, I cannot fathom."

Lord Toddington winced visibly at the open enunciation of the word *spy* and hastened to bring the conversation to an end. "Colonel Holt! The less the young lady knows about these matters—and about you—the better. Drusilla, you must promise to forget everything you have learnt tonight and on no account speak of it to anyone."

"You may be certain of my discretion, my lord," Drusilla assured him. Then, wondering whence she got her nerve, she quickly went on, "But I would beg you to call on me again if I can be of further service to you in these important matters."

Lord Toddington looked nonplussed. "My dear girl, in what possible way could you be of service to us? None that I know of. You must not think us ungrateful for the part you've played so far, but you cannot under any circumstances become more deeply involved. You are a guest in my house, and I would not have you subjected to further risk."

"As you wish," said Drusilla, swallowing her disappointment. "But, my lord, may I at least know the truth about the men who stopped our carriage?"

"I fear not, child. Such information cannot be divulged merely to satisfy your curiosity."

"I see," said Drusilla stiffly. It was obvious that she was to be written out of whatever drama was transpiring among the diplomatists. There was nothing for it, she supposed, but a dignified exit, and so she said as equably as she could, "I perceive that you have matters to discuss, so I'll take my leave. Pray remember, however, that I am as patriotic as either of you, and I do not forget my father's death at the hands of the French." She swept them her best curtsy. "And now I'll bid you gentlemen good evening."

Looking greatly relieved, Lord Toddington hurried her to the door, issuing yet another round of warnings about the necessity for secrecy and discretion.

MacRory Holt said nothing, but his wolflike gaze rested thoughtfully on Miss Drusilla Sedgewick as she made her exit.

Chapter Four

In the Salon of the Famous Madame de Staël

The next evening the Thornrose sisters and their secretary set off to a *souper* given by that formidable intellectual Amazon Germaine de Staël, in whose brilliant salon the literary and political wits of the Paris intelligentsia found their finest setting. Christabel, needless to say, was left at home, for this was not a setting in which she could be expected to shine—and besides, she announced loftily, more pressing matters claimed her attention this evening.

As the Thornrose party entered madame's salon, their hostess swept toward them, her full-figured person fully rigged with sundry trailing scarves and sashes, her elaborately sculpted brunet curls emerging from beneath her trademark turban. Whether Madame de Staël could be considered fair of face was a question that rested within the eye of the beholder. Men who were intimidated by her intellect (and most men were) found her decidedly unhandsome. But even the harshest of her detractors could not deny the soulful beauty of her great dark eyes. They were her best feature, and she used them to the fullest, gesturing with them as other women would gesture with their hands.

Madame's expressive eyes lit with pleasure as she greeted her English guests. "My dear Thornroses, how delightful to see you! I have not forgotten the days when I was a wandering exile in England, and you, the kind hostesses. But now I am at last able to repay the hospitality of my three Graces of reform, the so aptly named Faith, Hope, and Charity."

She kissed each of the sisters upon both cheeks, and then turned a penetrating glance upon Drusilla. "So this is the secretary with the excellent and learned French. You have, of course, read my novel *Delphine*?"

"Oh, yes, madame. In the original French."

"And my novel *Corrine*?"

"That, too, madame. In the original French, as well."

"And my *De l'Allemagne*?"

"Several times, in fact, madame."

Madame was pleased to approve these learned credentials and thereafter swept them off to meet with several persons prominent in the French abolition movement.

The subsequent discourse was all upon that subject, with Drusilla called upon now and again to give the Thornrose ladies the French word they sought. Madame de Staël, with the ease of long practice, sailed among her guests, subtly directing the flow of talk so that the conversation was both stimulating and relevant to the subject *du jour*.

Then it was on to the dining parlor to partake of the light repast that had been laid out. And such a centerpiece upon the table this evening!

It was a model ship—a model *slaver*, in fact—made to scale, complete to the smallest detail of the jewelry-sized slave chains. No one could partake a morsel without contemplating this miniature exemplar of the evils of slavery. Madame de Staël was, in her own inimitable way, making a statement, though what that silent statement might do to the appetites of her guests could only be wondered at.

Later in the evening, the Thornrose party walked through madame's mullioned-windowed solarium, where many exotic ferns and flowers grew in equally exotic pots. The *salonniers* were wont to congregate here as the evening advanced, and many elegant discussions were to be heard amongst the fronds and foliage.

Eventually madame sought out her English friends, saying, "I have only now heard of your secretary's escape from the brigands."

Drusilla felt herself coloring painfully. Was all Paris talking about her still?

"But how the little one is mortified!" apprehended their perceptive hostess. "Why so?" she demanded of the Thornrose ladies. "Surely it was a great adventure, and she is a heroine!"

"To us, yes," agreed Miss Faith.

"But," explained Miss Hope, "unkind talk is to be heard."

"About innocence blasted, virtue debauched, Spoiled Goods that will never sell on the Marriage Mart," elaborated Miss Charity with a specificity that caused Drusilla to wince.

Madame was immediately sympathetic, for her tempestuous love affairs with a series of famous men had made her the most gossiped-about woman in Europe, save possibly the Prince Regent's balmy wife, Princess Caroline.

"Alas," said madame to Drusilla, "I am too familiar with the tittle-tattlings that women must ever be subjected to in regard to their virtue. Walk with me a little, *ma petite,* and I shall give you some wise counsel."

(Madame de Staël was fond of giving wise counsel, sought after or not. Her literary counsel to Napoleon to cease playing the tyrant and abide by the Rights of Man had so infuriated the Emperor that he had had her exiled and her writings destroyed. But now it was Napoleon who was in exile, while Germaine de Staël queened it once more in her Paris salon.)

Linking arms with Drusilla, madame led her among the potted greenery. "So the evil-talkers distress you, child? It is so important to you, this Marriage Mart, this charade where the well-bred fillies parade themselves?"

"In no way, madame," Dru assured her quickly. "Yet one cannot help being oppressed by the slander."

"Bah! You must not regard it, I tell you! It will not do to let evil-talkers have the ordering of your life, for they will do it in a most beggarly fashion. Life should be a banquet, a festal board, a sumptuous repast spiced with earthly delights that you feast upon as a gourmand." (Madame was perhaps at this moment thinking of her latest lover, John Rocca, a most handsome cavalry officer twenty-two years her junior.) "But I tell you, child, that if you leave the ordering of your life to such as these, you will find yourself living on a diet of mean gruel and gnawed bones, for that is all the portion they will allow you. Do you comprehend my meaning, *ma petite?*"

"I believe so," replied Dru, who had not pored over *Delphine, Corrine,* and *De l'Allemagne* for naught. "You say, in effect, 'To thine own self be true.' "

Madame was pleased by her perspicacity. "I could not have put it better myself! And now," she decreed, surveying a knot of gentlemen who stood nearby, "I will find you a *beau idéal* to stroll with you and beguile you."

But the gentleman madame procured for this task left Dru decidedly unbeguiled, for that gentleman was the Chevalier Guy de Saint-Armand. As Madame de Staël's sashed and turbaned figure receded, the chevalier declared gallantly, "My heart is at your feet, mademoiselle."

"Really, sir?" Dru responded austerely. "Last night I distinctly heard you tell Lady Toddington that your heart was at *her* feet."

The chevalier was in no way abashed by this observation. "Ah, but did you not know, mademoiselle, that we

Frenchmen have an endless supply of hearts to lavish upon lovely women?"

"Oh, is that the way of it?" inquired Drusilla even more austerely.

"But of a certainty, mademoiselle. Pray conduct me to Lady Toddington, and I will show you how it is done."

"I regret to disappoint you, sir, but Lady Toddington occupies herself at home this evening."

(Christabel, who maintained a fervent belief in the cosmetic efficacy of dairy products, was, in fact, occupying herself with a milk bath and an egg-white facial. These undertakings involved a considerable amount of time and energy—for her servants anyway—as the peculiar ablutions required the procuring of numerous fresh eggs and the hauling upstairs and heating of enough milk to fill her half bath.)

The chevalier expressed surprise that her ladyship was content to remain at home alone. "For I know Lord Toddington and His Grace the Ambassador are gone hunting in the country with the Duc d'Angoulême."

Drusilla gave him a sidelong look. "You seem very conversant, sir, with the engagements of our embassy staff."

The chevalier shrugged well-tailored shoulders. "Say rather, mademoiselle, that I am conversant with the engagements of the royal family as printed in the court calendar. When you are a supplicant for royal favor, as I am, you must make it your business to encounter your benefactors at every possible opportunity."

Dru eyed him curiously. "On what account do you seek royal favor, Chevalier?"

"For the return of my family's lands, mademoiselle. Our estate was seized during the Revolution, and our *château* is currently"—his voice was cold with contempt—"owned by a certain rich *citoyen* cheesemonger named Dupee, who occupies it with his fat *citoyenne* wife and their numerous red-cheeked progeny. If the King would but order it, the estate could be returned to me, the scion of the family that lived there for five hundred years before the republicans thieved it. And yet"—he made an eloquent gesture of frustration— "His Majesty hesitates to dispossess too many of the rich *bourgeoisie* all at once, and so I must dance attendance upon the royal family to put my matter forward to their notice."

"And what," Dru asked thoughtfully, "will happen to the cheesemonger and his family if you succeed in your petition?"

"They will be turned out of possession, of course, and lose their purchase price. But at least they will still have their heads, a mercy not accorded my family in the Revolution."

"I see you do not forget the old wrongs, Chevalier."

"No, mademoiselle," vowed the chevalier, "I will never forget."

And with that, he took himself off, leaving Dru to reflect upon how hot the old hatreds still burned in La Belle France.

The rest of the evening passed for Drusilla in a manner designed to delight the heart of the most devout bluestocking. There was stimulating debate, learned pronouncement upon the great issues of the day, and numerous *bon mot*s tossed about. And if there was evil-talking about her, she was determined not to hear it, for it would not do to spoil the intellectual feast served up tonight by Madame de Staël.

At the salon's close, the Thornrose party headed home, surfeited on high converse. Despite the lateness of the hour, there was a rider going out the front gate of the Hôtel Toddington as they were entering. This was not unusual in itself, for Foreign Office couriers often arrived and departed at odd hours, bearing confidential diplomatic messages in their locked dispatch cases.

But the man coming out of the Hôtel Toddington this night was no courier.

It was the Chevalier de Saint-Armand.

Chapter Five

In Which Drusilla Becomes
a Student in the Great Game

For the next few days, Drusilla remained uneasy in her mind about the Chevalier de Saint-Armand. She was mortally certain that the handsome Frenchman had gone to the Hôtel Toddington in the hope of taking advantage of Lord Toddington's absence.

A subtle interrogation of Christabel elicited the information that the chevalier had, indeed, called but that Christabel had been unwilling to rise from her milk bath and wipe the egg whites from her face in order to receive him in her husband's absence.

It remained to be seen whether this rebuff would cool the chevalier's ardor. Drusilla feared it would not, and she greeted Lord Toddington's return from the hunting fields with extreme relief . . . relief that soon turned to surprise when, on his lordship's first night back, he sent a request that she join him in his study. Though puzzled by a summons at this late hour, she duly made her appearance.

Lord Toddington was not alone. Another man stood off to the side, one shoulder propped against a mantelshelf, his arms crossed upon his chest, his gaze hooded as he watched her entrance.

Drusilla's blood leaped with excitement when she saw that the man was the lean and green-eyed MacRory Holt, the man who had been Wellington's top intelligence operative in the

Peninsular War, the man whose absence Lord Toddington and the Lord Fitzroy Somerset loudly lamented, spreading it about that the daring Colonel Holt was rusticating on half pay at his estate in the Scottish Highlands.

But those lamentations had been a lie, she now realized, a falsehood put about to disguise the fact that the man who had once been called Wellington's eyes and ears was, in fact, back in France in some mysterious capacity.

Deep doings, indeed, among the diplomatists, and for what reason could they have summoned her here tonight?

Looking grave, Lord Toddington asked her to be seated, and once she had done so, the words he spoke caused a second tide of excitement to rise within her. "My dear, since last we spoke, circumstances compel me to reconsider your offer of the other evening. By now, you must be aware that I am more than a diplomatist, that I am also commissioned by His Majesty's government to supervise the gathering of secret intelligence in Europe. Colonel Holt is one of the confidential intelligencers who report to me, and he believes that our enemies have discovered what I am about. They have, in fact, already attempted to strike back at me."

"By kidnapping Christabel!" exclaimed Dru in sudden comprehension.

"Yes, but thanks to Holt's discovery of the scheme—and your unwitting assistance—the plot was foiled. But this does not mean they might not try again, and so I must ask you to help me safeguard my wife, to watch over her when I cannot."

Drusilla's rising tide of excitement subsided into a very sinking feeling. To be Christabel's secretary and interpreter was a chore—but to be her *keeper* on top of it!

Her crestfallen demeanor did not pass unnoticed by Colonel Holt, who spoke for the first time. "If you wish to be a player in the Great Game, Miss Sedgewick, you must first serve your apprenticeship."

"I'm afraid I don't know what you mean," she said stiffly. "What is this Great Game you speak of?"

A gleam like that of a sword came into MacRory Holt's eyes as he answered. "The Great Game is the name we call this intelligence-gathering venture of ours. For it is a great game, Miss Sedgewick, a game of bravado, bluff, and cunning, of moves and countermoves, of masquerading and unmasking, of secrets to be ferreted out, dangers to be dared—"

"Colonel Holt!" interjected Lord Toddington hastily. "You'll send the poor young woman into a swoon."

"Somehow I doubt that," said Holt with a faint, knowing smile, "but I'll cease for the moment."

"Really, my dear," resumed his lordship, "all we desire is that you accompany Christabel and be alert to her welfare. I'm certain you will encounter nothing more terrifying than expeditions to the shops."

I have been shopping with Christabel, thought Dru mordantly, *and it* was *terrifying.* But aloud she said, "Of course I will do anything you ask, my lord. Only, who are these enemies of yours that I must watch for?"

"Unreconstructed Bonapartists for the most part, but also Jacobins, anti-royalists, radical republicans. They all share a common goal, which is to unseat the Bourbons and reestablish a republic that would dominate the Continent once more. The brigands who abducted you were former soldiers of the Imperial Guard, recruited to the plot by a man who stood high in Bonaparte's secret police force."

"Excelsior?" hazarded Drusilla.

Lord Toddington nodded. "His real name is Henri Lazare, and he is devilishly cunning. Colonel Holt knows him

49

well from the Peninsula. A pity you did not get the fellow this time, Holt."

"We'll meet again, of that I'm certain." Holt's voice was offhand but edged for all of that.

"In the meantime," continued his lordship, "since Drusilla is now involved, we must have some secret means of communication amongst the three of us. A book code will serve, I think."

He paused to look at Drusilla questioningly. "You understand how this would work? The correspondents all have a copy of the same book, and the messages are in the form of numerical codes for pages, lines, and letters." At Dru's nod of understanding, he continued, "So it remains only to select the specific volume to be used. What books have you in your personal possession, my dear?"

"*Childe Harold's Pilgrimage*," offered Dru, saying the first title that sprang to mind.

It was a title that elicited a sardonic retort from Colonel Holt. "Of course! What young lady does not have a copy of *Childe Harold* these days? I, however, am not one of Byron's swooning admirers and have no matching copy."

"Then perhaps you should broaden your literary horizons, sir," suggested Drusilla sweetly, "particularly since it is said that more cantos are forthcoming."

"The situation's easily remedied," said Lord Toddington, stepping into his library. "I've several copies of *Childe Harold* on hand." He handed one of the vellum-bound volumes to Holt, who took it with a noticeable lack of enthusiasm.

Drusilla had a fleeting but vivid image of MacRory Holt sitting in his wolf's lair perusing Lord Byron's rapturously romantic verse in search of ciphering letters. It was a picture that nearly caused her to dissolve into laughter. Fortunately, she did not, though she was certain Colonel Holt knew that she was amused at his expense. She contented herself with smirking demurely at him and allowing herself to feel satisfied that she had repaid him somewhat for his earlier ungentlemanly behavior toward her.

"So we are agreed," Lord Toddington was saying, "that Drusilla is to watch over my wife. And one thing more, Drusilla: You are to do whatever you can to prevent Christabel from mentioning any association between myself and the island of Jersey."

Drusilla regarded his lordship with surprise. In London, Christabel had often complained about her husband's numerous and inconvenient trips to the tiny channel island of Jersey. These trips were indeed a puzzlement, since Lord Toddington had no maritime interests, and his estate was two hundred miles in the opposite direction. Christabel's intimates had come to suspect that his lordship was keeping a mistress there, but Christabel appeared to harbor no such suspicion. After all, what man who had the privilege of having access to her perfections would seek another woman?

So what *had* Lord Toddington been up to on the isle of Jersey?

Sensing that she was treading upon dangerous ground, Dru said carefully, "I believe Christabel may have mentioned your absences some few times in passing. But of what significance were these trips, my lord?"

Lord Toddington frowned. "That is not for you to be concerned with, my dear. Suffice it to say that we prefer that the subject not come up again. Christabel knows nothing of any of this business, nor do I wish her to. I won't have the dear girl worried that she may be the victim of a plot due to my position in the government. I leave it to you to be on guard for suspicious persons who might approach her."

51

Suspicious persons . . . like the Chevalier Guy de Saint-Armand?

Her thoughts must have shown on her face, for MacRory Holt asked sharply, "Has Lady Toddington been approached by anyone who aroused your suspicions, Miss Sedgewick?"

Choosing her words carefully, Dru answered, "The Chevalier de Saint-Armand's attentions to her seem to be . . . singular."

Lord Toddington's countenance stiffened. "By God, what are you saying, young woman?"

Dru went on hastily. "Not that Christabel pays him any heed; she is so universally admired that she shrugs off his gallantries. It has seemed to me, however, that he was extraordinarily determined to be in her company. And yet"—she regarded the two men doubtfully—"why would a chevalier of the *ancien régime* plot to undermine the monarchy?"

"Because," answered Colonel Holt, "he may not be the real Chevalier de Saint-Armand. The French aristocracy has been scattered these last twenty-five years. The chevalier would have been in leading strings when the revolution broke out. Who now would know the grown man on sight, and what better disguise for a republican spy than that of a returning *émigré?*"

"We'll find out soon enough," said Lord Toddington grimly. "I shall have the chevalier's *bona fides* looked into by our agents in London. If he should prove an imposter," continued his lordship in a voice that boded no good for the chevalier, "I shall know how to act. In the meantime, we depend upon you, Drusilla, to keep an eye on the fellow."

"I shall do my best, my lord."

"Excellent. You relieve my mind greatly in this matter of my wife's safety. And now I must ask you to leave us, as Colonel Holt and I have further matters to discuss."

"As you wish, my lord." She dropped a demure curtsy, but her eyes were shining as she told the two men, "May I say that I am pleased to have this opportunity to be of service to my country." *Even though,* she added silently as she took her leave, *it's only to shepherd Christabel to the shops.*

Nevertheless, the oddest feeling of excitement had taken hold of her—she, who was usually the most sensible of women. She was in the Great Game, if only in the smallest way, and for some strange reason this pleased her as nothing in her life had ever pleased her before.

Had Drusilla been privileged to hear the conversation that took place after she left Lord Toddington's study, she would have been considerably less pleased.

"I knew she would accept our commission," said MacRory Holt, satisfaction in his voice. "She's got a taste for the Game, our little Miss Sedgewick does."

Lord Toddington did not presume to dispute this assessment, for Holt was well known for his unerring ability to recruit confidential agents. Still, his lordship was curious about one thing. "You've always operated as a lone wolf, Holt. Why bring this young woman into the game now?"

"Because," answered Holt, folding himself into the wing chair opposite his lordship, "now I play a different game from my days as an Exploring Officer on the Peninsula. Now I move among the civilian populace, and I am in need of protective coloration."

Lord Toddington nodded in understanding. Blending in had always been a problem for Holt, both here and on the Spanish Peninsula. Though his ancestry was nearly as Gallic as Gael, in his looks he was all Scot. His lanky Scotsman's height and odd-colored eyes tended to mark him out, and he had a handsome face women remembered in their dreams.

The one and only time he had been captured during his many intelligence missions in Spain, it was his physical appearance that had put the French on his trail.

"So," observed Lord Toddington, "you think Miss Sedgewick will be of assistance to you?"

"I think that when I am in her company, men will pay less heed to me and more to her. Our coloring is so similar she could pass for my sister if need be, and she's tall enough not to make me look like a Long John when I stand next to her. And there's always something disarming about having a pretty girl at one's side."

"Well, as to that," allowed Lord Toddington with a shrug, "I suppose she's well enough for a Long Meg, but she's certainly no Christabel."

"That goes without saying," Holt agreed blandly, all the while giving inward thanks that this was the case. In his opinion, Lady Christabel Toddington ought to be packed off to her husband's stately home in Hampshire and locked away in the highest tower room, where she could do no more harm. He was mortally certain that the woman's loose talk had unmasked her husband as Britain's top spy master, whose job it was to dispatch confidential agents into France from a secret base on the isle of Jersey. MacRory Holt was also certain that the besotted Lord Toddington would hear nothing against his wife, so he kept his opinion to himself.

"But see here, Holt," Lord Toddington was saying, "I'll not deny that Drusilla might be helpful, but you must remember that she's no lightskirt, no *grisette* as we've sometimes hired in the past. She is from a good family—"

"Who wouldn't miss her if she dropped off the face of the earth tomorrow," interposed Holt dispassionately. "You as much as said so yourself, what with her parents dead and old

Lord Sedgewick and the rest of the clan not giving a hang about her."

"I'll warrant the Thornrose ladies will give a hang if something happens to her," countered Lord Toddington gloomily. "Not only is she their secretary, but the Sedgewicks and the Thornroses meet somewhere on the Thornrose family tree."

Holt was unimpressed. "From what I hear, there are Sedgewicks hanging from just about every family tree in England."

"My point exactly. The girl may be poor, but she's well connected. She's also a British citizen and a guest in my house. Were it not for my concern for Christabel, I wouldn't permit her involvement at all. Surely you can appreciate my concern."

"Yes," said Holt candidly, "though I doubt Miss Sedgewick would thank you for it. She's got a yen for adventure, despite those prim petticoats of hers. Moreover, she's hot to pay back the French for killing her father, and I swear she's one who has the nerve to do it. Remember, I've seen her tested in our kind of adventure as few women have been, and only one mistake did she make, about which I shall school her directly. Surely, my lord, you can appreciate the uses to which a young woman of her resources could be put."

Lord Toddington regarded him thoughtfully. "If she's all you say she is, then perhaps she won't care to be schooled and used. The young lady seems to have a mind of her own, her eagerness to mix it up with the French notwithstanding."

Holt smiled, a wolfish smile. "Leave Miss Sedgewick to me, my lord. I'll train her, and our cause will be the stronger for having her at our call."

After a moment of silence, Lord Toddington said heavily, "All right, Holt, I give you leave to deal with Miss Sedgewick however you please, provided my wife's safety comes first. I'll tell you, though, I don't like it above half. But be that as it may, if you believe that Drusilla Sedgewick is a high card dealt providentially into our hands, then we'd be fools not to deal her into the Great Game."

Chapter Six

In Which MacRory Holt
Comes Bearing Gifts

The note came two days later, slid under her bedroom door by
some unknown hand, though she was inclined to suspect
Grimthwaite, who had been in Lord Toddington's service for
twenty years and who, she suspected, was in the Game along
with his master.

Trembling a little with excitement, Drusilla carefully unfolded the rough copybook paper and found penned upon it a
series of numbers, written in groupings of three with a virgule
between each group.

She sat down at her writing desk, where *Childe Harold* lay
open, waiting to reveal all. Pencil at the ready, she studied the
first set of numerals: 9 4 15. This meant page nine, the fourth
line, the fifteenth letter, which turned out to be a T. Further
deciphering soon produced the following message:
TONIGHT. AFTER ONE. YOUR ROOM.

It was surprisingly easy work to get into her room by way
of the balcony outside her French windows. Balconies,
Drusilla was to learn, were to MacRory Holt what front doors
were to the rest of civilized society.

She might have expected that he would come that way, to
avoid alerting the household to his presence in her chamber.
Still, it sent a frisson up her spine to see him materialize so

suddenly and silently amongst the fluttering white curtains, like a wolf emerging from the mist.

Gesturing her to silence, he ran a quick, reconnoitering glance around her room and then moved immediately to check that her door was locked—as if, she thought dryly, she would be foolish enough to leave it unlocked while receiving a man in her room at one in the morning.

Was this man never off guard, she wondered, *even in a lady's boudoir?* And then she found herself wondering—most improperly—how many ladies' boudoirs MacRory Holt might have been in, and whether he had been there for business or for pleasure.

Satisfied that all was secure, he turned to face her. "The note I sent you," he demanded by way of greeting, "where is it?"

"Why . . . I burnt it," said Dru, taken aback and wondering if she ought to have kept it, even though it seemed most imprudent to keep such a message on hand. But then Holt gave her a brief nod of approval, and she perceived that she was being tested, and, as always, something within her spirit leapt to meet the challenge of this man and the strange and dangerous life he led.

"I've brought you some things you'll have need of," he told her, reaching into the pocket of his greatcoat to produce two glass vials of the type in which cheap scent was bottled and sold by street vendors. He set both vials down on her dressing table, and she saw that each contained a prettyish liquid, one garnet-colored, the other deep amber.

She picked up the vial containing the garnet liquid, uncorked it, and took a sniff—and then wished she hadn't. "It's . . . vile," she gasped, corking it hurriedly. "What is it?"

"Red-cabbage juice," answered Holt, a ghost of a grin

playing across his face at her discomfiture. "The other contains vinegar and water."

"But what am I do to with them?"

"Nothing for the moment. This is merely a precaution should our book code fail. Then, if need be, we can still correspond using the vinegar water for ink."

"Invisible ink! Of course!" exclaimed Dru, unaware of how enraptured she sounded.

MacRory Holt was aware, however, and smiled to himself.

Dru continued to enthusiastically demonstrate her knowledge of invisible ink, gleaned from the numerous Gothic tales she had read. "The paper is held over a candle flame to make the writing visible."

"Yes, but you'll find cabbage juice quicker and safer than candle flame," Holt told her. "All that's needed is to dip a quill feather into the vial, brush it across the paper, and the writing appears by chemical reaction. Better chemistry than playing with fire if you've a vital message to read."

"Yes, I see what you mean," agreed Dru, eyeing the vial of cabbage juice with new respect.

"Now," said Holt, briskly changing the subject, "have you an old, worn dress that can be put to rough usage?"

As it happened, Dru had plenty of old, worn dresses left over from the penurious existence she and her ailing mother had led before they were taken into the kindly bosom of the Thornrose family. She duly produced her olive brown poplin, wondering what Holt meant her to do with it.

The answer made her blush.

"Well, don't just stand there. Put it on."

"But . . . I've no dressing screen."

"I'll turn my back," said Holt impatiently. "Your maidenly charms will be safe from my gaze, I assure you. By the way, do you wear your garter above the knee or below it?"

Dru felt herself blushing even more hotly, if that were possible. "I fail to see what business that is of yours, sir."

Holt's expression iced at this rebellion, for he did not like to be told, in effect, that *her* garters were none of *his* business. "*This* is the business I'm about," he retorted, reaching again into his greatcoat pocket, "and the sooner you attend to it, the better off both of us will be."

She stared wordlessly at the object he held up to her gaze. It was a stiletto contained in a leather sheath that was surely—if she guessed aright—made to be hung on a woman's stocking garter.

Holt unsheathed the little knife, and she saw that the hilt was almost dainty in its fine workmanship, but the blade, though small, was sharp as a metal talon. And for the first time in the course of this whole amazing adventure, Dru was possessed of the awful feeling that perhaps she had got in over her head. But her pride would not let her waver, so when Holt sheathed the dagger and held it out to her, she took it in hand.

"You may as well put it on with the dress," said Holt. "The sheath goes above the knee," he added as he turned away to stand looking through her French window at the night sky.

Dru attacked the bodice buttons on her sprigged muslin, her fingers fumbling nervously, for never in her wildest dreams had she imagined to find herself undressing to the back of a gentleman not her husband.

Still perusing the view from her windows, Holt inquired conversationally, "And how is milady peagoose—Lady Toddington," he quickly amended—"keeping? Safe from the French fox, I trust?"

"For the time being, I believe so," answered Dru as she emerged from her muslin and dived hurriedly into the folds of the olive brown poplin. "The only places she goes without his lordship are afternoon calls upon the other diplomatic wives, and I do not think to encounter the chevalier there." After a second's hesitation, she dared to ask, "What will Lord Toddington do to Saint-Armand if he proves an imposter?"

Holt's shoulders shrugged in silhouette against the windows. "Charles Toddington will not have to do anything to Saint-Armand except denounce him to the *Chevaliers de la Foi,* who will then arrange for the duplicitous gentleman to die by defenestration."

Dru felt a sudden chill, which was not ameliorated as she picked up the stiletto sheath. "But who are these so-called 'Knights of the Faith' that they would be willing to kill Saint-Armand by throwing him out a window?"

"The *Chevaliers de la Foi* are a secret society of ultra-royalists who swear a blood oath to their grand master—the King's brother and heir, the Comte d'Artois. They've plotted for years to bring down the French republic, and now that the Bourbons are back in power, so, too, have the *Chevaliers* come to power—as the secret police force of the Comte d'Artois." His tone grew impatient. "I do not wish to hurry you at your *toilette,* Miss Sedgewick, but I have seen all there is to see from your windows."

"In a minute, sir," said Dru, hurriedly drawing up her garter ribbons. By happy circumstance, she habitually wore her garters above the knee, and the knife sheath settled snugly against her thigh. But the touch of the metal hilt caused her flesh to shiver.

"You may turn round now, sir."

He came and stood in front of her and looked her up and down consideringly.

Discomposed by this scrutiny, she advised him tartly, "It's all very well to give me one of these stocking-hanger stilettos, but you must be aware that I haven't the least notion how to use it."

"I am aware, and for now it is enough that you carry it as a spare weapon for my use."

"That sounds fine in theory, Colonel Holt"—despite her cool words, she felt her cheeks heating again—"but it seems impractical to have to raise my skirts should I need to draw the knife."

"An impracticality I'm about to remedy, Miss Sedgewick." Holt had his own knife in his hand now; it had simply appeared from up his sleeve. "Pray don't flinch," he admonished her as he took a fold of her skirt in hand and sliced through it . . . *and* through her best petticoat as well, Dru thought resentfully as she did her best not to flinch.

Still, she saw the utility of what he had done, saw how easily she could now reach the knife. And when Holt told her she must wear a pinafore over her dress, she saw the utility of that, also: She could get the dagger in hand without anyone seeing what she was about. Slowly, experimentally, she put her hand through the rent in her skirt and drew out her stiletto. It gleamed coldly in the candlelight of her room.

"So, my angel"—MacRory Holt's voice was soft, almost seductive—"do you like the pretty toys I've brought you?"

She swallowed, still staring at the stiletto in her hand. "They are hardly toys, sir."

"But you like them."

"I . . . yes, they will be useful, I daresay." She slipped the knife back into its sheath and looked up into his intent gaze. "Have you anything else for me?"

A small laugh escaped him. "Greedy for more, are we? Well, not tonight, I'm afraid. Besides"—his voice darkened abruptly—"we've done enough skylarking for one evening. It's lesson time now, starting with a review of your previous performance as Lady Toddington. A highly critical review, I'm afraid."

Dru felt her cheeks grow hot, but this time with outraged pride. "I thought I acquitted myself rather well, considering the circumstances."

"Up to a point," allowed Holt with a shrug. "But then you made one critical error that might have ruined everything."

"And what was that, pray?"

"You let yourself be goaded into telling the Emperor's Wolf that your father was killed at Corunna. Foolish, very foolish, my angel, for Lady Toddington's father is still quite alive, is he not? And well known in sporting circles, no?"

With deep chagrin, Drusilla was forced to acknowledge the truth of this criticism. Sir Toby Howard, Christabel's father, was very much alive and was, furthermore, master of the Sussex Hunt, which meant that his name often appeared in the sporting journals. Kidnappers on the lookout for his daughter likely would have known this fact.

Holt pointed this out in stinging language, adding with odious relish, "Had the Emperor's Wolf been real, he'd have eaten you up at that slip."

"I take your point," said Drusilla stiffly.

"Very wise, Miss Sedgewick. Now take a warning from me as well. This is no drawing-room intrigue we play at, no adventure out of a lady author's romance book. The danger is real. The stakes are high."

"I understand," said Drusilla promptly—too promptly for Holt's liking, it seemed.

"I wonder if you do understand, Miss Sedgewick. Pray consider our previous adventure. Do you comprehend that I, an officer and a gentleman, felt duty-bound to leave the daughter of a fellow officer captive in the hands of the enemy? Nothing mattered but that I had the opportunity to take Bonaparte's

Excelsior, Henri Lazare, out of the Great Game. To gain that prize I was prepared to sacrifice your safety and your virtue, and I would do so again without a moment's thought."

"I . . . see," said Drusilla, considerably sobered by this revelation.

"It's to be hoped you do, for I'll stand no missish nonsense from you. I give you fair warning: If you become an agent in this enterprise of ours, you'll find me no Sir Galahad."

Drusilla met those green eyes firmly. "I assure you, Colonel Holt, I had not so far imagined you a knight in shining armor, but I thank you for your warning."

"Then you're still game, Miss Sedgewick?"

"Yes," she said after the barest hesitation. "I'm still game."

"Somehow," said MacRory Holt, "I knew you would be."

The clock on the mantelshelf chimed twice, reminding Holt that he had other business to accomplish before Paris awoke. He swung his greatcoat over his shoulders and prepared to disappear over the balcony.

"By the way," he said before leaving, "your code name is Angélique." And then he was gone, slipping away to become one with the shadows in the garden.

Dru stood silently for a moment, thinking of the havoc MacRory Holt had wrought on her life. Thanks to him, she had a code book on her writing desk, invisible ink on her dressing table, a stocking-hanger stiletto on her thigh, and, worst of all, he had put her in a state of sheer female perturbation over the fact that he hadn't tried—not even once—to take a peek at her maidenly charms.

Until now, she had always considered herself a woman of superior sense. But it was becoming increasingly obvious that when it came to MacRory Holt and the Great Game, she had no sense at all.

Chapter Seven

In Which Christabel's Generalship Is Demonstrated

Lady Christabel Toddington, assisted by her long-suffering "secretary"—one Drusilla Sedgewick—was making an inspection tour of the British Embassy, which had recently been established in the Hôtel de Charost in the rue du Faubourg Saint-Honoré. Since the Duchess of Wellington, wife to the ambassador, had not yet arrived from England, and Lady Fitzroy Somerset, wife to the ambassador's secretary, was in an Interesting Condition, the position of Inspectoress General had fallen to Christabel. It was a commission she was determined to make the most of, and she sailed into the Hôtel de Charost every bit as commandingly as the princess who had formerly resided there.

It was one of the ironies of Restoration Paris that the British Embassy was now situated in the former residence of Napoleon's sister, the beautiful and hot-blooded Princess Pauline Borghese. The Borghese mansion had been put up for sale because Pauline was determined to join her adored older brother in exile. Her palatial home and its contents had been purchased by the British government, and Christabel was to make sure that all was in order upon this islet of British soil.

Christabel and Drusilla's arrival coincided with the unpacking of the newly arrived ambassadorial dinnerware

(Sèvres, gold-rimmed with polychrome fruits and flowers on a white background), of which Christabel was pleased to approve—except for the lack of creamers.

"One never thinks about creamers," she reflected philosophically, "until one wants some cream, and by then it is too late."

More creamers, noted the long-suffering secretary, whose head was still full of MacRory Holt and the Great Game.

They passed on to the pillared public reception rooms, the scale of which, to Drusilla's surprise, passed muster with the Inspectoress General. "The Borghese woman," Christabel allowed grudgingly, "had quite a good sense of proportion—for an Ogress."

Alas, the Ogress had no sense of décor to go with it. "There are altogether too many tassels on the cushions," declared Christabel, "and the cushions are actually laid on the floor for sitting upon, if you can credit that. The place looks like an Indian *seraglio,* and from what I hear of La Borghese, it wouldn't surprise me if she hadn't cavorted here with a sultan or two."

Whereupon Drusilla made the following notations: *Tassels off the cushions. Cushions off the floor. No cavorting with sultans in the public reception rooms.*

The ambassador's living quarters were next, and when Christabel began to speak of removing paintings from the walls, Drusilla felt obliged to protest. "Surely we must leave that for Her Grace to decide when she arrives."

"Except," countered Christabel tartly, "that Kitty Wellesley is incapable of deciding whether the sun will rise on the morrow. She is the worst ditherer I've ever met, and she has no French to speak of"—this from Christabel!—"so I cannot think how she will get on as an ambassador's lady. And do you know what her favorite pastime is?"

Drusilla was forced to confess that she had no idea what the Duchess of Wellington's favorite pastime might be.

"Knitting carpet slippers," answered Christabel, rolling her eyes heavenward. "She plies her needles constantly and turns out more carpet slippers than a Yorkshire stockinger. It all comes from marrying so late in life. She was a faded spinster of thirty-four and already eccentric when she married Wellington. You should make a mental note of that, Dru."

Drusilla did indeed make a mental note, but Christabel would not have liked it.

They trudged out into the garden park, which they found to be impressive in size, though bare and sere in this autumn season. As they wandered among fountains, fishponds, arbor trellises, and shrubbery, the Inspectoress General dictated many pronouncements about the proper arrangement of garden parks.

Drusilla was dutifully recording these pronouncements into her leather-bound notebook when Christabel came to such an abrupt, screeching halt on the path that Drusilla nearly trod on her heels.

"Look at those statues there!" commanded Christabel. "Did you ever see anything so unbecoming? Make a note to have them removed at once."

Pencil poised above her notebook, Dru leaned over to read the brass plaque affixed to the pedestal of the nearest offending sculpture. "But these are classical Grecian statues," she reported to the Inspectoress General, "brought back from Greece by Napoleon himself!"

"Humph! Stolen from Greece by Napoleon himself is more like it—as if anyone with taste would make off with statues of half-naked women guzzling wine."

"But Christa, these are bacchantes, female devotees of Bacchus, the god of wine. Running about half-naked and drinking from wineskins is what they are supposed to do."

"Not on British soil, they don't," said Christabel decidedly. "They must be got rid of immediately."

Get the bacchantes to a nunnery, wrote her secretary with a resigned sigh.

It was another excruciating hour before the inspection tour finally ended, during which time Christabel interrogated all the principal servants of the establishment with the vigor of Torquemada at his most inquisitory. Having properly terrified the domestic staff, the Inspectoress General and her secretary were finally departing when Lord Fitzroy Somerset approached them, asking leave to present the personable-looking, fair-haired young man in his company.

Leave to make the introduction was immediately granted, since personable-looking, fair-haired young men must necessarily be of interest to an inveterate matchmaker like Christabel.

The young gentleman's name was revealed to be Mr. Farnshaw Eggleston.

"Mr. Eggleston," his lordship further informed them, "hails from Wiltshire and is making a Grand Tour of the Continent."

Christabel pricked up her ears at this intelligence. Making the Grand Tour was a pastime much favored by young men of means—young *unmarried* men of means. Belle Toddington needed a young, unmarried man of means to remedy her greatest failure as a social arbiter: her inability to promote an eligible match (or any match at all, for that matter) for Miss Drusilla Sedgewick. A whole Season had already been devoted to this undertaking, and still Drusilla remained unwed—which relegated her to the status of an unfinished project as far as Christabel was concerned.

"And so Mr. Eggleston," chirped Christabel, "are you

touring alone or in company?" (By which inquiry she meant, *Are you encumbered with a wife, sir?*)

"I am in the company of," answered Mr. Eggleston, certainly unaware of how much Lady Toddington was anticipating the predicate of this particular sentence, "a learned divine familiar with the Continent. And learned he is, I must say," added the young man ruefully. "The old fellow can prose on by the hour about every building that has four walls and a ceiling. Seems like every Frenchie edifice we come upon is an architectural marvel."

Christabel beamed upon the unencumbered Mr. Farnshaw Eggleston, pleased to learn that he was wealthy enough to afford a bear leader.

It was upon the subject of this very personage that Mr. Eggleston next touched. "Unfortunately, my gentleman companion has succumbed to a temporary stomach complaint—too much rich food, if you ask me. So I am forced to stay on in Paris alone until he is recovered."

Christabel was more pleased than ever with Mr. Eggleston's traveling companion. "Then Miss Sedgewick and I shall see something of you, sir, while you are here. You must feel free to seek out our company as often as you like. In fact, Lord Fitzroy shall arrange for you to attend the Duke's upcoming reception in honor of the Comte d'Artois."

Fitzroy Somerset, secretary to the Duke of Wellington in wartime as well, knew a general's order had been given, and so hastened to say that this could indeed be arranged.

Mr. Eggleston was happily taken aback by the prospect of attending such an august affair. "I must say, I'd no notion of being invited to an entertainment where I might encounter royalty."

Christabel favored him with a sweetly predatory smile. "Oh, we shall keep you right royally entertained during your stay in Paris, Mr. Eggleston. Won't we, Drusilla?"

Once she and Christabel had gained their carriage, Drusilla ungritted her teeth sufficiently to say, "I know what you are about, Christa, and I won't have it."

Christabel was undismayed. "I might have known you would be disagreeable about this, Dru. Well, no matter. I intend to take charge of Mr. Farnsworth Eggleston for as long as he is in Paris. Possibly you will warm toward him once you have become more acquainted."

"I shan't warm to him, I tell you, so there is no point in taking charge of him on my account."

She was ignored, for Christabel's wandering wits had meandered down another, even more appalling avenue of inquiry. "If you and Mr. Eggleston were to marry, what will you call him in the way of a pet name? One can hardly suppose that once the bed-curtains are drawn for the night that you will continue to call him Farnsworth. Should it be 'Farnsie, my darling'? Or 'Eggy, my sweet'?"

The ghastly picture these musings conjured up caused Dru to groan audibly, this tortured utterance serving to recall Christabel to more immediate concerns. "I must discover Albinia Clatterbuck's direction in Wiltshire. She is certain to know all the county families and will doubtless be able to inform us of Mr. Eggleston's background and prospects. I shall write her at the first opportunity. Make a note of that will you, Drusilla, dear?"

Drusilla made a note. It read: *Strangle Christabel.*

"Hey there, Toddington! Move your laggardly arse, will you?"

"Ho, Toddington, you incompetent fumble-ribbons! Stir your stumps!"

Drusilla still had not got used to the custom the Parisian

coachmen had of addressing each other by the names of their employers. Their coachman, "Toddington," (who, until his removal to Paris, had been known as Alfie Pecksmith) was at this moment feathering his employer's carriage to a halt in front of the British Embassy. Since the conveyance was filled to capacity with the Toddingtons, the Thornroses, and their secretary, disembarking was a lengthy procedure, and exhortations from other drivers began to rain down upon them.

"Heave 'em out, Toddington, and get a move on!"

"Hey, Monsieur Slow-Coach, you're blocking the roadway!"

The cause of all the snarled traffic was the supper given by the Duke of Wellington in honor of the heir apparent to the French throne, the Comte d'Artois. The affair was also to be graced by the presence of the operatic *diva*, Giuseppina Grassini. The famed Italian songbird had agreed to warble in the Duke's main reception room, from which, it should be noted, all vestiges of the *seraglio* had been banished and everything was now shipshape and Bristol fashion.

Signora Grassini was an exquisitely beautiful woman with a voice to match, and it was widely rumored she had once enjoyed the romantic attentions of Bonaparte himself. She was on the Duke's arm tonight, however, a circumstance that roused Christabel to comment acidly, "If Kitty Wellesley has an ounce of sense, she will hie herself over from England without delay."

"Now, now, m'dear," soothed Lord Toddington, "when one is the conquering hero of an entire continent, it is only natural that lovely ladies will seek to be seen on your arm."

"But that is my point exactly, Charles. Being the conquering hero of an entire continent means that an entire continent's worth of females will be throwing themselves at your head."

"Just as you say, m'dear, and isn't that the young man

from Wiltshire that Fitzroy made known to you?"

His wife's frown changed to the avid expression of a well-bred bloodhound on the scent, and Dru thought resignedly that it was a wonder Christa didn't shout "View Halloo!" as she urged her party in the direction of Mr. Farnshaw Eggleston.

That unsuspecting gentleman hailed them cheerfully. "Glad to find someone who speaks English. Don't speak Froggie too well myself, so I don't know what the devil's going on half the time."

The Thornrose ladies immediately began making inquiries of Mr. Eggleston concerning several reform-minded persons who resided in Wiltshire, none of whom the young gentleman, alas, had the honor to know. Christabel then took the opportunity to mention that Drusilla was the favorite granddaughter of Lord Sedgewick of Sedgewick Downs, a personage whom the young gentleman, alas, did not have the honor to know, either.

Drusilla would have liked very much to escape Christabel's attempts to fix Mr. Eggleston's interests upon her, but after surveying the islands of guests scattered about the reception room, she saw none upon which she could safely beach herself. The company at this reception given by the hero of Europe for a Bourbon prince was quite intimidatingly Olympian, and no one, she felt, would be the least bit interested in chatting with mere Miss Drusilla Sedgewick.

Mr. Eggleston, she suspected, felt similarly intimidated, for he was moved to remark to Lady Toddington that these Frenchified entertainments certainly cast the humble gatherings of rural Wiltshire into the shade.

Christabel, who was determined that Drusilla would *love* rural Wiltshire regardless, immediately took Mr. Eggleston to task for being too severe upon his home county. "Your familiarity has doubtless bred a contempt that is not deserved, sir. Wiltshire has ever so much to commend it," declared Christabel, who had never actually been to Wiltshire and would have been unable to name any municipality of that distant shire. "Such striking scenery! Such local color and fascinating customs! And surely your neighborhood abounds with curious old legends."

Mr. Eggleston looked rather doubtful of this. "Why, as to old neighborhood legends, my lady, I can think of only one."

"Then recite it for us, sir!" commanded her ladyship brightly. "We absolutely insist upon it."

With a shrug, Mr. Eggleston complied. "Haven't heard it since my nursery days, of course, but as I recall, the legend chiefly concerns a hideous monster named Jenny Greenteeth. Supposedly, she lurks in a certain toad pond, and when she tires of her regular diet of pond scum, she roams about the shore, looking to devour lost boys or unwary milkmaids."

"How . . . quaint," said Christabel rather less brightly. "Isn't that quaint, Drusilla dear?"

"Wonderfully quaint," agreed Drusilla grimly.

A merciful *divertissement* occurred then in the form of the stir that heralded the arrival of the guest of honor, Charles-Philippe, Comte d'Artois, the youngest of the two surviving brothers of the unfortunately guillotined Louis XVI. The string orchestra struck up "The Lily of France," the lackeys cleared a path through the crowd, and the heir apparent to the French throne made his royal advance across the room to be greeted by the Duke of Wellington.

Drusilla looked with interest upon this Bourbon prince who, as grand master of the *Chevaliers de la Foi,* had intrigued unceasingly to recover his family's throne, in the course of which intrigues many of his family's enemies had gone sailing out of upper-story windows to their deaths. It seemed to Dru that the bitterness of a quarter-century's exile was strongly marked upon the face of the comte, and though reconciliation was supposedly the watchword of the reestablished Bourbons, the Comte d'Artois did not look like a man who was ready to be reconciled.

Mr. Eggleston, who was standing in her company, apparently agreed. "Sourest-looking Frenchie I ever saw," he observed in his downright way before asking her permission to depart upon the important business of finding out in which room the refreshments were being offered.

Christabel was much vexed at Mr. Eggleston's escape, for she had meant to serve up Drusilla alongside the cold collation. Her battle plan had called for the matched pair to go into dinner together, but she was prevented from carrying out this strategy by unforeseen circumstances in the person of Thomas Clarkson, another apostle of abolition who, like the Thornrose sisters, was traveling abroad, both to tour and to proselytize.

No sooner had Mr. Clarkson borne away the Thornrose sisters to discuss the latest development in their crusade than Lord Toddington was summoned from his wife's side to wait upon the Duke and the Comte d'Artois.

By then, Mr. Eggleston had vanished from the room, and Christabel took the opportunity to chastise Drusilla for letting him slip away. "If only you would exert yourself to be captivating, Mr. Eggleston might not be so eager to escape."

"I see no point," countered Drusilla, "in exerting myself to captivate when I haven't the least wish to capture Mr. Eggleston."

She was, of course, ignored by Christabel, who said decidedly, "Since neither of us is engaged at the moment, we shall simply contrive to encounter Mr. Eggleston in the dining parlor."

"In point of fact," said Dru, equally decidedly, "I am already engaged, Christa. I am on my way to join the Thornrose ladies and Mr. Clarkson. Mr. Clarkson is the author, you know, of *A History of the Abolition of the African Slave Trade.*" She did not bother to undertake the futile exercise of inquiring if Christabel had read the book but concluded in her firmest tones, "I am greatly interested to hear what Mr. Clarkson has to say."

She turned away from Christabel, preparing to flee, but then gasped and turned back just as quickly, for coming toward them was the one person whom she had hoped *not* to see tonight—the Chevalier de Saint-Armand—or the *faux* Chevalier de Saint-Armand, whichever the case might be.

"On second thought," she told the nonplussed Christabel, "perhaps we ought to seek out Mr. Eggleston after all."

Too late. The chevalier was upon them with remarkable speed, smiling gleamingly at Christabel with all those white teeth.

"My Lady Toddington, Mademoiselle Sedgewick. Well met."

Drusilla could not have disagreed more, but Christabel seemed as ready as ever to be diverted by the chevalier's gallantries. And though he said nothing untoward, nothing that the listening Miss Sedgewick need report back to her ladyship's husband, still the chevalier managed to breathe masculine sensuality like heat from a banked furnace. Without a doubt he had the Frenchman's knack for heating the blood and melting the bones of susceptible females.

Whether Christabel was susceptible, Drusilla could not ascertain, but there was another equally concerned about the possibility, for coming across the floor with the obvious intention of joining their threesome was Lord Toddington, and with him, the Comte d'Artois.

Drusilla felt a sudden tautening of her nerves. She knew instinctively that Lord Toddington had engineered this encounter in order to test Guy de Saint-Armand. Saint-Armand would be put to the ordeal of an interview with the Comte d'Artois, who often boasted that his princely nostrils could detect the odor of a republican spy at twenty paces. And if Saint-Armand betrayed himself in any way, the comte's fanatical followers in the *Chevaliers de La Foi* would soon have their knives out and the windows open for the false chevalier.

Dru cast a quick glance at the handsome Frenchman who stood by her side, the very picture of gay unconcern as the Bourbon prince approached. But if the chevalier was indeed a Bonapartist agent, he must surely know that in facing the Comte d'Artois, he was facing death.

Christabel, unaware of the currents of intrigue eddying about her empty golden head, was at her most vivacious as her husband presented her to the comte. Drusilla was also presented (as the favorite granddaughter of Lord Sedgewick of Sedgewick Downs), but only cursory attention was paid to her as befitted her status as a minor player in the drama.

Lord Toddington, his spy master's identity concealed behind his frank diplomatist's features, then begged leave to present the Chevalier de Saint-Armand.

The comte considered the young chevalier. "Ah, yes . . . we are entertaining a petition concerning the return of the Saint-Armand estates, are we not?"

The royal "we" came very naturally to the Comte d'Artois, Dru noticed.

"It is gracious of you to mention it, Your Highness," responded the chevalier smoothly, "but I would not tax you with the matter upon this festive occasion."

"On the contrary, Chevalier, the return of the rightful inheritances of our ancient nobility is a subject we are always eager to consider. We presume you have had the occasion to visit your estate? How do you find it?"

If you, in fact, have an estate to find. This was the unspoken thought that echoed in everyone's mind—everyone's mind, that is, except Christabel's. She was wondering why her usually cuddlesome Charles was looking so anvil-faced. Perhaps it was indigestion.

The young chevalier paused for a long moment, then answered the Comte d'Artois in a voice that was passionate with emotion. "I shall tell you, Your Highness, how I find my estate. I found it desecrated, vilely desecrated."

The comte's eyebrows rose. "How so?"

"I find that my family's ancient *château* is now owned and occupied by a tradesman, a dealer in cheeses."

D'Artois's hand flicked in an austere gesture of distaste.

"As for the lands granted to us in the time of Charles the Bald, they are now divided up into a hundred peasant farms."

"How tragic," the comte was heard to murmur, "to see the ancient demesnes parceled out to the Jacquerie."

"And what was once our stable for farm animals now becomes a school for the children of the peasantry."

"Well, as to that," remarked the Comte d'Artois with ponderous humor, "at least the inhabitants of your stables have not much changed."

From this remark, Drusilla divined that universal literacy, a favorite Thornrose cause, was one that obviously had not found favor with the Comte d'Artois. Or perhaps the Comte d'Artois sought to goad the chevalier, to catch a flash of republican anger in his eyes. But if the flash of anger was there,

Dru did not see it, and the chevalier's answer was perfection itself.

" 'Tis true, Your Highness, that there is little difference between the cattle and the peasant. However, when, by the King's graciousness, I am proclaimed rightful master of my estate, I assure you that the livestock will be back in the stable, where it belongs, and the peasant children will be back in the fields, where they belong."

"A laudable ambition, Chevalier, but at present we can address only the petitions of those whose estates have been kept intact. The reversion of estates held by multiple owners must wait until our rule is more firmly entrenched. In the meantime, we counsel you to make every attempt to buy back your estate parcel by parcel."

The chevalier bowed deferentially. "I have received this wise advice from other quarters, yet it makes my blood boil to think of chaffering with peasants for my birthright."

"We know full well the emotion of which your speak," intoned the comte, "and we look forward to the day when there will be a reckoning for the noble families who have been so grievously wronged. In the meanwhile," he concluded as he prepared to move on, "be assured, sir, that you have commended yourself to our notice, and once we take notice, we do not forget."

If the chevalier was indeed a Bonapartist agent, Drusilla did not think that the comte's parting sentiments would be at all comforting. But then, if the chevalier was who he seemed, he would doubtless be pleased, and so he seemed, turning to Christabel to remark, "That was a great stroke of civility on your husband's part to make me known to the comte."

"Yes, Charles is very thoughtful that way," said Christabel somewhat distractedly, for during the boring exchange between the chevalier and the comte, when no one was paying her any mind, her wandering concentration had been seized by the sight of Giuseppina Grassini, once again flaunting herself on the Duke of Wellington's arm, positively clinging to him like an Italian horseleech.

This was a sight that afforded Christabel no pleasure. Like many of her countrywomen, she nursed an unhappy suspicion that the Creator had unfairly endowed the dark and flashing-eyed Latin beauties with an exotic feminine allure that English ladies could never hope to match.

Closing her fan with a guillotine snap, she was once more the Inspectoress General of the British Embassy. "I had better see that all has been put in readiness for La Grassini's musical presentation. Obviously she is too engaged in flirting with the Duke to attend to such mundane matters. Do you care to accompany me, Chevalier?"

"To the ends of the Earth, my divinity!"

"No need for that, sir. We are only going as far as the music room." This remark was testily spoken, for Christa was in no good humor. "Do you come with us, Drusilla?"

Dru agreed resignedly that she would, for where the chevalier followed Christabel, it was clearly her duty to follow the chevalier.

Her mind continued to dwell, however, on the incident she had just witnessed, for she knew that it was she who had set events into motion by informing Lord Toddington of her suspicions about Saint-Armand. And if these suspicions were false, then the chevalier had been monstrously wronged.

But if her suspicions were correct, then Guy de Saint-Armand would prove a formidable foe. If he was a *poseur,* he had played his role to perfection just now, and he seemed every bit as cool and cunning as Colonel MacRory Holt.

Chapter Eight

In Which Drusilla Becomes
a Player in the Great Game

The next afternoon at teatime, Christabel flounced tempestuously into the sitting room, a copy of the *Le Bon Gen* magazine in her hand. "Look at this," she commanded, thrusting the journal under Drusilla's nose. "Look at this, and tell me if it means what I think it means."

The magazine was folded open to a drawing entitled *Voilà les Anglais*, which showed a dowdy pair of English tourists being mocked behind their backs by the fashionable French. On the opposite page, above a caption in French that read *Latest Fashions among the English*, there was depicted a bevy of flaxen-haired, apple-cheeked, bosomy ladies wearing costumes that looked to have come from the Tudor period.

"I'm rather afraid," said Dru, handing the magazine to the nearest Thornrose sister, "that it does mean what you think it means, Christa—that the editors are satirizing the wardrobes of the touring English. It is rather cleverly done, you must admit."

But this satire cut altogether too close to the bone for clothes-happy Christabel, whose beauty was of the flaxen-haired, apple-cheeked, bosomy variety. "I think it is odious and horrible and insulting to our country. Charles, you must bring it to the attention of His Grace."

Lord Toddington looked up from his afternoon copy of

the *Moniteur* and said mildly, "I doubt, my dear, that the Duke would find a caricature of our fashions of much concern, particularly when compared to the invective being heaped upon him personally in the press. Every time his name appears in print, he is referred to as the 'Duke of Villainton,' and we have a great fear that the journals are whipping up public sentiment against him to a dangerous extent."

"That's just what I mean, Charles! These French journalists have altogether too much license. I tell you I am not sorry for waiting until the beginning of the year to have little Charlotte brought over from London. I should not want our child exposed to such things."

"She's only four years old, m'dear," said his lordship soothingly. "I doubt that a satire on English fashion would much discompose her."

Christabel turned a gimlet eye upon him. "She is my daughter, sir, and I assure you, discompose her it would!"

"Just as you say, m'dear," agreed Lord Toddington, wisely changing tack, "but I fear that for the time being, we have no choice but to resign ourselves to suffering French hostility to both our fashions and our Duke."

The foregoing conversation proved eerily prophetic. Several days later, a hail of bullets whistled past the Duke of Wellington as he attended a military review in the Champs-de-Mars. The incident, needless to say, received mention in Lord Toddington's latest dispatch.

From the Rt. Hon. Lord Toddington to the Foreign Office
Private & Secret
Item: There is in Paris a growing class of dangerous men bent on stirring up trouble under the command of Excelsior.

Col. H. is instructed to redouble his efforts in the matter. . . .

At the same time, there came to Miss Drusilla Sedgewick a message by way of *Childe Harold*: TONIGHT. AT TEN. OUTSIDE THE BACK POSTERN.

A coating of white frost crackled beneath Dru's sensible shoes as she slipped through the back gate of the Hôtel Toddington. At first she saw no one in the deserted mews that ran behind the garden parks of the rue de Florentin. Moments later a mounted figure clopped out of the shadows—Holt, wearing a workman's coat and riding a poor sort of swaybacked mare. An English officer would disdain such a mount, but a country bumpkin, a *Jacques Bonhomme*, might ride into the city on just such an animal.

And "Jacques," it seemed, would have his "Jeannette" riding pillion, for Holt reached down and with one hand easily pulled her up behind him. Drusilla could not help but find herself most improperly aware of Colonel Holt's masculine lineaments, which came in the form of wide shoulders, a hard waist, and a horseman's powerful thighs. But since it was either cling to these lineaments or fall off his sorry steed, she felt she could hardly be blamed for taking an interest in them.

"Where are we going?" she murmured in French against his shoulder.

"To the Bonne Belle tavern down by the river."

"Why there?"

"Because I must find a man who doesn't usually want to be found, but when he is to be found, it is through a contact I have at the Bonne Belle."

"And what part am I to play in your search?"

"I want this man to have a look at you, and for you to have a look at him, for someday one of you may have to call upon the other for help. Aside from that, tonight you are to be nothing but window dressing, uninquisitive, closemouthed window dressing . . . unless, of course, I am forced to permit you to open your mouth and sing."

"Sing?"

"It's the custom in the riverine establishments for female patrons to sing a song if called upon. Refusing to do so would be considered bad form. You do know a French song or two, I presume."

"I know some of the classical ballads."

"I was thinking of something less literary, something more in the line of what you might hear in a barracks."

"You mean songs that are . . . not quite the thing."

"I mean songs that are very definitely not the thing."

"And what kind of female do you think I am," she asked in a chill voice, "that I would know such songs?"

"The kind of female," answered Holt, "who would be useful to me in a place like the Bonne Belle."

Drusilla sighed inwardly, remembering her youth in a rooming house on Thames Street where she had learned a number of things her mother would not approve of from the *émigré* boarders.

"I suppose I do know one song like . . . that."

"Somehow I thought you might," said Holt.

Dru fell silent, pondering the disquieting news that she might be called upon to sing the one and only naughty French song in her repertoire. Once again, she knew herself to be in over her head, and she supposed that before the night was over she would be in deeper still, led thither by MacRory Holt. Yet the thought of turning back never crossed her mind.

Their mount plodded steadily along through the intersecting mazes of mews, bystreets, and alleyways. The thoroughfares were turning meaner, for they were now deep in the river district, one of the city's less salubrious purlieus. Public drunkenness seemed to be the major neighborhood pastime. Beggars also abounded, some of them so pestiferous-looking that Drusilla could only be glad she had undergone the smallpox vaccination, that modern medicinal marvel the Thornrose ladies championed so ardently through their membership in the British National Vaccine Society.

Holt was now guiding their mount (Filbertine, by name) off the main thoroughfare and into a narrow alley that ended in a crude livery stable, the stalls built against the sides of the tenement building. The proprietor and Holt dickered spiritedly over the stabling fee. Eventually the transaction was concluded to their mutual satisfaction, with the liveryman accusing Holt of driving him into insolvency and Holt accusing the liveryman of extortionate pricing.

With Filbertine safely lodged, they went forward on foot, their destination, the Bonne Belle Tavern and Lodging House, which advertised itself to passersby by means of a painted wooden sign swinging beneath a lantern light. The tavern was situated in the last of a long block of row houses and was obviously a gathering place for the rowdier inhabitants of the neighborhood. Sounds of raucous mirth spilled out of the tavern, along with the strains of rollicking music, for the rivermen of the Seine liked to sing every bit as much as did the gondoliers of Venice.

Spilling out of the tavern along with the sounds of music and mirth came two drunken men trading fisticuffs and piquantly Gallic insults.

May God cut out your Adam's apple!

May the devil take off your whatnot!

The Bonne Belle was obviously no place to bring a lady,

84

and so of course MacRory Holt waltzed Miss Drusilla Sedgewick inside the establishment straightaway.

The interior of the tavern was dim and smoky and full of watchful eyes, all of which seemed to be following Holt and Drusilla's progress to a corner table. Dru tried to look non-chalant, as if she commonly frequented watering holes where bargemen, canal workers, and rivermen diced and sang and swore as they filled their tankards and themselves brimful of wine.

As for the women of the Bonne Belle, they struck her as being neither *bonne* nor *belle,* though some of them did strike her as being available for brief rental if the price was right. The belles of the Bonne Belle were meanwhile eyeing her and Holt back—eyeing Holt in the way women always eyed a handsome man, eyeing Dru as if sizing her up to see if she was *chanteuse* enough to hold on to her handsome man. The thought of eventually having to perform before such a rowdy crowd caused a cold feeling to settle in the pit of Dru's stomach.

She was temporarily distracted from that fear, however, when what looked like a snake hurtled onto their table. She almost—but not quite—let out a scream before she realized that it was actually an eel, thrown by a drunken crowd of eel-catchers at the next table. The nerveless Holt calmly picked up the writhing creature, pronounced it a fine spec-imen, and tossed it back.

A waiter named Gaspar came to their table bringing wine that Drusilla doubted she would ever be thirsty enough to want to imbibe. Holt and Gaspar engaged in cryptic con-verse, at the conclusion of which Gaspar took off his apron and went out the door as if on some errand. Holt picked up his wine and leaned back in his chair, eyelids half lowered over watchful eyes, which did not blink in the least surprise when, a quarter-hour later, they were joined at their table by a lithe and swarthy man who had a single gold ring glittering in his earlobe.

So suddenly had the man appeared that Dru could only think he had entered the back way. Holt was not in the least discomposed. He grasped the earringed newcomer's hand with evident affection and was greeted with equal affection in Spanish-accented French.

"Rory, my favorite *giorgio!*"

"Ramon, my favorite *gitano!*" replied Holt with a quick grin. "I've been seeking you for weeks, *compadre.* You make yourself hard to find in this great city."

Ramon spread his hands in a what-would-you-do gesture. "Alas, a *gitano* chieftain tarries not long in any one place. And the police of Paris are not *simpático.* A small disagreement over certain missing items of price requires me to disappear. The police are ordered to arrest me on sight, and there is a fat reward posted for the return of these items. Ah, well, 'tis a Gypsy's lot. Wherever we travel, the story is the same." His dark eyes flicked to Drusilla. "But I see you travel in fair company these days, Rory."

It was Holt's turn to shrug. "Things have changed since the Peninsula. Allow me to introduce Mademoiselle Angélique."

"A pleasure, Mademoiselle . . . Angélique," said the Gypsy chieftain with just the faintest unnecessary stress on her code name, which told Dru he was well aware that this was not her real name. "And so," he asked her then, "do you carry the knife of the great MacRory Holt?"

"Why . . . yes." The admission was surprised out of her. "But how did you know?"

"Because it is a trick I taught him in the days when we rode with the *guerrilleros,* one of many lessons I taught him as we sat about the campfire, eh, Rory?"

"I apprehend," said Holt dryly, "that you now propose to lower my crest by telling mademoiselle how you taught me the value of Gypsy fighting."

"But of course, for the story is too amusing to forego," answered Ramon, his dark, mobile face lit with a mischievous smile. "You see, mademoiselle, when our Rory here was but a boy lieutenant, he scoffed at the Gypsy fighting ways. So I took from our campfire a charred stick the length of a knife and challenged him to defend himself from me if as from one who attacks with a dagger. Eventually he disarmed me, of course, for he was a strong young bull, but not before his white shirt was so marked with charcoal that it could be seen he would be a gutted carcass had I come after him with a real blade."

Holt shook his head in rueful remembrance. "Ruined my last decent shirt, you scoundrel."

"And picked your Scotch pocket while I was at it," added Ramon reminiscently. "Ah, those were the days."

A burst of drunken song from a nearby table brought them back to the present, and after taking a deep draught of wine, Ramon asked, "So, Rory, what do you do here, prowling about Paris like a wolf among the jackals? Should you not be back in your craggy Highlands now that the Corsican is penned?"

"Whether the Corsican stays penned is the question, my friend."

"Ah, bah! So that is the game you play. Oh, there is much talk that *He* will return, that is true enough. But you know the French."

"I know," said Holt flatly, "that Henri Lazare is in Paris, and that he plots Wellington's death and Bonaparte's escape."

The Gypsy chief went still at the mention of Henri Lazare, and a hot glitter came into his dark eyes. "Tell me where Lazare is, and I will make an end to him."

"A pleasing prospect," allowed Holt, "only I don't know where he is. Remember that Lazare is on his home ground, with informants in high places and a city full of Bonapartist sympathizers to aid him. Furthermore, the French army remains Bonapartist to a man, as do the police, which is why the Bourbons have been forced to set up their own secret police."

Ramon considered this. "You are right, Rory. One cannot strike at Henri Lazare without certain knowledge of his whereabouts. He is four-faced, that one, like an ancient idol of the East that sees in all directions. You cannot easily get behind his back."

"And well I know it," said Holt grimly. "Don't forget, Lazare and I cat-and-moused about the Peninsula for three long years."

"I forget nothing of the evil of Henri Lazare," said Ramon, "not the ambushes, not the poisonings—nothing. I shall put out the word, not only among my Andalusian brethren, but to Gypsies of every nationality. We shall watch for Henri Lazare, for we are in many places and see many things, and in this matter, we would be an army of eyes and ears."

"My thanks, old friend," said Holt gratefully. "I sought you out in the hope you would do me just this favor."

"It is you who do us the favor, Rory, to put us on the scent of Lazare. Him, we have cursed. Him, we do not forget."

A shadow fell across their table. It was the waiter, Gaspar, who, Dru realized, was staring at her most particularly. Looking past him, she realized that the entire clientele of the tavern was staring at her as well.

"Mademoiselle," announced Gaspar in a voice of doom, "the patrons call for a song from you." He put down more wine before the two men and in a swift undertone told them further bad news. "Secret police agents have entered the tavern, and uniformed *gendarmes* are riding into the district. It would be well for Don Ramon to be away."

"Mademoiselle," said Holt loudly, "would be charmed to sing a song." Ignoring mademoiselle's look of frank horror, he went on in a voice that brooked no opposition, "Stand away from the table, my angel, so they can see you the better."

Dimly Dru understood that Holt meant for Don Ramon to slip away while everyone's attention—most particularly the attention of the secret police agents—was centered on the spectacle of Drusilla Sedgewick trying to entertain a tavernful of eel-flinging river denizens. Paralyzed by stage fright, a fear she had never until this minute realized she was subject to, she found herself unable to move despite the cries of *"Chanson! Chanson!"* that echoed throughout the tavern.

If only, she thought desperately as a cold sweat of fear broke out on her forehead, if only the earth would open up and swallow her . . .

Holt leaned close to her, his eyes hard, his voice soft. "Get up and sing, my angel, or I'll be forced to haul you out of that chair and beat you the way any other riverman would beat his woman if she refused to sing. If you won't give them a song, we'll have to give them a domestic drama instead."

Through her fog of fear, Dru saw that he meant what he said, that he wanted his old comrade safely away at any cost, and in her heart she bitterly rued the day that she had ever become involved with MacRory Holt.

Somehow she struggled to her feet and walked a few paces away from their table.

The roistering crowd fell silent. She opened her mouth, and sounds emerged that she hoped would approximate the song she had learnt in her girlhood from a French *émigrée* actress who had taken rooms in a certain shabby-genteel boarding establishment in Thames Street, London.

It was a typical piece of French ribaldry that she now attempted to sing, full of *double entendres* that invested innocent-sounding phrases with meanings that were far from chaste. The song's refrain was far from innocent as well:

Lift your skirts, Marietta, lift your skirts, Marietta.
Lift your skirts, Marietta, a yard above the knee. . . .

Among the kaleidoscopic worries that whirled through her brain was the fear that the song's humor (such as it was) might be over the heads of tavern-goers. But, no, she heard bursts of laughter, a series of guffaws, and, several eternities later, when she finally sang the last refrain, whistles and calls of *"Encore! Encore!"*

It seemed easier to do the bidding of the crowd than to disappoint them, so she stumbled through the song again. By now, her audience was convulsed with laughter, and she supposed that perhaps she possessed some hitherto undiscovered talent for musical comedy.

But when the last quavering note was sung, she turned around to discover that, in fact, *she* was the comedy.

Don Ramon, the Gypsy chieftain, had vanished, and replacing him in MacRory Holt's company—on MacRory Holt's lap, to be precise—was a bold-eyed daughter of the river. Her lips were whispering against Holt's ear, one hand was entwined in his thick brown hair, and the other slid caressingly inside his shirtfront. Holt appeared to be enjoying these attentions considerably. The patrons at the Bonne Belle were beside themselves with mirth as they beheld the spectacle of one of their resident belles snatching the hapless *chanteuse*'s beau.

To say that Drusilla was livid would not be putting too fine a point upon it. Here she was, the object of all eyes, dying a thousand deaths before an audience that would make an experienced *diva* quail, whilst Holt was sitting there cuddling this river doxy.

Hardly knowing what she did, Dru advanced on the couple, and when the doxy smiled up at her insolently, she lost the last shreds of her temper and pushed the girl off Holt's lap.

"You detestable pig of a man," she hissed at Holt—in French, fortunately, for most of the tavern habitués were attending interestedly to the melodrama, foremost among them the river girl, who bounced back to her feet, giving every indication of preparing to do battle.

(In this dreadful circumstance, Drusilla hoped that her late parents were not at this particular moment looking down upon her from heaven, because it was now apparent that all their efforts to raise her as a proper English lady had failed miserably.)

When the river girl came at her, fists cocked like a prize-fighter's, Dru, who was considerably taller and longer of reach, gave the petite pugilist a shove that sent her careering into the eel-catchers' table, knocking it over, in the midst, apparently, of a heated argument over a dicing throw. Tankards, coins, eel baskets, eels, eel-catchers, and the suspect dice went flying.

Holt, seeing that his Gypsy comrade was safely away, decided it was time to give thought to his and Drusilla's withdrawal, for he suspected that a typical riverfront brawl was now brewing in which every man, woman, child, dog, and cat could be expected to mix in.

He grabbed Dru's arm, shouting in French for the benefit of anyone who might be attending, "You win, my beautiful hussy!

I'm yours. Take me upstairs, and have your way with me!"

Ignoring the look she gave him, which told him quite clearly that she would much prefer to bounce a wine tankard off his skull, he slung her over his shoulder and mounted the stairs that led to the lodging-house portion of the tavern.

No sooner had the *chanteuse* and her impetuous beau made this dramatic exit than a squad of uniformed *gendarmes* burst into the tavern, scattering the patrons and knocking over furniture.

"Seize them! Seize them all!" shouted the sergeant, who, failing to discover the particular criminal he was after, had decided to arrest everyone on general principle.

The melee was properly joined then, for the rivermen of the Seine were a fractious lot who needed little or no encouragement to brawl with the police. Nor did they have any desire to be carted off to the Ministry of Police's notorious Temple Prison, where each dark cell was equipped with its own set of thumbscrews, the one remaining method of torture that had not been outlawed in France.

As the river folk struggled to get out of the tavern and the *gendarmes* struggled to keep them in, the sounds of chairs crashing and bottles smashing and the vociferous cries of the combatants floated upward to the second-story room where the *chanteuse* and her beau had taken refuge.

Though her exit had been an extremely mortifying one, Dru was glad to get out of the taproom of the Bonne Belle any way she could. She had a great many things to say to Holt, none of them complimentary, but she also realized that now was not the moment to voice them, not with a near-riot going on beneath their feet and police storming the building.

The bolt-hole that she and Holt had taken refuge in was a small windowless bedroom with no key in the lock—not that a lock would do any good anyway, Holt told her sourly, because the *gendarmes* would only smash in the door once they got the rowdy crowd downstairs in hand.

"Why are we hiding?" Drusilla demanded. "We've done nothing wrong."

"Except for being seen in the Ramon's company," snapped Holt, "and I don't care to have to explain that—or anything else—while I'm having the screws put to me in a prison cell."

Shouts and clatter resounded at the bottom of the stairs, and it was obvious that any second, the *gendarmes* would be up those stairs. Holt unbuttoned his shirt and in one smooth, long-muscled motion shucked it and his coat off his shoulders.

Dru's first thought was that she had been quite right to admire Holt's manly lineaments, for unclothed they were even more admirable. Her second thought was that the famous bayonet scar actually did exist, for she could see it curling whitely around his ribs. Her third thought came out in a startled squeak—in English. *"What are you doing?"*

Holt frowned at her fiercely for this linguistic lapse. He put the heel of his hand over her mouth, toppled her back onto the lumpy bed, and dropped down on top of her, his warm, heavy weight pressing her into the straw mattress. Shouts and crashes from down the hallway indicated that the *gendarmes* were now searching the upstairs rooms.

"Pray try to look engaged," Holt instructed her.

"Engaged in what?" Dru managed to whisper, looking up into the handsome face so close to hers, the oddly light eyes shining down into hers.

The answer came as Holt's mouth closed upon hers in a long, deep, wine-spiced kiss. Having never been kissed before, she had no defense against that kiss. Her hands slid up his arms to grip his bare shoulders, and her mouth clung to his.

She may have forgotten the *gendarmes,* but they had not forgotten their mission, and in the next instant the door flew open.

Holt lifted his head and shouted a curse.

A *gendarme* drew up short in the doorway, perceiving that he had discovered a couple *in flagrante delicto.* But seeing that the man was not the dark-haired Spanish Gypsy they sought, he backed out of the room, for he was not without a typical Frenchman's appreciation of *l'amour,* and it was obvious that this pair must have been otherwise engaged when the mischief was brewing downstairs. He was, therefore, content to shout gruffly at them before closing the door, "Everyone into the prison vans! By order of the Police Generale!"

"An order we'll be pleased to disobey, *mon ami,*" muttered Holt, rolling off Dru and reaching for his shirt and jacket. Dru got limply to her feet, feeling as if she had been scorched from head to toe by an infernal flame.

Holt was shrugging on his clothes and listening to what was happening down in the street where the protesting rivermen were being forced into horse-drawn police vans.

"We've got to get out the back," he told Dru.

They darted across the hall, only to find that all but one of the row of bedrooms were windowless. The happy discovery of that single window was considerably diminished by the fact that it was situated directly over the back entrance of the Bonne Belle, which was, at the moment, being guarded by four *gendarmes.*

Dru's heart sank. She was beginning to regard the Bonne Belle tavern as a species of hell from which she might never escape. Holt, a more practiced escape artist, was undaunted. He led her up a back staircase to the third story, which also boasted a window, which was connected to the rest of the row house windows by a narrow ledge.

"You can't mean for us to walk on *that?*" she hissed.

But Holt was serious. He was, in fact, insanely enthusiastic.

"Couldn't be better," he whispered, swinging a leg over the windowsill. "Come on."

He's enjoying himself, thought Drusilla bitterly as she gathered her skirts and climbed out after him. *The man thrived on danger.* And as unreasonable as it seemed, it was his way to force her to prove her mettle to him, no matter what kind of appalling situation she found herself in.

She knew better than to look down and could only pray that the *gendarmes* wouldn't look up to see the two figures inching along the ledge two stories above their heads. Every ten feet there was a window, and Holt hoped to get into one of the adjoining establishments this way. But one after another, they found the windows shuttered and bolted against them, either on account of the disturbance or the cold.

And what would happen when they reached the end of ledge and still had not got inside? This dire possibility was looming nearer and nearer when they discovered that the next to the last window shutter was unbolted and slightly open, showing a flicker of candlelight from within.

Gingerly Holt pushed the shutters inward, then vaulted over the sill, with Dru following. It was then that they realized they were not alone in the room, that the bedchamber—or more precisely, the bed—was occupied, the sheets billowing like foam upon a bounding sea of love.

Dru gasped and fixed her eyes ceilingward. The man and the women in the bed froze.

Holt was not abashed. *"Mille pardons, mes amis!"* he told the stunned couple on the bed as he pushed Dru—her gaze still determinedly averted—across the room and out the door.

The frustrated Romeo in the bed was not amused and

began shouting in French, "Intruders! Robbers!" at the top of his lungs as he sought his breeches.

Half a dozen heads popped over the railing of the stairwell that Holt had been about to descend. Altering course, he thrust Dru to the end of the hall and found a shuttered window, which he kicked open to reveal the first real stroke of luck to come their way this ill-starred evening.

Below the window was a hay wagon, drawn up apparently because the street ahead was crowded with prison wagons.

"We're in luck!" he told Dru. "Down you go now."

But Dru balked, panting out a garbled objection that hay wagons usually came equipped with pitchforks and scythes.

"Have to risk it," decided Holt, who evidently then decided she couldn't be trusted to risk it on her own.

Before she realized what he was about, he had picked her up and slung her, feet first, out the window. She felt the river wind whipping her skirts up in a way that ordinarily would have concerned her mightily had she not already been terrified of breaking a limb or being impaled upon a farm implement.

Neither of these things happened, fortunately, and an instant later, Holt thudded into the hay beside her. As they struggled to their feet, Holt's boot struck something, and a set of long iron prongs emerged from the straw less than a foot away from where Dru had landed seconds before.

"Found the pitchfork," Holt observed.

Dru shuddered, and was shuddering still, as they leapt from the wagon and made their way into the relative safety of the labyrinthine alleyways that surrounded the Bonne Belle tavern.

The reunion of MacRory Holt and his swaybacked mare Filbertine was touching to behold.

"Here you are Filly, girl," murmured Holt as he fed her a sugar lump. "Did they take good care of you, *ma belle?*"

Drusilla—bruised, aching, exhausted and nerve-shattered—leaned limply against the slatted walls of the stable, watching with increasing ire as Holt cosseted his mount just as if the ridiculous beast had borne him through dangers untold instead of merely idling about a nice, safe stall for the last few hours.

Didn't the ungrateful pig of a man realize, Dru fumed inwardly, *that she was the one who had just gone through dangers untold on his account?*

Feeling decidedly ill-used, she inquired with poisonous sweetness, "Are you not afraid that Filbertine may have taken a chill in the night air?"

"Oh, Filly's got a strong constitution," he replied breezily as he swung himself into the saddle. "She'd not have lasted long in my service otherwise." He grinned down at her. "And how is your constitution, may I ask? Not too worn down, I trust, by the evening's events."

"I believe," prevaricated Dru through gritted teeth, for she would rather die than admit the truth, "that my constitution is in tolerable condition."

"Somehow I thought it would be," he said with a knowing smile as he swung her up behind him.

Despite being bone weary, Drusilla forced herself to her best equestrienne posture and told herself sternly that she would allow herself no spineless slumping against those superb masculine lineaments.

Her thoughts, however, were not as easy to control as her posture. They kept turning, despite her best efforts, to those few moments in the bed in the Bonne Belle tavern where she had lain in Holt's arms and he had kissed her.

But with that memory also came the bitter knowledge that it was no true embrace in which he had held her, and that kiss was nothing but a spy's charade.

Chapter Nine

In Which the Plot Thickens

"You will never guess, my dear," declared Lady Christabel Toddington to her husband over a late breakfast, "what the Thornrose ladies will be engaged in while we are taking tea this afternoon with the Duchess d'Angoulême." From her ladyship's self-satisfied tone it could be safely inferred that she believed herself to have the more rewarding engagement.

Lord Toddington, a hearty morning trencherman, looked up from his laden breakfast plate with mild interest. "I confess, m'dear, I've never been able to guess what the Thornrose ladies will get up to next, so I fear you will have to put me out of my suspense and tell me."

"Well, you will scarcely credit this, Charles! Drusilla tells me they are going to call upon that French meat-embalmer fellow."

"Meat embalmer?" Lord Toddington had been on the verge of helping himself to another sausage but checked his fork in midair as he apparently thought better of it. "You mean that grocery purveyor, Appert? The one who preserves foodstuffs by boiling them in sealed bottles?"

Christabel beamed at him. "Why, yes, that is the very name Dru told me, now that I recollect. How clever you are to know that, Charles."

Lord Toddington sat back in his chair, looking thoughtful.

"What possible interest could the Thornrose ladies have in meat embalming?"

"I've no notion, really, though I hope they will not be foolish enough to actually eat any of the dreadful stuff." She made a moue of distaste. "This whole idea of *preserved* food is positively unsettling to one's stomach. It will never catch on."

"I'm afraid, m'dear, it has already caught on—in military circles, at least. Bonaparte was absolutely right when he said an army travels on its stomach. Tainted food and inadequate rations kill as many soldiers as do enemy guns. Good victualing can often mean victory before the first shot is fired. Bonaparte would have been well-nigh unstoppable had he been able to extend his marches by supplying his army with preserved rations."

"Well, then," observed Christabel brightly, "isn't it fortunate he was not able to do so."

"Oh, fortunate, indeed," said Lord Toddington of the British Secret Intelligence Department. "*Damned* fortunate."

The ride out to the Paris suburb of Massy was rendered most agreeable by the plush comfort of the Thornrose traveling carriage, an amenity especially appreciated by Drusilla, who was nursing sundry aches and bruises as a result of her previous night's adventure. In less than an hour, the carriage had left the city behind, and the Thornrose sisters and their secretary were disembarking before a walled manufactory identified by its archway sign as the HOUSE OF APPERT.

The establishment's founder, Nicholas Appert, was a man of many parts: vintner, pickler, restaurateur, brewer, baker, candy-maker. He was also an inventor whom the French government had officially proclaimed a "Benefactor of Humanity." Needless to say, any gentleman so styled would be of interest to the philanthropic-minded Thornrose ladies.

A young chemist's assistant in a leather apron showed them into a reception room. Displayed here were several copies of Monsieur Appert's famous opus, *The Art of Preserving All Kinds of Animal and Vegetable Substances for Several Years.* Framed upon the walls were press cuttings in which these same embalmed vegetables (carrots, peas, and asparagus, to be exact) were praised for "saving mankind from the tyranny of a seasonal diet by having brought spring and summer to winter." In a place of honor amongst these framed remembrances was an etching of Appert receiving his Imperial designation as a "Benefactor of Humanity."

In person, the Benefactor of Humanity proved to be a tall, thin gentlemen with a high forehead and a large balding cranium—a perfect illustrative specimen of the theory that the larger one's braincase, the more wits must be crammed inside. A passable knowledge of English was also contained in their host's impressive cranium, so Dru's translating duties were reduced to a minimum.

Having presented themselves to the scientific gentleman who had won their admiration, the Thornrose ladies proceeded to sing his praises—in triplicate, as was their usual habit.

"We are most impressed by your scholarly researches."

"We read your learned dissertation with much interest."

"We believe your hermetic process shows great promise."

"Your term *hermétique*," chimed in Drusilla, increasing the triplet to a quatrain, "is so cleverly apropos in its derivation from the Egyptian alchemical god Hermes."

"A little conceit of mine," said Monsieur Appert, looking pleased that the English ladies had grasped his classical allusion to Hermes Trismegistus, believed to have created a magical seal to make vessels impervious to outside influences.

"For you see, my dear ladies, I *have* managed to make my bottles perfectly airtight so no gas or vapor can enter or escape."

The ladies nodded wisely; then, on behalf of the assembled sisters, Miss Faith Thornrose delivered the highest encomium of all. "You are to be commended, sir, for publishing your procedures for the benefit of all mankind instead of secreting them under patent for personal financial gain."

Appert made a self-deprecating gesture. "But how should I keep my process *hermétique* to myself when the ravages of starvation are so cruel upon the human race?"

"That," said Miss Faith, "is exactly why we have sought you out, monsieur."

"It is our firm belief," went on Miss Hope, "that the lot of the poor would be much improved if the wholesome bounty of our English country gardens could be preserved and distributed in the city slums."

"It is our wish to found a society to accomplish this very thing," concluded Miss Charity.

Monsieur Appert's eyebrows rose inquiringly in his gleaming forehead. "But, ladies, do you not know that a factory for preserving foodstuffs in canisters of metal has recently opened in your homeland?"

The Thornrose ladies were indeed aware, but, alas, the metal canisters would not do.

"One must be an ironmonger to make them, and a hammer and chisel are needed to strike off the covers."

"Your sealed bottles can be used by the average householder."

"Now that hostilities have ceased between our countries, we had hoped that you would export your embalming bottles and machinery to England."

Their scientific host stared at them for an instant, a look of melancholy coming over his face. "Can it be that you gracious ladies do not know that this is most impossible?"

"Impossible? How so?"

"What can you mean, monsieur?"

"Perhaps you misunderstand us."

Appert shook his head. "My dear ladies, for nearly a year the House of Appert is"—he threw up his hands in a dramatic gesture—"boom."

"Boom?" inquired Drusilla with foreboding.

"Boom! An explosion in the middle of the night, and a great fire. By morning, the House of Appert, where once fifty workers came through the gates, is now down to the ground in ashes."

The Thornrose ladies exchanged stricken glances.

"But surely," exclaimed Dru, "you mean to rebuild!"

"Of a certainty, mademoiselle. Yet things are difficult in these unsettled times. Investors fear that one honored by the Emperor will not find favor with the monarchy. Still, we make some start already. Look for yourself."

He pulled back a brocade window curtain, and they beheld a large building in the beginning stages of construction. That a great conflagration had occurred upon the site was obvious, for numerous piles of charred beams had yet to be hauled away.

The English ladies resumed their seats in gloomy silence.

"Perhaps," Drusilla ventured hopefully to their host, "you have some other inventions that you might recommend to the ladies."

Appert's expression brightened. "I have lately had much praise for my newest *liqueur,* peppermint schnapps . . . but, then again, perhaps not," he added hastily, for it seemed likely that the somberly clad Thornrose sisters belonged to the one of those strange

English religious sects that forbade the drinking of spiritous liquors.

Then inspiration seemed to strike. Appert leapt to his feet and begged that the ladies might excuse him for a moment while he made all in readiness. When he returned, it seemed as if he meant to offer them refreshment, for his young assistant came after him, pushing a tea cart.

With the flourish of a *maître d'hôtel,* Appert removed the top from a covered bowl to reveal a heap of rather unappetizing-looking brown pellets, which he proceeded to drop into teacups of boiling water. The cups were handed round to the ladies, who stared somewhat uncertainly at the resulting infusion.

"But what is it?" Drusilla dared to ask.

"An invention for which I have much affection. I call it a bouillon tablet. It is the boiled-down essence of either beef or chicken. And it will last forever without spoilage. Drink up, ladies! Drink up!"

Not without some inward reservations, the ladies took tentative sips of their bouillon broth and found themselves pleasantly surprised.

"Why, one would think it came right from the stockpot."

"The beef has quite an amazing heartiness."

"It does not spoil, you say, monsieur?"

"That is the beauty of it, my dear ladies. It preserves the goodness of meat without any of the unfortunate ferments that despoil fresh flesh so quickly."

The ladies exchanged looks amongst themselves.

"Nourishing broths could be made easily from these tablets for those in the workhouses."

"The tablets could be given out in the rookeries along with our lye soap distributions."

"A charitable organization could set up its own kitchen to

make soup in the poorer districts. . . ."

The Thornrose sisters were off and running.

The sun was setting by the time the ladies returned from Massy in possession of a large tin of Nicholas Appert's bouillon tablets, along with detailed instructions for making more of the same. Again, the inventor gave no thought to deriving financial gain from his discovery. The ladies agreed that Monsieur Appert's generosity equaled his genius and that he very much deserved his Benefactor of Humanity award, notwithstanding the fact that he had received it from the bloody hand of the Ogre himself.

Christabel was waiting to greet them, and, after turning up her nose at the bouillon tablets, she hastened to remind them of the late supper she was giving that night.

Drusilla was dismayed. "Christa, I had much rather be in bed than dining with company at midnight."

Christabel looked at her critically. "You *are* looking rather heavy-eyed. I believe you have been gallivanting entirely too much of late."

If only you knew the half of it, thought Dru with a sigh.

Christabel's midnight supper had been hatched as an act of revenge against the wife of the Italian ambassador, who had unknowingly scheduled a rout on the same night Christa had been planning to entertain. The Italian hostess may have hailed from the land of the *vendetta,* but an aggrieved Christabel knew how to execute one in party form. The late supper was specifically designed to draw attendees away prematurely from the competing affair, and Christabel was happily contemplating the prospect of the signora's most sought-after guests whipping on their wraps and departing just when the rout was in full swing.

When the supper guests began to arrive, Drusilla was not surprised to discover that she was to be seated next to Mr. Farnshaw Eggleston. She had not expected it to be otherwise at an affair of Christabel's devising.

To give Mr. Eggleston his due, he was proving admirably oblivious to Christabel's matchmaking maneuvers. He had not a whiff of the suitor about him. His talk was all of rural Wiltshire, of the salmon in the streams and the gamecocks in the hedgerows, of his horse, Bounder, and his hounds, Darby and Doodles and Jenks.

"Proper hunting hounds, mind you, Miss Sedgewick, not any of these Frenchie poodle dogs that look as if someone's grandmother knitted them."

It had by this time been borne in upon Drusilla that Mr. Eggleston was a "galloping squire," one of those spiritual descendants of Squire Western, who felt that the epitome of human civilization had been reached in England's rural countryside. That Mr. Eggleston did not aspire to cosmopolitanism was obvious as he talked about the proposed course of his Grand Tour, the completion of which was now thrown into doubt thanks to the continuing illness of his bear leader.

"We'd have been in Spain by now, legging it through every moldering building and drafty cathedral we came across. Italy would have been more of the same, only worse—with paintings and statues—and Greece would probably have been the worst of all," he speculated gloomily.

"I daresay," agreed Dru with entirely spurious sympathy. "More paintings and more statues, and pottery on top of it."

"Pottery?" Mr. Eggleston sounded even gloomier than before. "Hadn't thought of that. Ye gods!"

Stifling an untactful impulse to laugh, Drusilla made so bold as to inquire, "Why undertake a Grand Tour, Mr. Eggleston, if you have no interest in the sights?"

The young gentleman sighed gustily. "To please my great-aunt, as it happens. I'm her heir, y'see, and she had the notion that my mind needed broadening and my address needed polish. And when your aged forbear, of whom you have great expectations, offers to send you on the Grand Tour, well, off you go, willy-nilly, whether you want to or not."

"Do you dislike Paris so very much, then?"

Mr. Eggleston shrugged. "Just seems very Babylonish compared to Wiltshire. And when all is said and done, I can't seem to warm to the Frenchies." His tone darkened. "Especially that one."

Drusilla followed his gaze to where Christabel was conversing animatedly with (whom else?) the Chevalier de Saint-Armand. "You don't care for the chevalier, Mr. Eggleston?"

"I don't care for the way Lady Toddington lets him dance attendance upon her."

Drusilla was in perfect agreement with the sentiment, but loyalty to Christa compelled her to chide Mr. Eggleston for speaking it aloud. "You refine upon the matter too much, sir. Christabel finds the chevalier an amusing rattle, that is all."

"Well, if she were my wife," said Mr. Eggleston in his bluff, countryman's way, "I'd run her amusing rattle off with a horsewhip."

Christabel sailed up to them then, laughing delectably on the chevalier's arm. Talk turned to the chevalier's recent encounter with the Comte d'Artois.

"Shall you do as the comte recommends?" Christabel asked the chevalier, curious. "Shall you try to buy back your land parcel by parcel?"

"It may come to that, my divinity," allowed the chevalier, "though doubtless the low-born churls will see fit to demand an exorbitant price for what should by right be mine."

"Then you had better find a rich wife as soon as possible," advised Christabel, always brutally practical when it came to matters of marriage and money. "You shall have to cease flirting with married ladies like myself and find an unattached heiress to court."

"I am of no mind to court heiresses . . . unless I find one who outshines your beauty—a thing I am certain is quite impossible."

"It will be difficult," conceded Christabel ingenuously. "Nonetheless, I shall keep an eye out amongst the young ladies in the hope of finding someone suitable for you. I have always enjoyed singular success in matchmaking—with a few minor exceptions," she added, throwing Drusilla a darkling look.

Christabel's attention was then naturally drawn to Mr. Eggleston, who had been standing by, somewhat stiffly. "And is your learned companion much improved, Mr. Eggleston?" she inquired in the fervent hope that the learned companion was not.

Mr. Eggleston's answer was all she could have hoped for. "He still does very poorly. I've begun to think I should send the old fellow home on a repairing lease."

"But can you continue on without him?" asked Drusilla doubtfully. Somehow she could not imagine poor, linguistically hobbled Mr. Eggleston venturing on alone through the Babylonish capitals of Europe.

"Oh, but Mr. Eggleston must stay in Paris," Christabel decreed before the gentleman in question could open his mouth. "Why, if you were to go on alone, sir, you might become lost and meet with an unhappy accident. And besides"—Christabel let fly her most imploring gaze at Mr. Eggleston—"you must attend all my luncheons and tell us more of quaint Wiltshire. We shall be desolate if you depart without doing so."

Jenny Greenteeth from the quaint Wiltshire toad pond could not surpass Christabel when it came to devouring lost boys, thought Drusilla mordantly as she watched Christabel turn the full force of her female charm upon Mr. Eggleston. That young gentleman was of course no match for Christabel and was soon heard to say in a bemused sort of way that perhaps he would stay on in Paris after all.

"And," put in the Chevalier de Saint-Armand, "I also would adore to hear your so quaint tales from your so quaint Wiltshire."

"Then you must lunch with us, too," said Christabel, blithely oblivious to the chevalier's subtle mockery, Mr. Eggleston's sudden scowl, and Drusilla's unhappy frown.

What an amiable foursome we shall make, thought Dru morosely. But she saw no escape from the ordeal.

Feeling thoroughly confounded, she excused herself from the midnight supper at the first opportunity and sought her room. But there she was confounded even more, for a warning from *Childe Harold* had been slipped under the door. It read: BEWARE APPERT.

Chapter Ten

In Which Drusilla Tours the Shops and Witnesses a Duel

"Do you know, Drusilla," observed Lady Christabel Toddington as their coach clattered toward that Mecca of shopping known as the Palais Royal, "people are forever telling me that you are a woman of superior sense, and now, at last, you have finally begun to prove it."

This rare compliment from Christabel caused Drusilla to bare her teeth in a false smile, for to her mind the only thing she had proven was that she had finally taken leave of her famously sensible senses.

It was all *Childe Harold*'s doing, of course. The latest deciphered message read: BECOME FAMILIAR WITH THE PALAIS ROYAL. Why she should receive such a command from Holt, she had no idea, and such was her lingering resentment at his cavalier behavior that she was greatly tempted to simply ignore his communication. But in the end she did not. The lure of the Great Game was too great, her fascination with the audacious man who played it, too strong.

She got herself to the Palais Royal by suggesting to Christabel that they tour the shops there. To forestall any appearance on the horizon of the dangerous Chevalier de Saint-Armand, she further suggested to Christabel that Mr. Farnsworth Eggleston be invited along to provide male escort. Christabel, of course, had been unable to resist the dual attractions of touring the shops while simultaneously furthering her scheme to have Drusilla drag Mr. Eggleston to the altar rails.

And so the expedition was arranged.

By day, the Palais Royal, with its shops and cafés and theatres, was considered to be the chief intellectual and commercial center of Paris. By night, the Palais Royal became the center of dissolute Paris. So famous were its fleshpots that a certain Italian libertine named Giovanni Casanova had noted in his memoirs that upon his arrival in Paris, he made straight for the Palais Royal without bothering to unpack. Drusilla, not being the sort of young lady who would have read Casanova's memoirs, had no knowledge of the bacchanal nighttime atmosphere that had drawn that libidinous gentleman thither. Her ignorance was shortly to be remedied, however.

They met Mr. Eggleston by the large fountain that graced the Palais Royal's central garden park. Also of their party was Christabel's worldly and practical little Parisian dresser, Annette, who was to guide them through the fashionable establishments situated in the Palais's four-story-high galleries.

As they strolled along the elegant arcade, Annette pointed out the sights. "But see, milady, we now encounter some of the *mannequins* that the *modistes* hire to promenade in their creations." She motioned to several sylph-like young women, who thereupon halted their progress to pose and pirouette to show to best advantage the exquisite fashions in which they were clad.

"Since these last ten years," Annette explained, "it is *passé* in Paris to use the little window dolls to display the gowns the way it is done in London. It is the living fashion dolls that are wanted now."

A very different sort of sight was to be seen at Monsieur

Baudin's cutlery shop at No. 177 in the Gallerie de Valois.

Annette's voice sank confidentially as she revealed, "This is the very shop where Charlotte Corday bought the knife she used to assassinate Marat in his bath."

"She assassinated a man in his bath!" exclaimed Christabel, no student of recent French political history. "Goodness! How immodest."

"An immodesty that earned her a trip to the guillotine, of course," observed Mr. Eggleston in his usual what-else-could-you-expect-from-the-French tone of voice.

Moving on, they perused such interesting attractions as a map maker's shop, a bookseller, a watch-and-clock shop, a confectioner displaying candies in boxes decorated by artists, several jewelers, sundry milliners and *modistes,* and finally a *corsetier*'s establishment, which Mr. Eggleston very properly declined to enter, choosing instead to patronize some nearby gentlemen's shops.

Meeting up with him later, they found him highly disapproving of the fact that many of the emporiums catering to men employed female *vendeuses* instead of male clerks to wait upon the customers.

"Pretty, flirting little devils, every one," was Mr. Eggleston's verdict on the *vendeuses,* "and out to make you purchase items you neither want nor have any use for." Seeing that the ladies' eyes were drawn to the package he now had in his possession, he added wryly, "Pray don't embarrass me by asking what sort of bagatelle I've bought. Just take it on faith that I don't want the blasted thing, and I've no use for it whatsoever."

The subject of refreshment had by now been broached repeatedly, but each time Christabel had vetoed the suggestion and flogged her flagging shopping expedition onward. Despite her Dresden-doll appearance, when it came to shopping, Christabel had the stamina of a dray horse. Nevertheless, she was eventually prevailed upon to consider stopping at one of the numerous cafés situated in this section of the arcade.

The first eatery they came upon was a prosperous-looking establishment called the Café Lemblin. But the very idea of their crossing the threshold horrified Annette. Their party, she assured them, would not be at all welcome.

"And whyever not?" exclaimed Christabel, amazed that there existed in all the world a respectable commercial establishment that would not welcome her, the wife of his wealthy lordship, and the acknowledged Incomparable of the London Season of '09.

"Because, madame," Annette explained, "the Café Lemblin is a famous gathering place of the Bonapartists, and they lash with their tongues the English on every occasion."

"Well, in that case," said Christabel with a sniff, "I'm sure we shouldn't wish to darken their doorstep."

"What about that place over there?" inquired Mr. Eggleston, pointing his cane at the Café de la Régence, an establishment that not only offered food but also rented chessboards and pieces to those who desired to while away their time with the game of kings.

But, alas, this café also had Bonapartist connections. Napoleon Bonaparte had been a well-beloved friend of the proprietor since his student days, when he would sit in the establishment moving chess pieces about for hours on his rented board, practicing, no doubt, for the great strategic challenges to come.

The next establishment that caught their eye was Le Caveau. The tinkling music that came out of it confirmed Annette's description of the establishment as one that catered to music lovers.

"Sounds a safe enough place for the ladies," opined their male escort.

But no.

"Only last week," revealed Annette, "there was an affray between those who favored the composer Piccini and those who preferred the composer Gluck. An admirer of Piccini ran a devotee of Gluck though with his sword, and the appetites of the diners were much discomposed."

"But are there not," inquired Dru, "any cafés that cater to monarchists? Surely we would be welcome there."

"Of a certainty, mademoiselle. There is the Café Valois at the end of the block. The monarchists assemble there, but always," she added, "they are fighting with the Bonapartists of the Café Lemblin."

True enough, for they found before the Café Valois a congregation of men arguing and gesticulating vociferously with—and at—one another with the typical incendiarism that Frenchmen reserved for political disputes. Obviously, it would not do for the ladies to enter there.

Mr. Eggleston, whose hearty countryman's appetite wanted feeding, was becoming increasingly hungry and increasingly exasperated. "What places, if any, are left to us, then?"

Fortunately they soon came upon Le Café de Chartres. Not only was this establishment pronounced most *convenable* by Annette, but it was also famous for its *vermicelle*. An hour later they emerged from the café, replete with *vermicelle* and in a much better temper.

The tempers of the habitués of the Café Lemblin and the Café de Valois were not in the least improved, however.

Mr. Eggleston craned his neck toward a crowd that was gathering on the park lawn midway between the two establishments. "By Jupiter!" he exclaimed to the ladies. "I believe a couple of these Frenchies are set to fight a duel right here in the public gardens."

The ladies promptly let their curiosity about this event overrule their good sense and so hurried along with the converging crowd to see what was happening.

Soon they saw the duelists: two young Frenchmen standing back to back, both stripped to their white shirtsleeves. One of the young men had obviously been a soldier of the now disbanded Imperial Guard, for he still affected the distinctive uniform trousers of a guardsman.

The other Frenchman was a civilian, his excellent figure distinguished by well-tailored inexpressibles and high, polished boots. He wore a fine cambric shirt and a fashionably tied cravat beneath an oh, so familiar face.

"Merciful heavens!" exclaimed Christabel. "It's the Chevalier de Saint-Armand!"

It was, indeed, though there was now no trace of the gay trifler about the chevalier. Gone was his social persona. His face was set hard, and his eyes glittered like black diamonds as he turned upon the tenth pace to face his antagonist. The young guardsman who was his opponent was in such a fury that he fired at the chevalier impetuously and precipitously—and missed.

The chevalier's response was not long in coming. He aimed his pistol and with exquisite deliberateness, shot the guardsman, the impact of the pistol ball knocking the young man to the ground.

Christabel squeaked and covered her eyes, and Drusilla, too, had to look away from the fallen figure, his shirt soaking red.

Mr. Eggleston was made of sterner stuff, however, and soon reported to them that it appeared to him that the chevalier's shot had hit high in his opponent's shoulder. "He'll live, I think," was Mr. Eggleston's verdict, "though 'twill be no thanks to Saint-Armand that the boy still draws breath."

The ride back to the Hôtel Toddington was a somber one despite the packages piled up on the seat beside Annette.

Mr. Eggleston felt compelled to observe in disgusted tones, "If these Froggies must be forever dueling over their Froggie politics, you'd think they'd at least have the decency to do it in some less public place."

Christabel shook her golden head in bemusement. "Who would have dreamt the chevalier would prove to be such a fire-eater on the dueling field?" A purring note of feminine admiration in her voice caused Drusilla's heart to sink—as if she hadn't already enough cause to feel heart-sunk where the chevalier was concerned.

Could it be that she had completely misjudged the man, that he was, in fact, the ultra-royalist he claimed to be? For if he was a secret Bonapartist, what would it profit him to come within ames-ace of killing another member of his brother-hood? Then the answer as to how this duel might profit the chevalier came to her: It would authenticate his royalist cre-dentials to anyone—such as the Comte d'Artois—who might be doubting them.

But was Guy de Saint-Armand ruthless enough to shoot another adherent to his cause in the hope of thereby ad-vancing their mutual cause?

Of course he was, she told herself grimly. Just as MacRory Holt was ruthless enough to deliberately leave a fellow offi-cer's daughter in the hands of her abductors simply to win a round in the Great Game.

She shivered, for suddenly the winter winds that blew along the Paris boulevards seemed quite mercilessly cold.

Chapter Eleven

Among the Grand Coquettes
of the Palais Royal

The winter moon spilled milky light down upon the white classical beauty of the buildings of the Palais Royal. It was cold that night, but Drusilla's burning resentment kept her warm.

MEET ME AT EIGHT AT THE PALAIS ROYAL FOUNTAIN she had been told—something easily ordered but not so easily accomplished. Were she a man, she would have had no trouble departing the Toddington residence at any hour she pleased. But a young lady had no such freedom.

Therefore, excuses had to be invented for her early retirement, serving maids had to be bamboozled, footmen and sundry servitors had to be eluded, and a carriage-for-hire had to be flagged down and the driver paid an exorbitant fare to transport her. It was quite an undertaking, and she was proud of having achieved a timely arrival well before the appointed hour. . . .

Only Holt was not there to witness her triumph, and she was mightily vexed.

In the meantime, she found the Palais Royal transformed.

All the shoppers, clerks, *mannequins*, and *vendeuses* had departed, leaving the first-floor shops locked and deserted. A few of the cafés remained open for business, among them the Café de la Régence, where the chess lovers could now rent two candles to set on either side of their chessboard as they played.

In contrast to the quiet of the first story of the Palais Royal, the upper floors were ablaze with lights and laughter and music. Quite a lot seemed to be going on behind those ranks of drawn curtains on the top floors. Quite a lot was going on round the fountain as well, and most of it had to do with ladies of easy virtue intent on enticing gentlemen upstairs.

Drusilla was wishing more and more fervently that Holt would arrive, but she supposed it would do no good to go looking for him. Doubtless he would materialize in his own way and in his own good time. In the meantime, she stood in the shadows and occupied herself with watching colorfully costumed guests emerge from their carriages to attend a masquerade at the Théâtre du Palais Royal.

She noticed, then, that a man had been eyeing her and now was about to approach her. Several men had already opportuned her, but she had given them the right-about in no uncertain terms.

She was at the point of putting some prudent distance between herself and the approaching stranger when the man's words arrested her progress. "I am commended to your notice by the colonel. Please to follow me, mademoiselle."

Relief overwhelmed her. Finally, a messenger from Holt, though she failed to understand why he should be jingling the coins in his pocket in such an obvious and significant manner. She obediently followed him to the far end of one of the galleries, which was deserted at this hour.

Seeing no one about, she felt it was safe enough to inquire in a low voice, "Where is the colonel now?"

But the man did not seem disposed to give her word of Holt's whereabouts. He did seem disposed to seize her in an embrace and attempt to bite her neck.

Frozen with a shock that her assailant doubtlessly mistook for acquiescence, for an instant she did nothing as the man continued gourmandizing upon her neck while his hands made free with her person. Her belated frenzied attempts to escape his embrace were then taken by her molester as evidence of amatory enthusiasm.

"So you want to play a little first, my pretty?" he muttered against her cheek.

"Let me go, you villain!" she gasped, completely forgetting about her knife in this dire hour of need.

The villain did not let her go, however, and, despite her panicked flailings was on the verge of forcing her down to the ground. . . .

Sometimes, even amidst the deceptions, machinations, subterfuges, skulduggery, and false colors of the Great Game, a young lady who has fallen into the clutches of a villain can count on her Sir Galahad putting in a timely appearance.

Out of the moonlit night came a male figure clad in dark, unexceptional clothing but moving with a speed and a ferocity that was quite exceptional. By main strength he wrenched the villain away from Drusilla's straining person, swung him around, and flattened him with a crisp right cross.

MacRory Holt, of course.

Giddy with relief at being rescued in the proverbial nick of time, Dru tottered toward the shelter of Holt's arms. But she found him Sir Galahad no more. Instead of cradling her in the tender embrace for which every rescued damsel yearns, Holt's hands fastened painfully on her shoulders. Dru now found herself being smartly shaken, and if her teeth did not rattle, it was not for lack of trying on Holt's part.

118

"Confound it, woman!" he grated out angrily. "I thought you had more sense! Whatever possessed you to go off alone with that lout?"

She wrenched away from his grasp, nearly as angry as he. "I only went because I thought he was your messenger. He said he was commended to me by the colonel."

The implication of this did not escape Holt. His eyes narrowed in the moonlight. "You're certain that's what he said?"

"Of course I'm certain," she snapped. "I'd never have gone with him otherwise."

But, of course, no apologies were forthcoming from MacRory Holt.

His attention was now centered on the fallen villain, whom he prodded to consciousness with his boot and then hauled upright. The moon was out from behind a cloud, and they saw that, as villains went, this one did not look particularly villainous. As he wobbled dazedly in Holt's sinewy grasp, they saw that he was a smallish man of middle years, who appeared to be quivering in terror from his disheveled neckcloth down to his polished shoes.

Serves him right, thought Drusilla uncharitably. She was also experiencing a deep sense of chagrin that she had not handled his boorish attentions with more finesse.

"What," demanded Holt, giving the prisoner a shake, "is this talk about a colonel?"

"Please, monsieur, I beg you," stammered the man, his face pallid except for the livid contusion on his jaw. "I meant no harm."

"Convince me of that," said Holt through his teeth, "and perhaps I'll let you live. Now, I'll ask you again, what is this business about a colonel?"

"A gentleman comes to me as I walk the arcade and strikes up a conversation about the women for hire in this place. He points to that one there and says she is a most avid of the grand coquettes."

"He said *what?*" gasped Dru, fairly certain that she was not being complimented.

"And I said that, yes, one could see by the swish of her skirts that she was quite a riggish little piece."

"How dare you, you—"

"Quiet," snapped Holt, taking a tighter grip on his unhappy prisoner. "To the point, monsieur. I'm losing patience. What else did this man say?"

"The gentleman informs me that mam'selle was well known for servicing soldiers and that if I commended myself to her from the colonel she would slake my desires shamelessly."

"Why, you vile, depraved—"

Holt cut in impatiently, his grasp growing more bruising still. "This informative gentleman of yours . . . tell me his looks and build and voice, and tell me quickly, or else I'll let mam'selle have at you."

"I t . . . tell you, m . . . monsieur," their captive stuttered painfully in nervousness, "this man was nothing out of the ordinary in build or feature. He was slight of stature, his hair black, his skin pale, his voice very soft. Please, I meant no harm. I only wished to purchase mam'selle's favors."

Holt, his mind already several moves ahead in the Great Game, shoved the fellow away in disgust. "If you know what's good for you, you'll get out of my sight before I change my mind about letting you live to see another day."

As the man staggered away into the night, Drusilla whispered uneasily, "Do you think it was Excelsior who set him upon me?"

"Who else? Though I can't fathom how the devil he knew who you were. So"—Holt's voice became thoughtful—"both

Lazare and I are abroad tonight in the Palais Royal, and neither of us the sort of man to withdraw and leave the ground to his old enemy. Come on then, my angel"—a note of excitement sounded in his voice as he hurried her toward one of the back entrances to the arcade—"I've a lurking-hole here that we can shelter in while we plan our next move."

As usual, Holt was long on orders and short on explanations, but Dru went with him without demur, wondering what sort of adventure she would have now.

The long galleries of the Palais Royal were well supplied with back staircases. On the third-floor landing of the least frequented stairway, Holt, after a swift look around, pushed open a narrow door, the outlines of which had been cleverly concealed within the grooves of the paneled wainscoting. So cleverly was this door cut into the wall that it was unlikely to be noticed by anyone not privy to the knowledge of its existence.

Hanging on a hook just inside the door was a lantern, which Holt lit to reveal a passageway so narrow, they were forced to proceed single file. At the end of the passage was a door and, hanging beside it, a knotted cord that dangled from a small hole cut in the ceiling. Holt gave the cord three tugs, waited a space of time, then gave it three more.

What could be going on at the other end of that cord, Drusilla had no idea, but evidently it served as some sort of signaling device.

"What is this place?" she whispered to Holt.

"Madame Solange's *maison de tolérance*," he whispered back, but then gestured her to silence before she could ask who was Madame Solange and what, exactly, did she tolerate.

Quick, light footsteps approached on the other side of the door, followed by three rapid knocks. Holt put his mouth to the crack of the door and, to Dru's amazement, hooted softly as an owl hunting in the woods in the depths of the night hoots. A soft hoot echoed in reply, and then the footsteps receded.

Dru shook her head with inward wonderment at the Gothic trappings of her latest adventure with Holt: concealed doors, hidden passageways, mysterious signaling devices, secret passwords (for she assumed that was the purpose of the birdcall), unseen listeners on the other side of locked doors. The goings-on in Mrs. Radcliffe's *The Mysteries of Udolpho* were nothing compared to this.

Holt's owl hoot must have done the trick, for the quick footsteps hurried back. There then came the sound of a bolt being shot, and the door swung open. Dru gasped at the personage who stood revealed before them—a very pretty, shapely young woman, who seemed to be having difficulty keeping her shapeliness confined in a corset and loose robe.

Surely, thought Drusilla, they had interrupted one of the famous *mannequins* of the Palais Royal at her *toilette*. But apparently neither Holt nor the young woman thought her attire—or, rather, the lack of it—worthy of comment, for neither spoke as they proceeded along a dark hallway.

Drusilla could now hear music, laughter, and the clinking of glassware and china. Passing though a curtained alcove, she caught a glimpse of a drawing room wherein more undressed ladies disposed themselves among well-dressed gentlemen, and it was now borne in upon her exactly what it was that Madame Solange tolerated at her *maison*. This was a place tenanted by women known variously as *filles de joie*, *femmes gallantes,* or grand coquettes, those beautiful heart-eaters and money-eaters for which the Palais Royal was so justly famous.

Their guide led them into a small anteroom and then left them, saying, "I shall tell madame you are here."

"This Madame Solange," Drusilla asked in a whisper when she and Holt were alone, "is she one of the grand co-quettes?"

"The grandest, I daresay," answered Holt, secret amusement sounding in his voice. But just before the door was opened to admit them into Madame Solange's parlor, his amused tone changed to one of warning. "You'll mind your manners around Solange, my angel, and not put on any stiff-necked lady's airs. I owe her my life, and I won't have her slighted."

"I'm not in the habit," retorted Dru, stung, "of being stiff-necked to anyone, no matter what their station in life."

"That's my good lass," said Holt, and for some reason his words took the sting out of the fact that she, Drusilla Sedgewick, had just been admonished to mind her manners in the presence of a fallen woman.

Madame Solange could indeed be said to be the grandest of the grand coquettes—in girth, at least. She was an extremely corpulent woman who nevertheless possessed a certain majestic handsomeness imparted by her perfect alabaster complexion and a magnificent head of elaborately dressed white-blond hair. Her shrewd grey eyes and generous mouth gave the impression of a woman whom life had made both compassionate and cynical, as if she had seen much of the world and found it both foolish and sad.

Madame received them from a brocade chaise longue upon which she was reclining *à la* Madame Récamier, although, needless to say, Madame Solange could easily have made three of that witty and beautiful society leader, Julie

Récamier. At the sight of MacRory Holt, madame's generous mouth curved into a smile.

"Rory, *mon homme brave,*" she greeted him, giving him her plump white hand to kiss. "At last you are come. We were beginning to despair of you."

"The young lady and I were delayed by a small misadventure," said Holt in his usual cool way. He motioned Dru forward. "May I present Mademoiselle Angélique."

Mindful of her manners, Drusilla made a demi-curtsy to Madame Solange just as she would to any older, distinguished woman.

Madame regarded mademoiselle with keen interest as she waved her guests into a pair of frilled boudoir chairs. Somehow, Holt managed to get his long frame folded sufficiently to take a seat opposite their hostess's languidly reclining bulk.

"So, Rory, I see that you have not forgotten the hidden ways of this place, nor the secret call of the *Chouans.*"

The *Chouans,* Drusilla recalled from table talk amongst the diplomatists, were pro-royalist insurgents who had revolted against Bonaparte's rule, and obviously MacRory Holt of the British Secret Intelligence Department was privy to their secrets.

Holt smiled at madame. "Nor have I forgotten how you hid me during the war when Henri Lazare had every policeman in Paris on my trail."

Madame's posture became considerably less languid at the mention of the sinister Lazare's name. "That is why I sent for you, Rory. Your Gypsy informant was right. Lazare does frequent the Palais Royal now that he has returned to Paris. I have twice seen him here. It has been fifteen years since I encountered him in the flesh, and now in the last few months I see him twice. It struck me as most passing strange."

Holt nodded in agreement. "When I got your message, I confess that my first thought was that your memory had played you false."

Madame Solange smiled a bitter smile. "You do not forget the man who burns your village, poisons your well, and takes away your menfolk in chains, never to return. And he is very little altered from when I saw him last. Strange," she went on reflectively, "that the years have marked him so lightly. His face is the same. Nothing of what he has done shows upon his person, whilst every sorrow that followed from his destruction of my family and our cause shows upon mine." She made a sweeping gesture that encompassed her terrific proportions and then fixed her shrewd gaze upon Holt. "Am I to assume, Rory, that Lazare was behind the misadventure that you and mademoiselle suffered this evening?"

"It was mademoiselle who suffered more than I," said Holt, his voice suddenly grim, "and, yes, Lazare was behind it. I'm certain of that now."

"And so"—Madame Solange raised exquisitely penciled eyebrows at him—"what will you do?"

"I want Lazare under my hand," said Holt in an iron voice. "He's the linchpin of a dozen plots to free Bonaparte and assassinate Wellington. I want him alive, but if I can't get him alive, I'll take him dead." He was on his feet now, pacing the length of madame's luxurious Aubusson carpet. "If only I had a dossier on his background such as he had on me during the war. If only I knew what draws him to the Palais Royal."

"Perhaps"—Dru dared to speak up for the first time— "he comes to meet with the Bonapartists at the Café Lemblin."

She had the satisfaction of seeing Holt pause in midpace to give her a brief look of approval that she would know this. "You've learned your lessons, I see, my angel. Yes, it's true that the Café Lemblin is full of republicans and

125

Bonapartists . . . which means the place is also honeycombed with secret agents working for the Comte d'Artois and the other countries of the Quadruple Alliance, among them the potboy, who happens to be in *my* pay. So far, Lazare has not been fool enough to openly stick his nose into the Lemblin. Something else draws him to the Palais Royal. It's not the gambling and it's not the women. So what is it?"

Madame Solange spoke from her chaise, as if she had been waiting for just the right moment to impart the important information she had discovered. "I think there is one who might know what brings Lazare here, if such a thing can be known. There is an old woman named Celestine, who for many years has been the attendant in the ladies' cloakroom at the Théâtre du Palais Royal. She knows much, has seen much. Judicious questioning might cause her to yield information. But be warned: In her old age she is talkative and guileless, and she might be likely to tell someone else that she had been questioned about Henri Lazare."

"Ah," said Holt, the course of the night's mission clear to him now, "I see why you wished me to bring a female accomplice."

Madame nodded. "Neither I nor any of my girls dare to question her. Celestine knows us all by name, and if she were to tell Lazare we were inquiring about him, I do not like to think what he would do. And, of course, not even the famous MacRory Holt could be expected to invade a ladies' lounge."

"True enough," agreed Holt, flashing his rare grin. "I'd rather face a troop of charging lancers than a bevy of ladies lounging."

Having deduced by now that *she* would be the one to invade the ladies' lounging room of the Théâtre du Palais Royal, Drusilla hastened to point out what struck her as a flaw in the plan. "There is a masked ball tonight at the theatre. To enter, one must have tickets and a costume."

"Solange will have arranged all," predicted Holt confidently.

His confidence was not misplaced.

Reposing on the table beside Madame Solange's chaise were two tickets to the masked ball. From that same table madame picked up a small brass bell and rang it. A serving maid named Marie soon appeared to listen to her mistress's orders.

"Bring a mask and domino for the gentleman, and as for the young lady"—madame's eyes rested with displeasure on Dru's worn brown poplin—"take away this little brown wren, and bring me back a bird of paradise."

Once "Mademoiselle Angélique" had been sent off in the keeping of Marie the maid, Madame Solange shifted her bulk on the overstuffed chaise in order to look at Holt more closely. "Rory, what do you mean to do with that pretty child you have trailing at your heels? Do you think to use her as bait to catch Excelsior in the honey trap?"

"Would it were that easy to bait a trap for Henri Lazare," said Holt regretfully. "But he's not one to let either his tongue or his trowsers slip for a pretty girl. I know that well."

"Not nearly as well as I know it," countered madame dryly, "I, who once offered him my youthful charms in exchange for the release of my menfolk—an offer that, as you may have guessed, he spurned."

"Now, this is a story," said Holt in surprise, "that you never told me before, Solange."

Madame sighed. "It is not a tale I care to bruit about, since it hardly redounds to my professional credit. Nor was I the only woman of the *Chouannerie* who sought to seduce the police agent Henri Lazare for the sake of her family or our cause.

All our efforts came to naught, however, for plot by plot, intrigue by intrigue, Lazare broke the spine of the *Chouan* rebellion in the Vendée. . . ." Her voice trailed away, and a shiver ran through her frame, causing a not insubstantial convulsion of flesh upon the chaise longue. "I still remember the eyes of that one as he watched my pleadings for my family and my poor attempts to offer myself to him. Like black ice in his snow-white face were the eyes of Henri Lazare. But then, my friend, you know that all too well, don't you?"

"Damnably well," agreed Holt grimly. "Don't forget, Lazare was Bonaparte's top agent in Spain, and after I was captured, he interrogated me every single day for weeks on end. As a captured officer I should have been exchanged or else sent to an internment camp. But instead he had me sent under guard to Paris. I knew then that I had to escape, even though I'd given my parole, because if Lazare ever got me into the Temple Prison, I'd never get out alive."

There was a brief silence in the parlor as both Madame Solange and MacRory Holt meditated upon their histories with that arch-master of cruel intrigue, Henri Lazare.

Then Madame Solange spoke. "Have you thought, Rory, of what might happen if the black-ice eyes of Henri Lazare were ever to fall upon your pretty 'Mademoiselle Angélique'?"

Holt hesitated for an instant, and Madame Solange thought she saw a troubled shadow behind his cool green gaze.

"Lazare has already seen her," he admitted, "though I don't know how he managed it. I never meant for that to happen. She was only to be window dressing, a honey trap perhaps, if I had need of one."

"I see," said Madame Solange thoughtfully. She then continued with professional detachment, "Had it been up to me,

I would have chosen for you just such a one as 'Mademoiselle Angélique' in her looks and manner. And have you made love to her yet, Rory?"

There was a deeper question within madame's spoken question, and the true answer within Holt's spoken answer was revealed to her by the forbidding tone of his reply—a short, bitten-off "No."

Oh, but you will make love to her, Rory, you will, thought shrewd Madame Solange, *for it seems to me that you are already a fair way to falling into your own honey trap.*

Drusilla was taken away to a large dressing room filled with wardrobe closets that contained a dazzling array of clothing, costumes, hats, shawls, and assorted other items of female frills and furbelows. The room was also filled with Madame Solange's *filles de joies* who were rummaging through their communal wardrobes in search of which finery to wear that evening. They regarded Dru curiously, and she regarded the pretty wages-of-sin earners with equal curiosity.

The maid, Marie, would have ordered the other girls out of the dressing room, but Dru hastily intervened. "Please do not interrupt yourselves on my account. I would be glad of your company and conversation."

Among the girls in the dressing room was the one who had answered the bell and who knew that Mademoiselle Angélique was not *their* kind of "adventuress." She now stepped out from amongst the clothes racks to demand suspiciously, "And why should you care to converse with us?"

"To become informed, of course," said Dru equably, "about life, love, men—subjects that must always be dear to the hearts of women."

This was Drusilla Sedgewick at her cleverest, showing

once again why MacRory Holt had been so entirely right to recruit her into the Great Game. Most other young ladies of good character would have vapored at finding themselves in such company, but Drusilla knew it was imperative to adapt to whatever surroundings she found herself in and learn quickly whatever there was to be learned. She also knew from her experiences in aiding the Thornrose ladies in their Magdalene rescue work amongst London's fallen women that it was want, not wantonness, that drove young girls into this sort of establishment.

Disarmed by her overture, Madame Solange's girls began to chatter away quite artlessly about themselves while Marie whisked out plumed and feathered raiment for mademoiselle's perusal.

"One is not born a grand coquette of course. . . ."

"One is born a fishmonger's daughter or a button maker's apprentice or a table girl in a tavern who grows tired of being worked from dawn to dusk for starvation wages . . ."

"But one must be born with beauty and love of a good time . . . "

"And acquire elegant manners and knowledge of the smart world . . ."

"One must have a sense of timing, of course. One must know when to be seductive, when to be gay, when to be sympathetic . . ."

"And always—always—make them give you jewels . . ."

"And never—never—let them give you horses, for the wretched creatures will eat you back into poverty . . ."

By the time all this worldly advice had been heaped upon her, Drusilla had been transformed from a brown wren into a feathered bird of paradise . . . but a bird with a secret talon, for accommodation had been made for her stiletto amongst the clinging gauze and colorful feathers of her skirt.

Drusilla been cherishing fond hopes that Holt might admire the glamour wrought upon her appearance by a plumed headdress, bare, feather-wreathed shoulders, trim ankles revealed below her immodest gauze skirt, and an artfully rouged mouth beneath her sequined half mask. Her hopes came to naught, however.

Holt spared her feather-bedizened person barely a glance, and with a brief "You'll do," he led her out the side door of Madame Solange's *maison*.

A crowd had gathered before the Théâtre du Palais Royal to watch the costumed guests disembark from their carriages. The male partygoers generally contented themselves with masks and dominoes. The ladies, however, burst forth from their conveyances like butterflies from a chrysalis, marvelously appareled as Turkish sultanas, classical goddesses, Chinese maidens, and Egyptian priestesses.

As the masqueraders entered the theatre, MacRory Holt and Drusilla Sedgewick entered along with them, masqueraders twice over.

Chapter Twelve

In Which Drusilla Plays Her Part
in a Masque of Danger and Desire

An English playwright of acid wit once wrote that the purpose of a masquerade was to bring together bashful people who were afraid to sin barefaced. There was nothing bashful, however, about the sinners congregating this evening in the entrance lobby to the Théâtre du Palais Royal.

A pair of crescent staircases led from the lobby up to the closed boxes in the balcony, where even more sinning was doubtless going on. The door to the ladies' cloakroom was situated beneath the right staircase, but at the moment the lounge was filled to overflowing with chattering females arranging themselves for the evening. Questioning the attendant would have to wait until later.

"We'll walk about first," said Holt, guiding Drusilla into the theatre, which had been cleared of benches to accommodate the dancers. The musicians were playing at their regular stations in the orchestra pit, the notes carrying easily over the noise of the crowd thanks to the theatre's excellent acoustics.

Set upon the stage proper were a number of curtained booths containing Curious Attractions brought in for the evening: a magician, a marionette show, several raffling booths, a pantomimist in whiteface, and the most curious attraction of all—the "Live Girl Mermaid Exhibited in a Giant Bottle."

Before *this* attraction, MacRory Holt paused.

In fact, nearly every passing male paused before this attraction, for the girl mermaid was very pretty indeed, with her long dark hair floating about her shoulders, and her lithe person costumed in a green waxed-canvas sheath sewn together at the nether limbs to form a giant fishtail. The décolleté bodice of the costume was adorned with glass brilliants that caught the light whenever the "mermaid" floated to the surface of the water in her giant bottle. As far as Drusilla could discern, the girl's main talent was to respire deeply in her tight bodice, sink to the bottom of her bottle, and smile fetchingly whilst simultaneously emitting air bubbles.

Holt seemed intrigued, however. "Tell me, my angel," he inquired in a thoughtful voice, "do you know how to swim underwater?"

"No," said Dru emphatically, "nor above water, either."

"Do you think you might be prevailed upon to learn?"

"Absolutely not," said Dru even more emphatically.

"Too bad," said Holt with a regretful shrug that left Drusilla wondering uneasily just what kind of aquatic undertaking he might have had in mind for her.

They meandered onward, circumnavigating the theatre while Holt, in his usual watchful way, made note of all the exits and the layout of the stage area.

"I suppose," he said finally, "we had better dance. You waltz, I presume?"

Dru murmured in the affirmative, and then, with her heart suddenly aflutter in her feathered bosom, she delivered herself into Holt's embrace, which in its effect upon her was like no other man's touch. She had waltzed many times during her London Season, having gained the permission of the almighty patronesses of Almack's to do so. But it was not until this moment, not until this dance, that she understood why the waltz was considered so dangerous to maiden hearts.

Until now she had never quite realized what it was to dance in a man's embrace, to feel the workings of his muscles beneath her fingertips, to move her body in perfect concert with his, to match him step for step in the gliding elegance of the waltz, to feel the shiver of desire his touch stirred within her.

To waltz, it was said, was to make love on the dance floor, and, oh, it could be so true, so true, if only Holt were as carried away by the music and the dance as she was. But then, she thought with an inward sigh, Holt was not the kind of man to be carried away by her or anything else. He was a man who had always walked alone, with only his own strength and skill and wits to keep him alive amidst the dangers and duplicities of the Great Game. It was his very self-sufficiency that made him so desirable, and she was sadly certain that she was neither the first nor the last woman to desire to tame this extraordinary man.

And what did he desire of her? The eyes that glittered green out of the black half mask told her nothing; the arms that held her close had doubtless held many another woman close as well.

Soon, too soon, the magical interlude of the dance was ended, and she was cast out of the circle of Holt's arms. Now he was once again the master of the Great Game, and she was once again his untrained recruit, brusquely commanded by her master to be about her next task, which was to search out, question, and bribe, if need be, a garrulous old woman named Celestine.

Drusilla found Celestine sitting upon a stool in the cloakroom amidst the billowing falls of silk and satin evening cloaks. The old woman looked up sharply as if suspecting Drusilla of intending to make off with someone's wrap.

Hoping to allay her suspicions, Dru held up a coin and addressed the woman with affectionate informality. "I am looking for someone, *Tante*. A man named Henri Lazare. I thought perhaps you might know of him?"

"Lazare the policeman? And what should you want with him, my pretty bird girl?" The old woman peered at her closely, taking in the details of her costume. "You may flaunt your fine feathers all you please, my girl, but I dare swear that in my day I was much prettier than you."

"I am certain of it, *Tante*," agreed Drusilla with becoming modesty. "But you were speaking to me," she went on in gentle reminder, "of Henri Lazare, were you not?"

"Was I indeed?" countered the old woman tartly. "I thought I was speaking of myself and of how my beauty brought me lovers aplenty without flaunting myself in feathers. There was Gerard, with his kisses of fire, though perhaps it is Etienne I remember so well, or Philippe, with the brave mustachios, who wooed me with kisses in the pleasure garden . . ."

Fearing that several decades' worth of osculatory reminiscences might be forthcoming, Dru hastily produced two more coins, which seemed to have the desired effect of focusing Celestine's attentions on the topic at hand.

"Henri Lazare, of the police office, you say? And I say Phaugh!" The old woman shook her head in digust. "A viper, that one is. I remember him all too well. I was a dresser at the Comédie-Française during the Terror. Into the troupe came a weasely-faced fellow named Lazare, who fancied himself an actor, but little did we know . . ."

"Yes?" said Dru eagerly.

"That he was also an agent *provocateur* sent by Robespierre and the Committee of Public Safety to trick royalist sympathizers into betraying themselves out of their own mouths. The Committee feared the power of actors to sway audiences, you see, and of course actors talk too much for their own good in any case . . ."

The old woman's voice trailed off, leading Dru to fear that her informant's attention might be wandering. She slipped Celestine another coin, which encouraged the attendant to resume her narrative with a heavy sigh, as if these memories were not so happy as the memories of Etienne's kisses of fire.

"One day soldiers came to arrest all those whom Lazare had secretly entrapped. Those players who had not said their lines to Lazare's liking went to the guillotine. The remaining players came to the Palais Royal and formed a new troupe, which acts here still. You might almost say that Henri Lazare is the founder of this troupe, and ofttimes over the years I have seen him come here, though, of course, the plays are not so good as they were in my day. . . . "

"Yes, yes, of course," agreed Dru, endeavoring to conceal her excitement over the vital intelligence she had just obtained. This was the first time that she had ever attempted to bribe someone for information, and the process seemed to have gone swimmingly. She dropped another coin into Celestine's hand and departed in hasty search of Holt.

She left the old woman staring after her, trying to remember one more fact about Henri Lazare she felt was worth remembering. And that fact, which Celestine remembered too late to tell the pretty bird girl, was that Henri Lazare was here, tonight, attending the masquerade at the Théâtre du Palais Royal.

"An actor, eh?" mused Holt. "Well, I can't say it surprises me. All confidential agents must of necessity be mountebanks and *poseurs,* or we'd none of us live very long." His gaze went up to the stage and the exits on either side of it. "Let's have a look backstage. Perhaps I can bribe a stagehand to keep an eye out for Lazare."

They edged away from the crowd and slipped though the heavy velvet curtains that led to the cavernous backstage area—and found themselves suddenly transported to ancient Troy.

Looming all around them were the set pieces for the theater's current production of *Helen of Troy*: the towering facade of the Trojan horse, ready to be drawn through the city gate, and beyond that display, the topless towers of Ilium, which were situated on rolling stage floats. Dangling everywhere were the pulley ropes that connected to the hoists, winches, sandbags, and flywheels that powered the stage machinery of this famous theatre.

They soon discovered that the backstage was deserted of workers on this masquerade night. Dru took advantage of the private moment to ask Holt a question that had been on her mind but which she had been prevented from voicing by the evening's rush of events. "Why did you warn me against Nicholas Appert? He seems a genuine humanitarian and very agreeable."

Holt laughed sardonicly. "I doubt he'd be so agreeable if he knew you were associated with the British saboteur who blew his precious cannery to kingdom come."

Dru stared at him, stunned by this revelation. "*You* caused the explosion? It wasn't just an unfortunate accident?"

Holt grinned his rare grin, obviously proud of himself. "Six barrels of gunpowder with lit fuses hardly qualifies as an accident, my angel—and the entire operation carried out even though every policeman in Paris was on my trail."

"But . . . but why did you do it?"

"To deny the French army the use of embalmed rations, of course."

"But . . . to destroy the entire factory?"

Holt swung around to face her, a dangerous glint in his eyes. "Do you presume to judge me in these matters, my angel?"

Dru sensed his anger but stood her ground. "It's only that it seems a wretched waste to destroy an important scientific—"

Holt was no longer listening, however. His head had snapped up, and he was looking past her with such a fierce expression that his previous anger seemed no more than a passing summer storm. His eyes were keen and wary, his rangy body filled with a springy tension as if he meant to launch himself at some enemy.

Dru felt a sudden chill crawling along her spine. She whirled around to look where Holt looked—and saw that they were not alone.

A man had come out from among the towers of Troy and now walked toward them, a man with a pale, passionless face that showed nothing as the dance music sounded in strange accompaniment to his advance. Dru knew instantly who he was: Henri Lazare, formerly of the Emperor's secret police, Henri Lazare, arch-intriguer, merciless torturer, master poisoner, machinator *extraordinaire*.

If MacRory Holt was a wolf in the Great Game, then Henri Lazare was a ferret. He had very black hair, thick as an animal pelt, a cold, dry voice he never raised, and a specialist's nose for human weakness. He was of less than average height, with small delicate hands, and those of his prisoners who had the misfortune to watch him peel off his gloves soon learned that he had a surgeon's knowledge of nerves and pain.

But this knowledge would do him no good now against MacRory Holt, for if it came to a fight of male strength against male strength, Holt, the younger man and the battle-hardened soldier, must surely win—and both men knew it.

Check, you bastard, thought Holt triumphantly as he twitched his knife from up his sleeve. "So, Lazare, I find you at last, and this time it is I who will be the interrogator and you, the prisoner."

"Do you think so, indeed, Holt?" The man who called himself Excelsior spoke in his dry, precise voice. "You are too quick to declare yourself victorious. Not all the Dramatis Personae of our little masque have yet appeared. Allow me to direct your attention to stage left."

Holt's eyes flicked leftward, and Drusilla's did too, and her heart misgave her. Four men with pistols dropped from—where else?—the Trojan horse. The men wore half masks and dominoes, but once they began speaking, Dru knew them instantly. Once upon a time she had hung upon their every word when she was their prisoner in the woodlands of Picardy, and she could only pray they did not recognize her now through her feathered disguise.

MacRory Holt, however, they recognized all too well.

"We know you now for what you are, Scotsman."

"You are not the Emperor's Wolf, as you said."

"You are the Duke of 'Villainton's' wolf, Wellington's eyes and ears."

"But now we shall put out the eyes of 'Villainton's' wolf and cut off his ears."

Dru shuddered and reached for her stiletto as Henri Lazare stepped closer. "Your knife, Colonel Holt. Throw it down or my men will shoot."

Trapped! thought Holt with grim fury. Playing for time, he said, "How did you know I would be here?"

"You set your Gypsy bloodhounds on my trail. But even

the canniest bloodhound can be lured with a false scent and followed back to its master. I knew you would come here looking for me, and tonight I let you find me."

Damn you, Lazare, for the cunning swine you are, thought MacRory Holt.

At last! The wolf at bay, thought Henri Lazare. Aloud, he said, "You are my prisoner. Toss aside that knife, or my men will shoot."

"A pistol shot will bring everyone running," Holt pointed out.

"Perhaps. But you and the girl will be past caring."

"You waste your shot on the girl. She knows nothing and is near to fainting away as it is."

Taking her cue, Drusilla moaned dramatically and began to wilt and wobble on rubbery knees—no great feat of acting, if the truth be told—and then sank into a swoon. Holt caught her up and swung her onto a scenery float and took the stiletto that she had ready to slip into his hand.

"Your knife, Colonel Holt," repeated Lazare as Holt turned back to face him.

With his hands half-raised in an attitude of surrender, Holt walked forward and tossed down Drusilla's dagger. The men holding the pistols relaxed their guard, and, scenting victory, one of them stepped forward to retrieve the knife, carelessly placing himself directly in the line of fire between Holt and his own comrades.

Holt reacted instantly to his enemies' tactical error, shoving the nearest wheeled set piece toward the man and then slashing with his own knife the rope-and-pulley contrivance that dangled beside him. The severed ropes whipped upward, and the walls of Troy came tumbling down—in the form of a scenery flat, of course, but still with a gratifyingly loud crash, and close enough to Lazare's pistol-wielding cohorts to cast them into confusion.

An instant later, heads thrust through the curtains and the music dwindled to a stop. But those responsible for the theatrical disaster had already lost themselves in the growing crowd.

They kept to the shadows and *slunk*—there was no other word for it—back to Madame Solange's *maison*.

That Holt was in a black humor over their misadventure was obvious to Drusilla. He'd said nothing to her other than ordering her curtly to go to the wardrobe room and get back into her clothes. By the time she had divested herself of her feathers and turned back into a brown wren once more, she had the distinct feeling that something new was afoot.

Two meaty fellows were waiting outside madame's parlor. Like madame, they were former *Chouan* insurrectionists, strong-armed bludgeon men Holt occasionally used to perform certain commissions requiring much brawn and not too much brains. They stood back respectfully to let Drusilla pass, but she felt a growing sense of unease as she did so.

In her absence, Holt had related to Madame Solange in a few bitter sentences the tale of how Henri Lazare had bested him tonight.

Madame was philosophical. "Still, you have survived; you live to fight another day."

"So you say, Solange, but it wasn't my life only that was at risk tonight."

Once again Holt remembered the fear that had possessed him when he realized that Drusilla was with him in the closing jaws of Lazare's trap. It was the kind of fear he would never feel for his own skin, the kind of fear that could turn him aside from cool, uncaring purpose if he let it.

He had been a fool to involve her, he saw that now. Yet

who could blame him for seeking to recruit a young woman of her pluck and resource, especially when all that pluck and resource came wrapped up in such a pretty packet? But lissome figure, long legs, chestnut curls, and hazel eyes notwithstanding, Miss Drusilla Sedgewick would have to be dismissed, and so he told her when she came back into the parlor.

"The Game becomes too dangerous," he said without preamble. "I must have you out of it."

Dru's eyes widened in shock. "I don't understand what you mean," she said, though it would have been more accurate to say that she didn't *want* to understand what she feared he must mean.

"I mean, my angel, that there'll be no more of these dangerous adventures for you, and no more of Byron's puling poetry for me."

Drusilla stared at him, stunned by this cavalier dismissal. She had cooperated in everything that had been asked of her. She had strapped on a stiletto at her country's call; she had taken every risk at Holt's side; she had made an idiot of herself in front of drunken eel-catchers; she had even gone shopping with Christabel, for God's sake! And now she was being sent packing without so much as a by your leave.

Pride in herself which she had never known she possessed was mortally offended by this treatment, and hot protests rose to her lips. "I've never heard of anything so unfair! Why, I saved your life tonight!"

"And well I know it, my angel. So I'm going to return the favor and save yours. Don't you understand what has happened?" he demanded fiercely. "Our four friends from Picardy must have seen you loitering about the fountain and pointed you out to Lazare as the false Lady Toddington. But they can't be sure of what your game is, so Lazare devises a test. He finds some unfortunate fellow who likes the swish of your skirt and sends him over to you with a message from the colonel. By going with him the way you did, you confirmed your association with me beyond any doubt. You might as well," he concluded bitingly, "have handed Lazare a calling card that read 'MacRory Holt's female accomplice.' "

Drusilla bit her lip in chagrin as the full magnitude of her blunder became clear. And now, Holt meant to drum her out of the Great Game in disgrace because of it.

"But you can't simply dismiss me as if I were an unsatisfactory servant," she protested.

"I can, and I will," said Holt. "I dealt you into the Great Game, and, by God I can deal you out at any time I choose."

From her chaise longue Madame Solange watched with interest this most unusual lovers' quarrel.

Dru glared up at Holt. "I think the real reason you dismiss me is because I, the mere apprentice, failed to swoon admiringly over your destruction of Nicholas Appert's cannery."

A bad mistake, "Mademoiselle Angélique," thought the watching Madame Solange, *to take that tack with Rory. You discount an exploit of which he is most proud.*

"I don't give a damn for your swooning," grated Holt, "as long as you're safely back where you belong and out of my business."

"And what if I don't choose to be discarded so ruthlessly?"

"That choice isn't yours to make. The only choice you have is whether you will agree to go of your own free will like a sensible woman or whether I will be forced to truss you up like a Christmas goose and have those hulking fellows outside drop you over the back wall of the Hôtel Toddington."

Drusilla turned a questioning look at Madame Solange to see if she was acting in concert with the perfidious Holt.

Madame shrugged apologetically. "Rory calls the tune

143

where you are concerned, mademoiselle. If he wishes you trussed up and dropped over a wall, then that is what will be done."

But privately Madame Solange allowed herself leave to think, *You serve this girl badly, Rory, this female of your own peculiar kind, with whom I think you could have made a match unparalleled.*

Drusilla forced herself to take a deep, calming breath and surrender to the inevitable with dignity. "I perceive I am outnumbered. Very well, madame, you may inform your hulking fellows that I will cooperate. And as for you, Colonel Holt"—she turned to face him, shooting hazel-eyed arrows of accusation into his watching gaze—"I only hope that your commanders in the Great Game reward your loyalty far better than you have rewarded mine."

And then she was away, the hulking fellows on her heels to make sure she did not go astray before hiring a carriage to take her home.

In the silence that followed her departure, Madame Solange remarked to Holt with studied neutrality, "A young lady of decided character, I would say."

"A young lady of too damned much character altogether, I would say," growled Holt. "I never should have recruited her into this enterprise, and I've only myself to blame. But you'd think she'd have the sense to see that she is well out of it after tonight's debacle."

"You ride yourself too hard," Madame Solange told him consolingly. "It was a draw, not a debacle, and Excelsior can take no more satisfaction from tonight's work than you can."

But in this Madame Solange was wrong. Although Holt had slipped through his fingers, Henri Lazare was by no means dissatisfied with his night's work, for he had learned something of vital importance about MacRory Holt. Always before, Holt had been a lone wolf, a man apart. But now it seemed that the wolf had taken a mate.

Henri Lazare, that connoisseur of human frailty, that vivisector of human hearts, smiled darkly to himself. To think of the great MacRory Holt falling prey to the fatal malady of love! This female, whoever she was, had the besotted Scotsman crowing like a barnyard cockerel about his destruction of the cannery at Massy, a mysterious occurrence the cause of which had never been conclusively proven—until tonight, when Holt had convicted himself of the crime in his own words.

That the usually cool and closemouthed Holt would boast of such an act to this woman argued blind trust in and foolish infatuation with her. That the woman came so quickly to Holt's aid with her own dagger argued the companionship of a matched pair. The knife that Lazare now held in his gloved hand confirmed it.

It was a Gypsy stilleto of fine Toledo workmanship—the kind of knife a Gypsy man would give his woman to carry. That knife and all it betrayed about Holt had been left behind this night. Oh, yes, thought Henri Lazare, there was much wisdom to be divined from the silken hiss of a stiletto being unsheathed along a satin thigh.

There was a new stake on the table in the Great Game, a living stake.

And so the order went out to all of Henri Lazare's confidential agents, to all the secret cells of plotters who did his bidding, and when it was decoded that order read: FIND MacRORY HOLT'S WOMAN

The most well-furnished of the well-tenanted bedrooms in Madame Solange's *maison de tolérance* had been given over to

Holt's use. A crackling fire burned on the grate, and beside it was a canopied bed fitted with sheets of white linen and a coverlet of royal blue eiderdown. An embroidered dressing gown lay on the bed, and in a curtained alcove was a copper half bath filled with steaming water.

These accommodations were infinitely more comfortable than Holt's Left Bank lair, which had been selected for its unobtrusive appearance, the attached stable for Filbertine, the stout, iron-studded door, the long gallery for practicing knife-throwing, and the secret basement escape tunnel down to the Seine. These attributes aside, Holt's riverside lair was damp and poorly furnished, and the bed he slept in was cold and lonely.

Madame Solange soon joined him, running her chatelaine's eye over the room to ascertain that all was in order. Satisfied, she joined Holt at the window out of which he had been staring broodingly at the glittering lights of the Palais Royal. The lamps were still lit even at this late hour, for the gambling and wenching went on every night until dawn.

"It is beautiful, *non?*" she observed. "But it is not real, you know. It is a counterfeit, a cheat. The gamblers counterfeit the game of life, and the *filles de joie* counterfeit the game of love. My simple cottage and my young husband and our wheat fields in the Vendée were far more real than any of this."

Holt nodded, but Madame Solange knew his mind ran to something—*someone*—else, and about that she meant to console him.

"The girls," she told him, "are casting lots for who should come to you tonight."

His eyebrows shot up. "I am so much of a prize, then?"

She laughed that he did not know it. "But of course you are, *mon homme brave*. You are handsome, kind, very much a

146

man, and, what is more, you are a genuine hero, and heaven knows we get few enough of them in this place."

But when Holt merely laughed and shook his head, she made him a different offer. "There is another you might prefer, the one I spoke of to you a few moments ago, the one who bears some resemblance to 'Mademoiselle Angélique.' "

Holt paused, tempted a little, and then said, "But she, too, would be a counterfeit and a cheat, would she not? So I think I'll pass."

Solange shrugged, not entirely surprised. "There is not enough hot French blood in your rock-ribbed Scots body, Rory. But as you will, my friend. I will see to it that you are not disturbed."

She went away, then, to tend to the business of her establishment. As for Holt, though he slept in a bawdy house surrounded by the most beautiful grand coquettes in Paris, he slept alone.

Chapter Thirteen

In Which Drusilla Dines
at the Bonaparte Club

"Devil of a fellow, that Holt," proclaimed Major Ivor Leslie to the table at large. "Why, he was no more than a puppy-faced lieutenant when he single-handedly saved the entire British army from starvation at Torres Verdes."

Drusilla's wandering mind snapped to attention at the mention of the very man whose image she had been trying desperately to banish from her thoughts these last few weeks. It shouldn't have surprised her, she supposed, that Holt's name had come up at this regimental dinner party hosted by Lord Toddington. But what did surprise her was her own foolish yearning to hear more of the exploits of the man who had initiated her into the Great Game and then cast her aside when she became inconvenient.

"So there we were," went on the major obligingly, "camped on a mountain in Portugal with the Frogs below, aiming to starve us out. Holt volunteers to sneak through the French lines and buy up all the supplies he can from the locals—not only to feed us, but also to deny the supplies to the Frogs. And, by God, if he doesn't do it. Every night for weeks, he somehow got cattle and wagons of corn through the French cantonments. I don't mind saying that to us hungry fellows it seemed as much of a miracle as the feeding of the five thousand with the loaves and fishes."

148

Drusilla smiled politely at this feeble witticism whilst at the same time thinking acidly that being hailed as a miracle worker at such a young age must surely have given MacRory Holt a good conceit of himself—a conceit that lingered to this very day, in her considered opinion.

Christabel was intrigued. "I should certainly like to meet this famous Colonel Holt if he ever travels to Paris," she remarked, blissfully unaware that she had already met the famous Colonel Holt under what could only be described as liver-curling circumstances, when he waylaid the Thornrose carriage in the Picardy woodlands.

" 'Tis a great pity that he was retired on the half-pay rolls," said Lord Toddington, who had, of course, seen to this personally. "His talents must certainly be wasted in the backwoods of Scotland," added his lordship sententiously, a statement that caused Dru to observe sourly to herself that it was no wonder Lord Toddington was successful as a diplomatist. He lied so beautifully.

From the other end of the table, Captain Cameron Graham, a fellow Scot, felt obliged to continue the paean to his countryman by relating how Holt—"as an escaped prisoner of war at large in Paris, d'ye ken"—had worn his British uniform, bold as brass, passed himself off as an American officer, and still managed to send vital intelligence back to Wellington, even though he was on the run in the enemy's capital—"with every man's hand turned against him and no safe place to lay his head, d'ye ken."

Hearing this, Drusilla was hardput not to roll her eyes heavenward in disgust. *What utter poppycock!* she fumed inwardly. After all, she now kenned very well where Holt had lain his head whilst he was on the run in Paris, and she doubted he had suffered any hardship whatsoever in his accommodations. In fact, she was certain that Madame

Solange's girls had seen to Holt's comfort in every particular. Indeed, they were probably still doing so, she reflected bitterly.

It was just as well (she told herself yet again) that she was out of this dubious business of intelligence-gathering. It was a daft thing for her to have done in the first place, and she was resolved to do no more daft things from now on. Not even if the famous MacRory Holt came to her and begged her on his hands and knees to reenter the Great Game, not even if he took her in his arms and kissed her and told her he couldn't do without her . . .

Yuletide and the beginning of the New Year of 1815 came and went. And so did the Duke of Wellington. Increasingly alarmed for the Great Man's personal safety, the British Foreign Office removed him from his ambassador's post in Paris and dispatched him to Vienna as the British plenipotentiary to the Congress of Vienna.

With the conquering hero departed and the attention of the entire European continent centered on Vienna, Parisian society had gone "cursedly flat." This, at least, was Christabel's opinion, vehemently expressed as she sat with Drusilla in the library one February morning, reviewing the cards of invitations Grimthwaite had brought in along with the morning post.

"There's not an invitation here worth considering," complained her ladyship as she tossed aside the last of the engraved pasteboard cards. "There's no one left in Paris but encroaching mushrooms with too much money and too little breeding. I vow, there were so many rich cits at the ball last night, 'twas no better than a guildhall meeting. And they simply won't understand that one doesn't talk about money. One just has it. It was most dispiriting."

Even more dispiriting was the news contained in a letter from Miss Albinia Clatterbuck, the Wiltshire informant commissioned by Christabel to inquire into Mr. Farnshaw Eggleston's bloodlines and finances. Miss Clatterbuck reported that although Wiltshire fairly teemed with Egglestons, the only Farnshaw Eggleston she knew of had been deceased for at least a decade.

Christabel's china blue eyes glazed as she attempted to apply deductive reasoning to these sketchy facts. "It's obvious, Dru, that your Mr. Eggleston is a relation—"

"He is not *my* Mr. Eggleston," struck in Drusilla wearily.

Christabel continued her cogitations, unheeding. "Obviously, your Mr. Eggleston is a relation and a namesake of the deceased gentleman of the same name. After all, what parent would burden a defenseless infant with the name Farnshaw except to flatter a rich relation. But this still doesn't tell us whether or not your Farnshaw is going to be able to keep you in any sort of style."

"Christabel, I keep telling you that Mr. Eggleston is not going to be called upon to keep me in any style whatsoever."

"Oh, it is just like you to be provoking when I have received nothing but bad news in the post," said Christabel crossly.

But if the contents of the morning post were bad, the contents of the afternoon post bordered on tragic. Drusilla came into the library to collect the Thornrose ladies' correspondence and found Christabel pacing the room in high dudgeon.

"Just look at this!" Christabel commanded, waving an unfolded letter before her, rather in the manner of a barrister presenting evidence for the prosecution. "I knew the wretched man would do something like this. I warned ev-

151

eryone concerned that a leopard doesn't change his spots, that dissipation ran in his blood, that he could no more rid himself of his amorous propensities and behave like a gentleman than—"

"Christa!" broke in Drusilla, thoroughly alarmed. "Who on earth are you talking about?"

"The Earl of Brathmere, of course. Who else would I be talking about?"

Drusilla's heart sank and she was grateful that the Thornrose ladies were not present to hear whatever it was that their beloved niece Verity's bridegroom had done. The three Thornrose ladies had been cherishing high hopes that their reform-minded niece, Verity Thornrose, now the Countess of Brathmere, could successfully reform the rake-hell Earl of Brathmere. But perhaps that was not going to be the case after all.

"I warned Verity about that man," reiterated Christabel, "and I told her she must treat his trowsers with saltpeter, as it is a well-known remedy for gentlemen with randy habits. But she only laughed at me and said that it was an old wives' tale, and now look at what that unregenerate satyr has done, and poor Verity married to him only six months."

"And just what, exactly, has Lord Brathmere done?" asked Drusilla, although by now she was fairly certain she did not want to know.

Christabel's bosom swelled indignantly. "The babe is due in June," she stated darkly. "Need I say more?"

Drusilla gasped. "Verity wrote of this to you?"

"Well, of course she wrote to *me*, her oldest and dearest friend. She wanted me to hear it first from her, as she was sure others would write me of it sooner or later."

Drusilla sank down on the nearest settee. "Oh, poor Verity. What a state of mind she must be in!"

"Oh, well, as to that," said Christabel bitterly, "Verity is, of course, ecstatic."

"Ecstatic?" repeated Drusilla, uncertain whether Christabel was essaying satire or whether her vocabulary had broken down completely under the stress of the awful news. "Verity is ecstatic that her husband has fathered a child by another woman?"

Christabel looked at her blankly. "Who said anything about Brathmere fathering a child by another woman?"

"You did!"

"I most certainly did not!"

"You most certainly did, too! You just did! If not, then what is all this talk about licentious habits, leopards not changing their spots, and Brathmere being an unregenerate satyr?"

"And so he is!" declared Christabel roundly. "What else do you call a man who gets his wife with child after only six months of marriage?"

Drusilla shook her head, trying to clear her Christabel-beclouded brain. "Then . . . all this fuss is because Lord Brathmere has gotten his wife with child? But whatever is wrong with that?"

"It is a great inconvenience to me," snapped Christabel. "*That* is what is wrong with it. Verity writes me that she is unable to travel due to her Interesting Condition and therefore will be unable to bring little Charlotte to us. Not only am I missing my daughter dreadfully, but now I must find someone else to bring her over—no easy task, I assure you, because a child of four cannot be consigned into the care of just anyone. And all because that odious Brathmere couldn't keep his inexpressibles buttoned!"

Drusilla drew a deep breath. "Christabel, you must promise me something. You must promise to let me be the

153

one to tell the Thornrose ladies the news about Verity. They are not so young as they used to be, you know, and it wouldn't do to say anything that would cause them a shock."

Christabel bridled at the implication. "Why, as if *I* would ever say anything to shock those dear ladies. The very idea is absurd!"

The twilight shadows were lengthening in her bedroom when Drusilla woke abruptly from an after-tea nap. She had taken to her bed this rainy February afternoon not out of any particular need for sleep, but out of sheer *ennui*. Christabel was not the only one finding Paris cursedly flat at the moment.

Even the fascinations of the anti-slavery campaign had begun to pall. She was at the moment engaged in the onerous task of translating Mr. Wilberforce's "Letter to the British People Concerning the Abolition of the Slave Trade." Mr. Wilberforce was a worthy man but not a pithy one. His "letter" ran to four hundred pages and had to be bound in book form. At the moment it lay on her writing desk awaiting her attention. And say what you will, William Wilberforce was no Lord Byron and his tome was no *Childe Harold*.

In the midst of these glum musings, Dru sensed a presence in her room.

She sat up with a stifled gasp and saw that her tapestry-covered armchair was occupied by a long-legged gentleman whose booted feet were propped up on her fireplace fender in the manner of one who felt very much at home in her bedroom.

"You!"

"In the flesh," said MacRory Holt.

"How did you get in here?"

"Not as easily as usual, my angel. Particularly"—he

sounded irked—"since you'd seen fit to lock your balcony door against me."

He sounded for all the world, thought Dru, like an irate husband whose wife had locked him out of the bedroom. "You can hardly complain about being locked out," she reminded him coldly, "when you made it clear that you had no further use for me."

Holt removed his booted feet from the hearth fender and stood. "I apprehend from your unwelcoming tone that you're still piqued about that. Well, unruffle your feathers. I'm forced by circumstances to let you back into the Game one more time."

"Oh, are you, indeed? This means, I presume, that once again you find it expedient to hide behind my skirts whilst you conduct one of your missions."

"Just so, my angel. As it happens, I'm in dire need of your skirts tonight, so I've brought you a few trinkets, which I hope will smooth my way back into your good graces."

"And what makes you think I'll accommodate you for the sake of a few trinkets?"

"And how can you know you won't," he countered reasonably, "until you've seen the trinkets?"

He came to stand beside her bed, and she was suddenly aware of how positively wanton she must look, sitting amidst a froth of white sheets, her hair loose upon her half-bare shoulders, her bosom barely contained within her thin lawn underslip. At least she hoped she looked wanton—just a little, anyway. After all, what woman wants to look sensible whilst clad in gauzy underthings and frothy sheets.

And she could swear that Holt, too, had abruptly become aware of her dishabille amongst the gauze and froth, and for just an instant she thought she had a glimpse of how hot those cool green eyes of his could be. But it was only an instant, for he whisked her dressing gown off the trunk at the end of the bed and tossed it to her. "Put that on, my angel, and come see what I've brought you."

Despite all her sensible resolutions to the contrary, Drusilla soon found herself seated in her armchair by the fire, her bare feet tucked beneath her dressing gown.

From up his sleeve Holt slid out a stiletto as beautiful as a jewel in its fine workmanship. "To replace the one you lost when we came up against Lazare," he told her. Next, like a stage magician producing a silk scarf from up his sleeve, he pulled out a folded length of lavender from one of the capacious pockets of his coat. It proved to be a pinafore embroidered with violets at the hem and pocket.

"Green is more your color, I'd say," he observed critically as he handed it to her, "but it's a pretty enough trifle for tonight's work. And," he added, sliding a small packet out of his breast pocket, "I thought you might do with some earbobs as well."

Drusilla took the packet, doing her best to disguise her eager curiosity. A gift of jewelry from MacRory Holt! Who would have thought it? She unwrapped the brown paper and saw that the earrings were of pressed tin, hammered into the shape of . . . She held them up to the light and looked at them more closely, not quite believing what she saw.

"They look like . . . guillotines."

"And so they are," nodded Holt. "They were once the highest kick of fashion among the fair *citoyennes* of Paris. But no more, needless to say. Now the street markets are full of only *fleurs-de-lis* and white cockades."

Drusilla stared down askance at what were certainly the most outlandish earrings she had ever seen. "If they're not being sold anymore, then where did you get these?"

"From a diehard *citoyenne* who marched halfway across

the world as a *vivandière* in Bonaparte's army. I got them, along with a certain document I needed, off her corpse."

Drusilla abruptly put down the earrings. "You robbed these off a dead woman?"

"By no means. I bribed an undertaker to do it for me."

"I don't suppose you happen to know what this diehard *citoyenne* died of?"

Holt shrugged. "The undertaker didn't say and I didn't ask."

Well, thought Drusilla resignedly, *so much for gifts of jewelry from MacRory Holt.*

With no little dread, she dared to ask him where, exactly, one might be expected to wear guillotine earrings.

"Into the lion's den, that's where," answered Holt, his eyes wolfishly alight at the prospect. "Tonight, my angel, you and I attend a banquet at the Bonaparte Club."

The mission at the Bonaparte Club was this: Gain entry to the charity banquet being given there tonight for wounded veterans and for the *viviandières,* those intrepid women who had marched along with Bonaparte's army to serve as nurses, seamstresses, cooks, victualers, and of course, concubines.

Into the lion's den, indeed, for MacRory Holt. But Drusilla could not see the profit of it, and she told him as much as she watched him put on his disguise before her dressing table mirror.

"Even if the Bonaparte Club is awash in conspirators—"

"You may be sure it is," interjected Holt grimly.

"Surely they won't be discussing their plans at the banquet board. I don't see what you hope to gain."

"Insight," answered Holt, "into the state of mind of the enemy and, if I'm lucky, a chance to nose around the club's headquarters, a thing I've not been able to accomplish yet.

They're damned careful about who gets through the door—which leads me to believe they have something to hide."

Dru shook her head. "I only hope you are right that this disguise of yours will gain entrance for you on my ticket." For along with the deceased *viviandière's* earbobs, Holt had also acquired her banquet ticket, and he meant to have Drusilla take him in as her father, a wounded veteran.

Holt's disguise for the evening consisted primarily of the false "peeper patch" of a professional beggar—an eye patch cleverly constructed so that the wearer could see most of what went on around him yet still appear to be blind. Holt's other eye was shaded by a heavy scar constructed from theatrical putty. Anyone on the lookout tonight for the "Duke of Villainton's" green-eyed wolf would have to look hard at Holt to find the resemblance. A dusting of white hair powder had turned his brown hair a dirty grey, aging him enough to be Dru's father, which, as it happened, was his pose, tonight.

Drusilla, in the meantime, had tried to dredge up her old sensible self, the sensible self that had sworn most determinedly that never again would she mix into another of Holt's intelligence-gathering intrigues. But after an internal debate of perhaps thirty seconds, her sensible self was quite thoroughly vanquished.

And so here was Miss Drusilla Sedgewick, with a Gypsy knife in her garter and a dead woman's guillotine earrings in her earlobes, back in the Great Game for the sake of England and MacRory Holt.

The Bonaparte Club was situated in a fashionable commercial district and boasted a large public meeting room where rows of trestle tables and benches had been set up to accommodate the banqueters. The generous and festive meal—and the wine-imbibing that accompanied it—was well under way to judge from the noise emanating from the establishment.

But first she and Holt must get past the two burly men who served as doorkeepers and ticket takers. These guardians were necessary, since tonight's banqueters had been chosen by lottery out of the thousands of penurious veterans and *viviandières* who would have liked to attend.

At the door to the club, Dru handed over her winning ticket and, smiling up at the two ticket takers through her lashes, prettily requested that her dear papa, himself blinded in the wars, be allowed to enter with her, as she did not wish to leave him unattended.

The younger of the men smiled back at her in a friendly way. The older one leered.

"And what," inquired the leering fellow, "will you do to make it worth our while to let in your 'dear papa,' mam'selle? A kiss from that pretty mouth of yours is what we'll have to charge you to let the old fellow at the trough."

"If that's your pleasure, sirs," said Dru with a sprightly smile, for she did not think a genuine *viviandière* would object to this too strenuously.

So she stood on tiptoe and bussed the younger fellow lightly on both cheeks in what her mother had always called "kissing in the French manner." But when she tried to do the same to the older fellow, it was obvious from the way that he seized her chin and ground his mouth against hers that he had French kissing of quite another variety on his mind.

But Holt was instantly shouldering against the lickerish ticket taker with a feigned clumsiness while at the same time demanding in a querulous, elderly man's voice, "What manner of banquet is this where an old soldier's daughter is beset by louts demanding that she barter her kisses? I'll make a ripe tale of this, see if I don't."

"Oh, get along inside with you, then," growled the man, obviously afraid of the fuss that might result. "There's no need to make such a noise about it."

"Yes, Papa, *do* come along," urged Drusilla, and she tugged Holt away, leaving the door warden nursing his bruised shoulder and wondering how such a battered and bedamned-looking old fellow could have such a solid heft of muscle to him.

The din of three hundred hungry French souls dining on the type of viands they did not often get to sample in their straitened existences was considerable. Tricolor cockades, sashes, shawls, and earrings were much in evidence, as were eagle-shaped coat buttons copied from the battle standard of the Emperor's *Grandé Armée*. Also to be seen were representations of bees—Napoleon's personal heraldic device—and violets—his favorite flower and the device he had bequeathed to his young son, the King of Rome.

Drusilla saw immediately that her earrings and her violet-bedecked pinafore were exactly right for the circumstances. She had to give Holt credit. When he took a lady into a lion's den, he saw to it that she was properly dressed for the occasion.

With Holt stumbling in her wake in his best invalid fashion, Drusilla eventually found them bench space between a one-armed *grenadier* and a wooden-legged *chasseur*. Sitting across the table from her and Holt were two weathered dames, former *vivandières,* who were reminiscing nostalgically about how rich the corpse plunder had been after the Battle of Wigram.

But most of the talk that floated up and down the trestle

table was of the present, and bitter talk it was, of the wrongs being done to the soldiers of France by the restored monarchy.

"The Emperor's best officers," related the one-armed *grenadier,* "are banished from Paris, their only crime having been to fight for their country in the late wars."

"And it has been decreed," put in the wooden-legged *chasseur,* angrily banging down his tankard, "that from now on, only the sons of the nobility will be admitted to the military academies and the polytechniques."

"*Mon dieu,* I can tell you worse than that," said one of the leathery-complected *viviandières.* "L'Hôtel des Invalides for old soldiers has been closed and all the decayed gents put out on the streets with licenses to beg."

There was a muttering up and down the table, and then, a scarred and maimed sergeant was on his feet crying out that he wished to propose a certain toast that was already known to them.

"Do you believe in our Savior?" he shouted.

"Yes, and to His Resurrection!" came back the answering shout from the crowd.

It was both a toast and a prayer for Bonaparte's return.

Another old soldier stood up, and much to Dru's amazement shouted "*Vive le Roi!* Long live the King!"

But the crowd knew the answer to this catechism also.

"*Du Rome! Du Rome!*" they responded, for Napoleon's infant son was more king to them than the Bourbon who now sat on the French throne. And as for that particular royal gentleman, he came in for a few toasts as well.

"Up with King Louis—up to the gibbet!"

"Hail to King Louis *le cochon,* Louis the Pig!"

"Here's to Louis, *Roi Panáde,* Louis, King of Slops!"

Drusilla cast a sidelong look at Holt, who, of course, was drinking and toasting as lustily and seditiously as everyone else. He must certainly be getting an earful of insight into the enemy's state of mind tonight, she thought. Looking around the banqueting room, it seemed to her that the women gathered here would be happy to take up a spot of knitting beneath the guillotine, while the men were looking forward with pleasure to seeing Bourbon heads roll once more.

Selections of martial music were now being played, and speeches—of the rabble-rousing variety, no doubt—were also to be delivered by various club officers. Holt felt no need to sit through the oratory, as every incendiary word would appear in the anti-monarchist newspapers tomorrow.

And so a certain invalid veteran accompanied by his daughter went slightly astray in the Bonaparte Club in their search for a breath of fresh air . . .

Most of the doors they came upon were unlocked, and the rooms beyond showed nothing other than what one would expect to see in such a place. But then, beneath the basement stairs, they came upon a locked door, a circumstance that caused Holt's eyes to gleam speculatively.

While Drusilla held a candle, Holt took out a small pouch of locksmith's tools—or, to put it more precisely, lockpick's tools. After some twisting and twiddling with the various delicate little implements, he heard the lock click and pushed open the door.

"Hello," said Holt softly after he'd carefully closed the door behind them, "what have we here?"

What they had was a printing press.

"Well, well . . ." Holt was almost purring. "And right on their own premises, too. Let's see what the blighters have been up to."

What they'd been up to was producing a pro-Bonapartist

broadsheet, bundles of which had already been run off and stacked against the wall.

The colored drawing on the broadsheet depicted a bouquet of violets, and artfully sketched in amongst the blossoms were the faces of the Emperor, his son, and the Empress Marie-Louise, that plump Austrian virgin who had been sacrificed to the Ogre for political reasons and who had produced the eaglet King of Rome with such admirable dispatch.

The caption below the drawing read, *Flowers of the spring so dear to the French, you will give us back our glory and our peace.*

Drusilla, who had learned a thing or two about tracts and pamphlets in the employ of the Thornrose sisters, was impressed by the visual appeal and artistic execution of this clever polemic on paper.

Loud voices and a pounding of what sounded like an army of feet on the stairs above their heads promptly ended their reading and galvanized them into defensive maneuvers.

Drusilla snuffed the candle between her fingers, and she and Holt pressed themselves against the wall behind the door to the storage room. If any of the men coming down the corridor were to try the door and find it unlocked, she and Holt would be in real trouble. She felt Holt's body next to hers, his arm across her wildly beating heart like an iron bar, and she knew he was preparing himself to attack their discoverers out of the dark if it came to that.

The footsteps grew louder, and a gleam of light shone under the door, then disappeared, then returned as someone bearing a lamp moved up and down the corridor. For the first time in her life, Drusilla understood that strange impulse that sometimes seizes the hunted to step out of one's hiding place and give oneself up, discovery being preferable to the awful suspense of awaiting capture as the footsteps come nearer and the light shines brighter.

163

But she bit her lip in the unbreathing silence and con-
quered that panicked urge with a good dose of British feminine common sense: *You simply cannot be apprehended in a
Paris basement wearing tin jewelry. It's just not done.* And eventually, after several eternities, the footsteps receded, and the
light dimmed into blackness.

She then discovered to her chagrin that she was clutching
the breast of Holt's shirt in a convulsive grip and that her icy
hand was covered with his warm one. Holt, who had spent a
good deal of his adult life hiding in bolt-holes with ruthless
men on his trail, must have known what she was enduring.
Once the corridor was quiet, he pulled her against him in a
swift, hard embrace, and his lips brushed her hair in the
briefest of kisses.

But when she lifted her face breathlessly to his, he merely
laid his finger across her lips to signal her silence. It was probably a rule of the Game, she thought dismally, that no real
kissing was allowed.

The ride home on Filbertine (oh, yes, she was part of the
night's adventure, too) was oddly lulling to Dru. Or perhaps
it was the wine that she had indulged in when she and Holt returned to their place at the banquet table. Several more toasts
had to be drunk, and Dru had felt sorely in need of drinking
them after her adventure in the basement.

As they jogged through the night-darkened streets, Holt
was more taciturn than usual. Dru had no doubt that he had
been sobered by the industry of Britain's Bonapartist enemies, as well as by the evident stupidity of Britain's Bourbon
allies.

But, as it turned out, there was something else on his
mind, something she had no notion of until she had slid off
Filbertine's back and was preparing to slip through the pos-

tern gate into the Hôtel Toddington.

Holt's voice was harsh as he leaned over the saddle and admonished her, "Don't ever barter your kisses again the way you did tonight. Not even for my sake—do you understand?"

He urged Filbertine off into the night mists, leaving Dru wondering if it was remotely possible that she had caught a glimpse of that green-eyed monster, jealousy, looking out of MacRory Holt's handsome face.

Chapter Fourteen

The Violets Are Blooming

Several days later Drusilla set off in the company of her three employers to tour the famous orphan asylum maintained by the French Legion of Honor. Praised as one of the most enlightened institutions of its kind, the Legion orphanage was an attraction that could not fail to interest the Thornrose ladies. However, upon arriving at this worthy institution, they found the front door locked and the premises empty of orphans.

Vigorous knocking finally brought forth an aproned matron, who, when asked to explain the absence of orphans, unleashed a spate of nearly incoherent lamentations and agitated hand-wringing.

"Do you mean, my good woman," inquired Miss Faith, "that the orphanage is no more, and the orphans are scattered?"

"Why, only a week ago," observed Miss Hope, "we were informed that three hundred orphans were in residence here."

"Surely one cannot scatter three hundred orphans in so short a time!" expostulated Miss Charity.

But that was exactly what had happened. The Legion of Honor, founded by Bonaparte, had recently attracted the unfavorable notice of King Louis's military ministers. Even worse, the Legion's orphan asylum had also attracted the ministers' unfavorable notice. The upshot was that the orphanage was ordered closed and the orphans remanded to the doubtful charity of their individual parishes.

The Thornrose ladies greeted this news with indignation, but there was nothing to be done except return to the Hôtel Toddington to dictate letters of protest to the appropriate French authorities.

As their carriage clattered homeward along the city's boulevards, it struck Drusilla that a great many men abroad today wore nosegays of violets in their lapels, and a great number of ladies had draped themselves in violet-colored shawls and adorned their bonnets and shopping baskets with silk violets. Flower sellers sat among banks of violets and did a brisk trade with the passing *boulevardiers,* while at every turn, the window boxes of the buildings boasted new clusters of violets.

All of Paris, it seemed, was abloom this March morning with the Emperor's favorite flower.

"I knew it was only a matter of time," proclaimed Christabel triumphantly when Drusilla returned, "before we wore down Mr. Eggleston's resistance and convinced him that he was enamored of you whether he knew it or not. You must confess, Drusilla, that he has shown marked attention to you of late and will shortly be swooning at your feet. You cannot deny it."

Indeed, Drusilla could not deny it. Mr. Eggleston, she feared, was about to fall at her feet out of sheer exhaustion, run to ground at last. That was the only reason she could think of to explain his sudden partiality. Certainly she used no arts to attract him, and yet he had begun to seek her out with an assiduousness he had not previously shown. Tonight, for instance, he had quite unabashedly invited himself to accompany her and the Toddingtons to the

Comédie-Française, where they were to view the much-praised production of *The Destruction of Pompeii.*

This tragedy in five acts, featuring the acclaimed actress Mademoiselle George, was currently the talk of Paris. Though Christabel generally disliked tragedies ("They never end happily, you know"), she was making an exception for this one. So much praise had she heard of the fearful verisimilitude of the stage effects portraying the volcanic eruption of Vesuvius that she was determined to see the play herself.

"I am persuaded the evening will not be dull," she predicted confidently. "The exhibition of pyrotechnics at the theatre is said to be unrivaled."

As it turned out, for once Christabel knew whereof she spoke.

In the private box hired for the season by the British Embassy, Mr. Farnshaw Eggleston engaged in earnest and labored flirtation with an unreceptive Miss Drusilla Sedgewick.

Christabel smiled complacently at this burlesque. As for the drama unfolding below her on the stage of the Comédie-Française, Christabel found that almost as tedious as Drusilla was finding Mr. Eggleston's wooing. So harrowing were the tragical sufferings of the characters and so lengthy and tormented were their declamations about their sufferings that Christabel was moved to whisper to her husband, "I can only think it a mercy that Vesuvius shall erupt and put a period to so many unhappy existences."

But, alas, Lord Toddington was not privileged to witness their volcanic demise. Just as the final act began, he was unexpectedly summoned back to the embassy by one of Fitzroy Somerset's young clerks, who had been sent in search of him.

Christabel was not pleased. "How vexing that you must leave, Charles. This is too bad of Fitzroy, and I shall certainly tell him so when next I see him."

Lord Toddington looked up gravely from the note the clerk had brought him. "Fitzroy writes that it is a matter of vital urgency, though what the particulars of it can be, I've no notion. In any case, my dear, I'll leave the carriage at your disposal and beg that you enjoy the rest of the play as best you can."

No sooner was he gone in a swirl of black evening cape than there came a knock at the box door which heralded the entry of a certain French gentleman whose timely appearance revealed that he had been keeping a close eye on the activities of the Toddington party.

The Chevalier Guy de Saint-Armand sauntered in, clad in flawless evening attire, his black curls in fashionable disarray upon his nobly handsome forehead. Drusilla stiffened at the sight of him, while Mr. Eggleston scowled openly. Christabel brightened, however, for the chevalier was a very winning fellow who had about him now the additional cachet of having perpetrated violence upon another man in a public duel.

After engaging Christabel in some flirtatious nonsense that ended in his kissing each rosy finger of his divinity's little hand (Drusilla's fingers were not so honored, needless to say), the chevalier disposed himself on a theatre chair and crossed one elegantly clad leg over the other.

"So, my friends," he informed them expansively, "it is *bonne chance* that you are come tonight. Now we shall have some adherents to the Lily of France in the War of the Blossoms."

Drusilla and Christabel exchanged puzzled looks while Mr. Eggleston snapped in impatient annoyance, "What the devil are you speaking of, Saint-Armand? We know nothing of any 'War of the Blossoms.' "

The chevalier raised his eyebrows in amazement. *"Non?* But it has been raging all this month in the theatres of Paris. Can it actually be that you have not heard of it?"

"But we have not!" exclaimed Christabel, concerned that some modish new caprice of the French *beau monde* might have escaped her notice. "You must tell us at once, sir."

"I shall do more than tell you," said the chevalier expansively. "I shall draft all of you into this War of the Blossoms. From this moment on, you are beautiful soldiers in the cause of La Belle France."

But being a beautiful soldier for Froggie land held no brief for Mr. Eggleston, who snorted audibly, then ostentatiously turned his attention to the stage as the chevalier undertook to explain to the two ladies the significance of the War of the Blossoms.

Not, it seemed, since the days when the White Rose of York had contended against the Red Rose of Lancaster had there been such a floricultural passage of arms as there was now between the royalists' *fleurs-de-lis* and the violets of the Bonapartists. The rivalry had lately spilled over into the theatres, with those actresses who favored the royalists accepting only bouquets of lilies, while those actresses loyal to the Emperor would have nothing but violets. The audience reaction to these floral standards was being accorded a great significance in the press, Saint-Armand informed them.

At which point Mr. Eggleston broke in prosaically, "Vesuvius has begun to spew, ladies. Don't think you'll want to miss it."

Indeed they would not, for great alarums and diversions were now taking place upon the stage. The actors were entering, exiting, and emoting amongst thunderings, flashings, toppling statues, and whirling fizgigs, while offstage bellows blew large quantities of smoke and ash over actors and scenery alike.

"That's surely not woodsmoke they're puffing about," remarked Mr. Eggleston in his usual practical way. "If it was, Mlle. George would be smoked as a haddock by the end of the play."

That lady was meanwhile expiring affectingly on a stage littered with volcanic debris and resounding with the rumblings of Vesuvius. It was to the famed tragedienne's credit that she could win back the audience's attention so completely from the stage effects. By the time she had delivered her last speech and the curtain had fallen over her still form, many in the audience were weeping openly.

And now for the second drama of the evening.

Out came the supporting players to take their bows, amongst them several actresses carrying white lilies. There was applause but also many shouts of "Sycophant! Toadeater!" Then Mlle. George appeared, her arms filled with violets. The crowd went wild with approbation and calls of *"Vive l'Empereur!"* filled the air, resounding throughout the theatre.

Mr. Eggleston could not resist a gibe at the chevalier. "Blossoms ain't falling your way tonight, eh, Saint-Armand?"

"That actress George has won them over," snapped the chevalier. " 'Tis well known that she was once the Corsican's mistress."

"Really? You don't say!" exclaimed Christabel, staring down at Mlle. George with enlivened interest. "I vow, every time I turn around in Paris, some female is pointed out to me as being one of Bonaparte's mistresses. The city must be positively chock-a-block with the Emperor's light-o'-loves."

"And every last one of 'em must be in the audience to-night," put in Mr. Eggleston, who was beginning to be concerned about the high temper of the theatregoers. "I think we'd best withdraw, ladies. We make a target of ourselves simply by being in this box."

That was all too true, for it was from this very box, in this very theatre, that the Duke of Wellington had made his first public appearance in Paris in the company of the French royal family. This had not been forgotten, apparently, for now fists were being shaken up at them, and calls of "Down with Villainton!" were to be heard. Someone in the audience even had the temerity to hurl an orange in their direction.

Christabel's eyes widened. "Good heavens! Perhaps we had better leave," she agreed, and she began to arrange her cloak, her reticule, and herself for departure.

Eggleston rose to his feet, clapped the chevalier on the back with false *bonhomie,* and said in a tone of undisguised mockery, "Well, Saint-Armand, looks like it's up to you to man the ramparts and give those 'violets' what-for. I'm sure you'll do the pretty lily-flowers proud."

"Your concern touches me deeply," snapped the chevalier, his dark eyes stabbing venomously at the Englishman.

Drusilla had been standing with the gentlemen (it took her only one quarter of the time to arrange herself that it did Christabel), and she felt the enmity flash between the two men like a drawn sword. A half-formed intuition leapt into her mind that perhaps there was more to the pair's dislike of each other than she knew, but the thought went astray in the flurry of their hurried departure from the Comédie-Française.

It would not be fair to say that the Toddington party fled incontinently from the Comédie-Française, but on the other hand, they did not exactly stand on the order of their departure, either.

"Well," said Christabel, once they had conveyed Mr. Eggleston to his lodgings and safely reentered the grounds of the Hôtel Toddington, "we shall certainly have a deal of news to tell Charles when he returns from the embassy."

But Lord Toddington had already returned from the embassy, and it was he who had all the news to tell. He came quickly down the hall toward them, his face so harshly drawn that they stopped short at the sight of him.

"Charles, what on earth is it?" demanded Christabel. "You look positively bilious."

"Bonaparte," he said, summing up the dire news in a single word. "Bonaparte has escaped from Elba and has landed in the south of France. It is believed that he intends to march on Paris."

Christabel succumbed to hysterics. As the news spread across the city, so did many another English lady sojourning in Paris have hysterics—and not a few gentlemen as well, if the truth were known.

This was not to be wondered at. For an entire generation, British nursery maids had been terrorizing their infant charges into good behavior with admonitions like: *If you cry in the dark, Old Boney will come and snatch you away,* or *Tell a lie, and Bonaparte will cut out your tongue and fry it for breakfast meat.*

No nursery tales of this sort were needed for Drusilla, of course. She knew from a young age the name of the Ogre who was responsible for her father's death at Corunna. And now that Ogre was on the loose once more.

"They will stop him at Grenoble," predicted Lord

Toddington. "You may depend on it."

But they did not stop at him Grenoble. The Fifth and Seventh Regiments of the Army of France deserted from the service of King Louis and declared their allegiance to the Emperor.

"They will stop him at Lyons," said Lord Toddington. "The Comte d'Artois is marching there personally with reinforcements for the city garrison."

But the garrison and the reinforcements defected to the Emperor, and d'Artois barely escaped with his life.

When news of this reached Paris, a mob of citizens gathered at the Victory Column in the Place Vendôme and raised a huge sign, upon which they had printed with a fine Gallic sprightliness of humor: *FROM NAPOLEAON TO LOUIS XVIII: MY GOOD BROTHER, THERE IS NO NEED TO SEND ME ANY MORE SOLDIERS. I HAVE ENOUGH.*

Indeed, all across France, the various units of the French army were declaring for the Emperor at an alarming rate, and the French populace was giving vent to their anti-Alliance feelings in ways that had begun to make their British guests feel most uncomfortable.

"They've lost their Frenchie wits just like they did in the Revolution," opined Mr. Eggleston when he came to call at the Hôtel Toddington and told how some cheeky Frog had posted a pro-Bonapartist broadsheet right on his, Farnsworth Eggleston, Esquire's, chamber door. "You mark my words, they'll be rolling out the tumbrels and sending *aristos* to the guillotine next. Best watch your step, Saint-Armand." (The chevalier had also come to call). "There's probably a basket over at the Bastille with your name on it."

"I do not find you amusing, monsieur."

"I wasn't trying to be amusing, Chevalier."

Bonaparte's progress toward Paris was to be faithfully chronicled in the headlines of the *Moniteur*.

The Cannibal Has Left His Den.
The Corsican Wolf Has Landed in the Bay of San Juan.
The Tiger Has Arrived at Gay.
The Wretch Spent the Night at Grenoble.
The Tyrant Has Arrived at Lyons.
The Usurper Has Been Seen Within Fifty Miles of Paris.
Bonaparte Has Been Advancing With Great Rapidity.
Napoleon Has Spent the Night at Fontainebleau.
His Imperial Majesty Napoleon is at the Gates of Paris.

And so the bewitchment of the French people was complete, with the wizard and warlord Napoleon poised to reascend the Imperial throne he had vacated some ten months before.

Somewhere between *The Usurper Has Been Seen Within Fifty Miles of Paris* and *Bonaparte Has Been Advancing With Great Rapidity*, Christabel decided that Paris was becoming inhospitable.

"When Bonaparte takes the city," she predicted gloomily, "we shall in all likelihood be ravished by *grenadiers*."

"Why *grenadiers* in particular?" asked Drusilla, curious. "Why not *voltiguers,* or *cuirassiers* or *chasseurs?*"

Christabel shot her an annoyed look. "If you're going to be in one those provokingly *plausible* moods of yours, you may as well excuse yourself, for I won't listen. And I'll have you know that I am not the only English female in Paris who fears for her life and her virtue should the Ogre take the city—"

She broke off abruptly as Grimthwaite opened the door to

admit Lord Toddington. His lordship's entrance caused much surprise, for he had been engaged in round-the-clock consultations, the subject being, needless to say, how to counter the relentless advance of the Grand Disturber.

Christabel greeted him with some anxiety. "What is it, Charles? Why are you here at this hour of the afternoon? It's not more bad news, is it?" Of late, all the news had seemed bad to Christabel.

"On the contrary, m'dear," said her husband, seating himself beside her and taking her hand in his. "I believe I bear good news. I have received orders from the Foreign Office to remove myself and my staff immediately to Belgium."

Because, thought Drusilla, though of course she did not say so aloud, *the Foreign Office could not afford for the custodian of so much confidential intelligence to fall into the hands of the enemy.*

Christabel was delighted beyond anything. "Oh, when can we leave, Charles? I beseech you, my darling, let it be as soon as possible."

Lord Toddington smiled at her indulgently. "We will go as soon as the household can be made ready to move. I have written ahead to have a house rented for us on the rue Ducale. It will not be what we have here, of course, but I fancy it will suit us well enough."

"Oh, my darling, this is wonderful news! We shall be away from Paris—and we shall not be ravished by *grenadiers* after all," she added brightly as she departed to give the Toddington house staff their marching orders.

Drusilla lingered, screwing up her courage to ask Lord Toddington a question, even though she knew it was against the rules of the Game to do so.

"My lord, have you heard anything from Colonel Holt?"

Lord Toddington frowned at her mention of Holt's name, and looked around quickly to make sure they were not overheard. "Colonel Holt goes his own way, my dear. When he wishes us to know his whereabouts, we will hear from him."

And with that rather cryptic and not at all reassuring statement, Drusilla had to be content. She would have been even less reassured had she seen the dispatch that Lord Toddington sent off to London that same evening.

From the Rt. Hon. Lord Toddington to the Foreign Office
Private & Secret
Item: I have heard nothing from Col. H. in more than two weeks and suspect the worst as regards to his safety.

Christabel was a marvel of efficiency organizing her household to fly before the Ogre's ravening horde, which by this point numbered some eighty-thousand men. That Bonaparte seemed to be able to raise an army literally out of the dust was causing no end of tremors among the crowned heads of Europe. Humbler folk were equally fearful, and the British community in Paris was fast making preparations to leave the country.

The Toddington evacuation was proceeding apace. The Thornrose ladies, with their minimal wardrobes and orderly habits, were the most easily mobilized to depart. They were dispatched ahead of the general exodus in order to take the journey at a slower pace that would be kinder to their aging joints.

Drusilla was left behind in order to aid Christabel in closing up the Toddingtons' Paris establishment.

In one matter, Christabel had undergone a change of heart. The Earl of Brathmere—who previously could not be enough detested for depriving Christabel of her daughter's presence—was now looked upon as the savior of the Toddingtons' little Charlotte.

"I can only thank Providence that my angel is safe in

London with Verity and Brathmere and not here in the midst of this dreadful crisis," said Christabel fervently.

The blessings of Charlotte's absence had been borne in upon Christabel as she had watched one of the young embassy undersecretaries load his harassed-looking wife and several small howling progeny into a cramped and overloaded traveling chaise. The young paterfamilias did not look to be in for a comfortable journey.

Overhead, the main chimney of the Hôtel Toddington bellowed forth black smoke at a prodigious rate. Lord Toddington was burning all the reports in his confidential files, many of which had been authored by MacRory Holt. It would not do to have them fall into the hands of the enemy.

If only, thought Drusilla with a sigh, she could be sure that Holt himself had not fallen into the hands of the enemy.

He had been much on her mind this morning as she had packed the portmanteau she would keep with her in the carriage. Into it she had put her few valuables, which somehow had come to include the things associated with MacRory Holt: her knife, her copy of *Childe Harold*, her vials of red-cabbage juice and invisible ink. The guillotine earrings she had tucked into the black velvet case that held her grandmother's pearls, even as she called herself several kinds of fool for doing so.

As she set down her portmanteau beside the mammoth pile of Christabel's luggage, a flash of color caught her eye, and she saw a Gypsy wagon drawn up outside the wrought-iron gate.

"Christabel, look!" she exclaimed. "What do you suppose those Gypsies want?"

Christabel spared the wagon a distracted look. "They probably want what Gypsies always want—to pick your pocket while they tell your fortune."

"I believe," said Drusilla thoughtfully, "that I must have my fortune told."

Christabel's attention was on her baggage, however, and she did not see Drusilla walk through the gates and approach the brightly painted wagon. Seated upon the diver's box was Don Ramon the Gypsy chieftain, who hailed her with a wave.

"Hola!, señorita. You come in good time."

"And how is that, Don Ramon?"

"Our mutual *camarada* has need of a woman's touch, and you, it seems, are the woman he is calling for."

"I beg your pardon?" whispered Drusilla, not sure she had heard aright.

The Gypsy chief gestured impatiently. "You must go to him. We have brought your bag."

A grinning *gitano* boy of perhaps ten deposited her portmanteau on the road beside her and said proudly, "The *giorgios* are as the blind, Don Ramon. I took it easily."

"Well done, spratling. Now put it in the wagon for the pretty lady."

"But wait," protested Drusilla, "I can't simply leave with you."

Don Ramon's face hardened. "Then you will not answer Rory's call?"

Drusilla spread her hands helplessly. "It's not that I don't want to, but—"

"Then decide now, señorita. The guardsmen will come soon to chase us away, and I do not think they will let you accompany us."

This was true, Drusilla knew. Even though Lord Toddington was aware of her association with Holt and the Gypsies, he could not very well let her ride away in a Gypsy wagon while his wife and half the embassy staff were watching.

MacRory Holt was calling for her.

"All right, I'll come."

"Hurry then!" ordered Don Ramon. "Into the back of the wagon, and we'll be away."

It was not until some time later—after Don Ramon's wagon had departed and Drusilla had mysteriously disappeared—that Christabel comprehended the awful truth.

Her secretary had been stolen by Gypsies!

Chapter Fifteen

A Gypsy Idyll

In a flowery meadow beside a curving bend of the Seine, Don Ramon's band of Spanish Gypsies had set up camp, their colorfully painted wagons drawn into a circle. Stepping down from the wagon in which she had been riding, Dru saw that she was now amongst people whose menfolk favored flat hats and drooping mustachios, while the women affected head scarves, elaborate jewelry, and ruffled skirts of many hues.

Compared to the brilliantly attired *gitanas,* Drusilla looked drab as a squab in her grey traveling dress, but this did not concern her at the moment. Her thoughts were all of MacRory Holt and why he had sent for her. Upon this subject Don Ramon had been singularly unforthcoming, saying only that the matter rested entirely in the hands of Catalona the *drabardi.* This exotically named personage was, as it turned out, the elderly woman who served as the Gypsy band's healer, wisewoman, and matchmaker.

That MacRory Holt was in the hands of a Gypsy healer was a matter of grave concern to Drusilla. That MacRory Holt was in the hands of a Gypsy matchmaker—to this Drusilla gave no thought at all, although perhaps, she should have.

Catalona the *drabardi* and her patient were situated in a marvelously painted wagon of red and purple. Wooden steps led up to the door, which opened into a candle-lit interior decorated with strange motifs and redolent of aromatic herbs.

Drusilla noticed nothing of the décor, however. Her attention was centered upon the man who lay sprawled on a narrow shelf of a bed that was far too short for his long-legged frame. It was Holt—gaunt, unshaven, stripped to the waist. He lay frighteningly still, his face and chest streaked with fever sweat.

Beside him sat an old woman, her grey locks streaming from beneath an embroidered scarf as she leaned over to bathe his forehead with cold water. She peered up at Drusilla with dark, snapping eyes and said in strongly accented French, "So you are here at last, girl! Would that it were sooner, for his sake."

"What has happened to him?" whispered Drusilla, almost afraid of what the answer might be.

"This," she said, turning over Holt's limp forearm to show an angry red slash from elbow to wrist. It was not a deep wound, but it had a look about it that Drusilla did not like.

"Is it infected?" she asked as calmly as she could.

"It is *poisoned*," said the old woman. "Poisoned from the knife that cut him, the blade dipped in some cunning brew."

No need to ask who had concocted the cunning brew. "Excelsior" had done it. Henri Lazare, who had a compendium of poison recipes that Lucrezia Borgia would have envied. Henri Lazare, who killed the Emperor's enemies with poisoned snuff and poisoned wine and poisoned knives. It was Henri Lazare who had laid Holt low—of that, Drusilla was certain.

She must have said the Frenchman's name aloud, for the old *gitana* quickly nodded. "Aye, Lazare brewed the bane, but he did not wield the knife himself. It was his hired *bravos* who set upon Rory in a dark alley. Lazare would never go against Rory *mano a mano.*"

As if sensing that he was being discussed, Holt moved on his cramped bed, muttering deliriously.

"He must have a physician," said Drusilla.

"He has *me*," said the old Gypsy woman, her eyes flashing with affront.

Drusilla bit her lip, in a quandary over what to do next. Holt was wounded, poisoned, trapped in a country that would shortly be ruled once more by his mortal enemies. She knew of no English doctor she could summon, and what French physician could be trusted in this time of turmoil? For the moment, it seemed that Holt must be dependent on the curative skills of Catalona the Gypsy healer.

Catalona's further diagnosis of the cause of Holt's fever did not make Drusilla feel any better about this situation.

"It is not the poison that oppresses him. That I have cured. Already I have leeched the bane from his body," proclaimed the *gitana* healer as she lit another incense stick. "No, it is the curse that fevers him, and no *giorgio* butcher-doctor can heal that."

"A . . . curse, you say," repeated Drusilla, who diplomatically refrained from adding that, as far as she was concerned, this was utter bosh. "Curses are not a thing that we *giorgios* easily understand," she said at last.

The old woman nodded, the coins sewn into her head scarf jingling faintly as she did so. "He has been cursed," she repeated with finality. "The evil eye has been put upon him. And you, little girl with the two names, it was both your names that our Rory called out in his fever dreams. Do you know what it means when a man calls out a woman's name in a fever dream?"

Drusilla shook her head, and the Gypsy was obviously disgusted at her ignorance. "Bah! This is a thing that, if you do not understand it at once from the heart, you probably never will. But it is enough that you are here with him, even if you have no knowledge of these matters."

"You think he will recover, then?" said Dru, hopeful in spite of herself. She smoothed back Holt's hair, noting how innocent he looked with his brown locks in boyish curls around his damp forehead.

The Gypsy healer was watching her with sharp, dark eyes. "Now that you are here," said the old woman with certainty, "the curse will be lifted." She picked up her bag of herbs and tied it shut with an air of finality, as if her work was done. "You will sit with him tonight, for my old bones must go to bed with the sun. He will be better tomorrow, for it is the curse not the poison that weakens his marrow."

It was not at all sensible, Drusilla knew, to think that this could be true. Still, she found herself praying most fervently that the Gypsy healer's diagnosis was correct.

Sometime during the night Holt's condition took a turn for the better. Drusilla could not say exactly when this occurred, for in spite of herself she had dozed off in the rush-backed chair at his bedside. Several hours before dawn, she snapped awake to find Holt stirring. Laying a hand across his forehead, she found to her immense relief that his fever had broken.

She turned to light another candle, and when she turned back, she found that Holt had propped himself up shakily on one elbow and was staring at her incredulously.

"What the devil are you doing here?" he croaked by way of greeting.

"I'm here either to nurse you or undo the curse upon your

head," she replied with a wan smile. "I'm not altogether sure which it is yet."

Holt shook his head as if this was past his understanding. "How could Toddington have been fool enough to let you come?"

"He did not exactly let me," Dru admitted, "though I am certain he will divine where I am and conceal my absence as artfully as he has concealed the fact that you have been skulking about Paris these many months." Hoping to forestall further inquiries about how she came to be here, she put a tin cup of water into his hand and saw with satisfaction that he had the strength to hold it to his lips and drink down the entire contents.

When he had finished, he looked up at her, his gaze suddenly sharpening. "Bonaparte? Does he still advance?"

She nodded. About this matter there could be no dissembling. "He still advances toward Paris. Lord Toddington has removed to Brussels."

Holt groaned faintly. "I've got to be rid of this buffoon's costume and get my own clothes back." For the first time Drusilla noticed that Holt was wearing loose, brightly striped Oriental trousers, of which he was apparently not fond. Later, she learned that Catalona, who knew Holt well from the war years on the Peninsula, had taken the precaution of impounding his clothes and boots to ensure his cooperation with her healing endeavors.

Holt levered himself into a sitting position, panting from the effort. "You must help me to leave here, my angel. I should be out reconnoitering Bonaparte's advance."

"I have no intention," she told him in her firmest voice, "of helping you escape your sickbed. Besides," she added in practical afterthought, "I fail to see why you need to reconnoiter in any case. News of Bonaparte's location is in the press every day. The journals tell everything there is to know about the situation."

Holt absorbed this information in silence and then summoned up a painful smile. "So, MacRory Holt, famous Exploring Officer, is rendered superfluous by a mob of journalists. Is that what you're saying?"

"Only for the time being," she said soothingly. "In the meantime, you must do all you can to get your health back."

She put her palm to his naked chest, and through the layers of muscle, she felt his heart beating strongly and regularly and not, thank heavens, racing erratically as it had last night when he was in the grip of a fever. He looked up at her, his eyes greener than highland grasses, and her breath caught in her throat as she thought of how irretrievably her life was now bound up with his.

Gently but firmly she pushed him back down on the bed, for she intended to take full advantage of her female prerogative to bully the man she loved for his own good. "You're in no state to do anything but rest at the moment, and I'm certain Catalona will not return your breeches until you are improved."

"Women," muttered Holt, but he did not try to get up again. Just when Drusilla thought he might be on the verge of falling back asleep, she heard him mutter, "It will be war again. You know that."

"I fear so," she agreed, "and so you must be recovered by then, for Wellington will surely have need of his 'eyes and ears' once more."

This was the beginning of Drusilla's strange, happy, and all too brief idyll amongst the Gypsies. Once again she adapted easily to an existence that no well-bred English young lady of good family had any business adapting to with such alacrity. But then, she told herself ruefully, perhaps she had never really had the makings of a proper English lady, after all, and was only just now discovering that.

She was housed in an eye-dazzling little wagon painted all over in lavender, yellow, and orange. Also residing in the wagon were two other young girls, Lita and Josefina, who uncomplainingly made room for one more in their wagon, for that was the Gypsy way.

The two girls, both younger than she, were shy of her at first, watching her silently with big dark eyes. Dru set out to win them over—and soon did—by showing that she expected no special favors and by working as hard to meet Holt's needs as any Gypsy woman worked to maintain her man.

She also impressed the girls with her fashionable appurtenances—specifically, her stocking-hanger stiletto. They eyed it enviously and expressed the hope that their betrotheds might one day bestow such a love token upon them.

Though barely out of childhood, both Lita and Josefina were already promised as brides to young men in Don Ramon's band. Drusilla was not certain whether she was supposed to be chaperoning them or they, her, but in all events, they rubbed along well enough together despite the close quarters, her lack of Spanish, and their lack of French.

MacRory Holt was meanwhile devoting himself to getting back his strength and his breeches. He was not an easy patient to nurse, Drusilla discovered. In fact, he was quite horrible.

"What, mutton gruel again?" he growled when she brought him more of the same.

"It is strengthening to the blood and kind to the digestion," she reminded him, quoting the wisdom of Catalona the healer. In truth, Holt's invalid's fare varied very little from what the rest of the Gypsies ate, which more often than not was a lamb-and-vegetable stew served over a dish of saffron noodles.

"I want my clothes, and I want my riding boots," he demanded as he had demanded every day for the last week.

"I don't know where your clothes are, and I don't know where your boots are," she answered as she had answered every day for the last week. "Now eat your gruel."

"I'm not going to eat any more of that blasted gruel, I tell you. I want some real food."

Dru had been expecting this. Day by day, as Holt's strength had increased, so had his obstreperousness. Today she was prepared to bargain. "If you eat your gruel now, I shall bring you some *hotchi* from the festival tonight. It is a famous delicacy, I believe."

Holt smiled at her slowly—quite an evil-looking smile, in Drusilla's opinion. "So," he said silkily, "you're eating *hotchi* tonight. Fortunate you."

"Whatever do you mean?" she asked, vaguely alarmed.

"*Hotchi,* my angel, is whole roasted hedgehog, quills and all."

"Oh," said Drusilla somewhat greenly. Here was one Gypsy custom that she did not think she could take to, after all.

"I'll tell you what." Holt swung off his sickbed to stand before her in his ridiculously striped sultan's trousers, his arms folded across his bare chest. "Bring me my breeches and riding boots, and you may have every last drop of my mutton gruel for your dinner tonight."

Dru bit back a laugh and shook her head. "I am sorry, sir, but I cannot be suborned by a bribe of mutton gruel, even under the threat of having to dine on hedgehog instead."

Holt was not amused. He was, in fact, frustrated nearly out of his mind by being clapped up as a helpless convalescent. It was slow torture to him to be sick and weak while Bonaparte rode in triumph across France.

In his frustration, he had even gone so far as to contemplate sneaking out in the dead of night, stealing clothes off a clothesline, boots off a wagon step, and Drusilla out of her wagon. And if Dru would not cooperate in his clandestine departure, he intended to gag her and toss her over his saddlebow until they were a safe distance from the camp.

But in the end he could not. He owed the Gypsies his life, and stealing their possessions and fleeing in the night would have been a sad repayment of their hospitality. Besides, he had such outsize feet—even for a man of his height—that he doubted he could find another pair of boots in the entire encampment that would fit him. And the prospect of riding barefoot through enemy-held territory daunted even MacRory Holt.

Drusilla, meanwhile, had put down his tray and paused in the doorway with a sunny smile he found infuriating. "I'm sure," she advised him, "you will eat your gruel once you consider how hungry you will be if you don't."

"Confound it, woman!" Holt's roar showed that he was, indeed, making remarkable strides toward fitness. "When you come back, you had better have my breeches in hand, because I refuse to wear these blasted . . . pantaloons for another minute. Not another minute longer, do you hear me?"

"Really," chided Drusilla, "you are being quite childish." Though, at the moment, Holt looked anything but childlike, striding toward her, tugging purposefully at the drawstring of his pantaloons.

Dru prudently withdrew from the wagon and marched off to complain to Catalona that Holt was being quite impossible and needed an airing. The elderly *gitana,* who was sitting with Don Ramon, the Gypsy *Jefe,* under the festival awning, allowed that perhaps Holt might be let out for the feast to-night, and Drusilla went away satisfied.

Don Ramon turned to the elderly healer, his dark eyes clouded with bewilderment. "With respect *drabardi,* what is this game you play with Rory and the señorita?"

"I play no game, *Jefe,*" said Catalona, very innocent. "It is only that after what he has endured, Rory's blood is sluggish and wants stirring. The spirit of the festival and flamenco will do him good."

Don Ramon shook his head. "This curse that you say Lazare put upon him . . . I know Lazare put poison in Rory's veins and would put a knife in his back if he could. But I had never thought the Frenchman one for casting curses."

Catalona raised her grizzled brows. "And did I say that it was Lazare who put this curse upon Rory? Did I name the name of anyone who has put the curse upon him?"

Don Ramon looked puzzled. "Then he was not cursed?"

Catalona shrugged elaborately. "When a man calls out for a woman in the night, would you say he is blessed or cursed?"

"Such a man could certainly not be said to be blessed," conceded the Gypsy chief.

"So then he must be cursed. And to remove the curse, he must be given what he yearns for."

Don Ramon considered this and then suddenly began to laugh. "You are a cunning woman, Catalona, and I am profoundly glad that you are our *drabardi* and nobody else's."

Breeched and booted at last, Holt went to the festival. Here, under bright lanterns and flickering torches, he beheld Miss Drusilla Sedgewick dressed in a gypsy costume of drawstring blouse and ruffled skirt, her chestnut curls cascading from beneath her head scarf.

Watching her, Holt once again congratulated himself for recruiting this particular young woman into the Great Game. She had more than justified his expectations and his training. Indeed, he felt rather like that Pygmalion fellow of Greek legend.

He studied her as she passed among the Gypsy throng and thought with proprietary pride that she moved amongst these strange people as gracefully as if she were waltzing at Almack's. Though perhaps that was not the best comparison to make, for he felt distinct displeasure at the thought of her waltzing with overdressed dandies whilst all the real men (like him) were away fighting the war.

Fortunately, there would be no question of that tonight. Only the flamenco dancers would dance at the festival. Already they were arriving, along with singers and musicians and several other neighboring bands of Spanish Gypsies who would share in the festivities.

Feeling uncharacteristically lighthearted, Holt went after Drusilla with the intention of squiring her about the festival and challenging her to sample *hotchi*. He was willing to bet she would eat it and turn green before she would let him best her at such a dare.

"But where," asked Dru in disappointment, "are the fortune-tellers?"

Holt shook his head. "You won't see any here. The Gypsies don't tell fortunes amongst themselves, only to *giorgios* for money. But come and watch the dancers. I don't think you'll be disappointed with them."

He led her to a platform of polished wooden planks set up at the center of the encampment. The women who mounted the makeshift stage to dance to the throbbing flamenco melodies soon became whirling columns of rainbow-colored ruffles as they stamped and clapped and twirled their skirts.

The flamenco they performed was the *Faraona*, which, according to Gypsy legend, was the very dance that Salome performed before King Herod in her seven veils. The dance still had the power to seduce, to judge from the heated enthusiasm of some of the male observers. But Holt knew that though Gypsy women danced like she-devils, their chastity was highly valued, and any attempt to trifle with them would bring the knives flashing out.

Despite the colorful sensuality of the women who danced before him, Holt found that tonight his senses were filled with an awareness of Drusilla. She wore no exotic perfumes, yet the clean, fresh scent of her was in his brain as she stood in front of him, her slender form molded against his by the press of the crowd. His eye could just make out the curving line of her cheek that led down to her long, slender neck, to where her collarbones pointed the way to the enticing valley between her breasts . . . which in his opinion that Gypsy drawstring blouse did a quite inadequate job of decently covering.

Almost as if she had sensed the intensity of his gaze, she turned her head and darted him a gay smile over her half-bare shoulder, and a strange new fire was kindled in his belly. And then, in a moment of stunning self-realization, he divined the truth: that it was Drusilla's chastity he desired to trifle with, and no one else's.

"Rory, *amigo!*"

The sound of his name brought Holt out of his lustful reverie with a start—a most atypical exhibition of nerves for someone so famously nerveless. He turned to find Don Ramon at his side.

"You and the señorita must come to my wagon at once,"

said the Gypsy chieftan, looking grave. "We have news from Paris."

That news had come in the form of the latest edition of the *Moniteur*, brought to the encampment by one of the Gypsy men attending the festival.

"My apologies for the fish scales, my friend," said Don Ramon. "It's the only use we have for *giorgio* newspapers."

Holt took the creased paper and read grimly, with Drusilla looking over his shoulder.

Momentous events had been taking place out in the great world beyond their *gitano* paradise. King Louis had fled Paris, along with his *émigré* court and all the currency in the national treasury. And now, according to the headline in the newspaper: *His Imperial Majesty Napoleon Enters Paris Tomorrow and Will Address His Loyal Subjects at the Tuileries.*

Holt crumpled the paper in a cold fury. "He has taken Paris without a fight, without a shot being fired."

"There will be fighting enough now," said Don Ramon somberly.

"Aye," said Holt, "and sooner rather than later, unless I miss my guess. You'd best head your wagons back to Andalusia, my friend."

Don Ramon nodded in agreement. "When *giorgios* make war upon each other, it is best for *gitanos* to make themselves scarce. That lesson we have learned to our sorrow. But what will you and the señorita do now, Rory?"

Holt's answer was crisp and unhesitating, the exact shape of the intelligence mission they must accomplish having taken shape immediately in his mind. "The señorita and I will watch the Emperor's military display in Paris tomorrow, and I will gauge the number of troops at his command and see how many of his old generals have returned to his service.

Then I will put the señorita on the *diligence* so that she may take this information to Brussels."

Don Ramon frowned at this. "Surely you don't mean to stay on in Paris, Rory?"

"For the time being, that is exactly what I mean to do."

"Then you are a fool," said his friend bluntly. "Lazare will have the knife out for you again. He will have a free hand against you now, for he is sure to stand high in the councils of the Corsican."

Holt nodded in cool agreement. "Shouldn't wonder if he's not made Chief of the Paris Police as a reward for his efforts."

"All the more reason for you to leave the city as soon as possible, *amigo*. Let some other do your snooping for you."

"I don't mean to be run out of Paris before I'm ready to go," said Holt with a shrug.

"*¡Dios mío!* Rory, you are mad! Señorita, help me plant some *prudencia* in this thick Scots skull."

But Drusilla only shook her head resignedly, knowing it was useless. Their Gypsy idyll was over, and the dogs of war were loose and snarling round them now.

Chapter Sixteen

The Return of the Ogre

Paris: Bonaparte's city soon, though not quite yet.

Drusilla and Holt rode into Paris together, as they had before, on Filbertine, the swaybacked mare. But the Paris they entered on this morning of March 20, 1815, was vastly altered from the Paris of the restored monarchy that Drusilla had entered some seven months before.

Now the tricolor of the Revolution was raised everywhere, to flutter alongside banners sewn with Imperial bees, and pennants depicting the war eagles of the Imperial Guard. On the great public buildings, signs mocking King Louis had been nailed up, the most restrained of them bearing the slogan: *A large fat hog to be sold for one Napoleon.*

Overnight, the Bourbonist emblems had disappeared from the streets of Paris. Traversing the city, Drusilla and Holt saw not a single royalist lily and only one white cockade, and that was tied to the tail of a black dog.

They unsaddled Filly at another of the alley stabling places that Holt always seemed to know of, this one selected for its proximity to an inn from which the *diligence* would leave the next day. It was a stroke of good fortune that Dru had the vial of invisible ink in her portmanteau, for it would allow Holt to transcribe his report in minute detail instead of trusting only the bare bones of it to her memory.

"How is it, my angel," he asked her with a smile as he remembered her gallant attempt at bawdy minstrelsy at the Bonne Belle Tavern, "that you always manage to fulfill my needs?"

Except, of course, that one burning need that seemed to steal upon him at every turn of late, as it did at this moment as he watched her sitting on her heels on a straw-strewn stable floor rummaging through her portmanteau. What, he wondered, was there about such a picture that could make him want to take her face between his hands and kiss her mouth?

Drusilla looked up to find his gaze upon her face. "I thought I had better wear these," she said with a smile, producing her guillotine earrings. She had come to regard the little pieces of beaten tin as a good-luck token, for had they not carried her unscathed through her adventure at their enemies' table in the Bonaparte Club?

But putting on earrings without the aid of a mirror presented difficulties that few men could appreciate, and after watching her snag the sharp-edged pieces of metal several times in her long, shining hair, Holt found himself saying, "Here, let me help you."

He gathered her curls together in hands that trembled slightly with eagerness to touch her and thought ruefully that his little apprentice had mastered her master quite thoroughly with a single smile.

They concealed Holt's saddlebags and Drusilla's portmanteau amongst the hay bales, then walked together toward the royal palace at the Place du Carrousel in the Tuileries gardens. It was here that the newspaper dispatches had said that the Emperor would arrive today to re-enthrone himself as the true monarch of France.

Already a great crowd had gathered. Tricolor cockades, some of them as large as soup dishes, were for sale everywhere. Holt bought two of a somewhat smaller size and pinned one to his coat and one on the bodice of Drusilla's grey traveling dress.

Protective coloring, thought Dru, who soon felt in need of it, for a wild rumor was sweeping through the crowd that the English had assassinated the Emperor at Fontainebleau.

Angry, mobbish shouts of "Death to the English!" and "Death to Wellington!" rose to the sky, and the two British agents secretly in the tumultuous multitude shouted as loudly as anyone else as they stood side by side, hand in hand for courage and comfort in the midst of their enemies.

Then a courier arrived from Fontainebleau with the message that the Emperor was not assassinated, that he would be in Paris within the hour.

The temper of the crowd changed at once to wild jubilation, and an awful truth became evident to Holt: *The French people won't fight for the Bourbons, but, by God, they'll fight for Bonaparte.*

In anticipation of the Emperor's return, there now drew up before the Tuileries a procession of fine carriages bearing members of the Napoleonic military nobility. The men who stepped out of the carriages wore the gorgeous, bemedaled uniforms of the Emperor's service. Their wives were dressed as for a great *fête,* wearing the silks and diamonds and jeweled tiaras that had caused such heart-burnings amongst the *émigrée* ladies.

Holt made mental notes of the marshals and generals who had declared their support for Napoleon. Marshal Davout, General Excelmans, and several others he recognized immediately. As for those officers he did not recognize, the crowd helpfully shouted their names as the men ascended the monumental marble staircase to the palace, for the French public knew by sight the soldier-generals who had marched behind Napoleon to conquer half the world—and to kill the father of Drusilla Sedgewick and many a friend and comrade of MacRory Holt.

Another carriage disgorged a passenger, and the name Lavalette was murmured by the crowd. Drusilla felt Holt tense beside her like a racehorse at the starting gate, and she knew why this should be so, for she recognized the name as well. Lavalette had been Bonaparte's Postmaster General—the sort of postmaster who had opened and read the public mails to such helpful effect that Bonaparte had once called him "my eyes and ears in Paris."

And then Drusilla felt the cold hand of fear clutch at her heart, for disembarking also from Lavalette's carriage was Henri Lazare, his ascendancy to the high councils of the Emperor now publicly confirmed as he took his exalted place amongst the other dignitaries. Beside her, Holt's lean wolf's jaw clenched to see his old enemy standing above him on a marble pedestal of victory while MacRory Holt skulked secretly in the crowd below, licking his wounds in defeat.

A new trepidation seized Drusilla at the look on Holt's face, for she had now begun to guess what was in his mind. And surely Henri Lazare must sense the burning green gaze fixed on him from out of the surging crowd, and surely he was staring back at the two of them, his eyes dark and malevolent and plotting . . .

The church bells had begun to peal, and rising like an ocean wave from the direction of Fontainebleau came the shouts of *"Vive l'Empereur!"* rolling down the boulevards of Paris in prolonged echoes as the carriage bearing the Emperor approached.

Mesmerized in spite of themselves by the spectacle of the

return to power of their country's great enemy, Drusilla and Holt watched as the crowd, nearly delirious with joy, surrounded the Emperor's carriage despite the frantic efforts of his escort to clear a path. Bonaparte was at this moment in dire danger of being loved to death by his subjects, but his marshals and generals rushed forward to raise him to their shoulders and carry him safely into the palace.

A speech was impossible in the midst of the joyful tumult, but the crowd was satisfied simply to see with their own eyes that the Emperor had indeed returned, that he was once more in the bosom of his people. Paris had decked herself out like a bride at her wedding, and the bridegroom had arrived.

But there was an unwanted guest at the wedding, and that was the man known as "Villainton's" eyes and ears.

Drusilla sat on a hay bale, chin in hand, watching Holt write out his intelligence report by lantern light. His pen raced across the foolscap with the speed of a man used to seeing his words vanish into nothingness the instant he penned them. It was nearly dawn when he finished and folded the sheets of paper into a square small enough for her to slip into the bodice of her traveling dress.

"There's one fact I didn't commit to paper that I'll trust to your memory alone. . . ." He stopped for a moment, forcing his gaze away from the sight of her slipping the tiny packet into her bodice. "You must tell Lord Toddington," he resumed, "that Berthier was not at Bonaparte's side tonight."

"Berthier?"

"Bonaparte's former Chief of Staff, his right arm for nearly twenty years and"—he grinned faintly—"the only man on the face of the earth, apparently, who can read His Napoleonic Majesty's abominable handwriting. Boney gave him a title and a castle in Saxony as a reward for his services, and if

Berthier should not rally to his old commander's side, it will be a very much to our advantage. You'll remember all this, I trust."

"Yes, but . . ." She trailed off, not quite having got up the courage to say what she intended to say, to do what she intended to do.

He looked at her sharply. "Well?"

"I . . . I wish that you would come with me now, or let me stay here to guard your back until you are ready to leave the city."

"Don't be ridiculous," he snapped. "You leave on the first stagecoach out of Paris."

"And"—she took a deep breath—"what if I should refuse to go?"

"Why, what's this, my angel? Insubordination?" Holt's voice was silky, but his eyes were hard. "I think you forget who is the master and who is the apprentice."

"There is no point," she told him sturdily, "in your trying to bully me on that score. The apprentice has seen the master in striped sultan's pantaloons and has quite lost her awe of him."

Holt almost smiled at that. "You may be as cheeky as you like, my angel," he said lightly, "but your *derrière* will still be on the *diligence* in the morning."

She stepped closer to him, looking intently up into his face. "Then swear to me that you're not staying behind to make one last foolish play against Lazare."

Holt frowned. This, of course, was exactly what he meant to do, though he fancied that the play he had in mind was not foolish but bloody clever.

"Rory, please . . ." She stepped very close to him, her slender figure barely visible in the dawn light. His nickname, which she had never presumed to use before, was upon her lips; her hands had fastened onto the breast of his jacket. "How can I let you send me to safety while you stay behind in a city filled with your mortal enemies? Either leave Paris with me, or let me stay and help you."

Her words were comradely enough; a man could almost say them to a fellow soldier before a dangerous mission. But between men and women there existed a language beyond mere words, and the language spoken by Drusilla's bewitching young person told Holt very clearly that she meant to unleash all the womanly lures at her command against him.

And potent lures he was finding them, too, with her face turned up so close to his that the creamy skin of her cheek almost touched his chin, her heavily lashed hazel eyes gazing into his, her mouth, lush and expectant, awaiting his.

By God, if the little baggage doesn't mean to seduce me into letting her stay with me, thought Holt, his blood kindling at the very thought, for the Great Game wasn't the only game into which he had been craving to initiate her.

"Don't try your virgin wiles on me, my angel," he warned her hoarsely. "You'll get more than you bargained for, I promise you that."

"Shall I?" she whispered softly. But her eyes challenged him. "Shall I, indeed?"

He could hold himself in check no longer.

Without speaking, almost without thinking, he caught her to him and covered her mouth with his own, and not with any tentative first kiss, either, but with the demanding, full-blooded, tongue-fencing kiss of a man who finally, after a long struggle, had let his desire slip the tether of duty.

Her mouth welcomed his, just as her body welcomed his caressing hands. She bent supply to his embrace as his lips slid along the long, elegant neck that was so much a part of her willowy beauty.

201

The honey trap was sprung at last—and never was there a more willing victim than MacRory Holt. . . .

Sometimes in the dreamy depths of the night, Dru had tried to imagine what it might be like to be Holt's lover, to have all the virility of his lean frame and the ingenuity of his keen mind lavished upon her woman's body and her woman's heart. And now as the summer dawn slowly lit this Paris stable, she found that her misty dreams had become suddenly, dazzlingly, and overwhelmingly real as Holt's arms wrapped hard around her and he kissed her with hungry passion.

All of it was deliriously physical and far beyond her maidenly imaginings, and but for the iron arm across her back, she thought she must fall under the storm of kisses.

And then she did fall—into the hay piled in the stable. Though she had forgotten their surroundings entirely, Holt had not, for what man with a willing maid in his arms could forego a bed of sweet-scented hay spread invitingly at his feet.

He tumbled her down into that bed of hay, smothering her laughing protests—which were really no protests at all—with quick, light kisses. His hands were quick as well in their desire to feel her naked, one ardent, questing hand sliding slowly up the silken length of her slender leg, the other attempting to work his will on the polished buttons of her bodice.

But then the tether of duty gave MacRory Holt a swift, painful, and timely jerk as one ardent, questing hand discovered the knife that he himself had given her while the other hand felt his folded message concealed within her bodice. He froze for an instant and then, with a painful groan, rolled off her and got to his feet to stand staring down at the young woman tumbled in the hay, her face still flushed with passion from his kisses.

Holt's face, however, was stony with self-denial. "You look like a slattern. Get up and make your dress presentable," he ordered her in a voice of granite, and if there had ever been any molten emotion beneath his stony-eyed expression, Drusilla could see no sign of it now.

She shot to her feet, her own emotions a thoroughly molten mixture of thwarted romantical yearnings and outraged female vanity. How dare he say she looked the slattern when he had just done his uttermost to divest her of her clothes, to say nothing of her virginity? But before any of her furious words could gain utterance, she saw with a sinking heart that neither her pleadings nor her wanton behavior had swayed him from his course.

He was seeing to Filly now, checking the contents of his saddlebag. She watched him take out his small arsenal of pocket pistols. One went into each side pocket of his workman's coat. The third was hidden in a special leather pouch sewn on the inside of his jacket, for he was broad-shouldered enough that the concealed weapon did not spoil the line of his coat and give the stratagem away.

There was only one reason he would fully arm himself like this, and her great fear was that his bitter anger over the defeat of his life's work would overrule his usual cool judgment. And against Henri Lazare the tiniest misstep, the smallest misjudgment, could be fatal.

"I'll follow after you," she threatened him in her desperation. "I'll follow after you instead of getting on the stage."

"No, you won't," he said, not bothering to turn round as he refastened his saddlebag. "You're a patriot, and a soldier's daughter, and in the end you'll obey my orders and do your duty."

"And what about your duty?" she questioned him. "Surely it doesn't include some mad scheme of personal revenge?"

She was ignored—and no man, she was certain, could ignore one so maddeningly well as MacRory Holt when he had a mind to do so.

"I'll use the money you gave me for my *diligence* ticket to hire a carriage to follow you."

This got Holt's attention away from his horse. He didn't doubt that in the long run he could elude her pursuit, but what good would that do if she had no money for her ticket to Brussels?

"And you taught me," she reminded him, "how to follow a mounted rider from a hired carriage. The instant you leave, I'll use my ticket money to hire one and be after you, and then we'll see how good a teacher you were."

"I can see," said Holt slowly, "that I've taught you too much and too well. But," he added, moving against her with sudden, cunning swiftness, "I didn't teach you *everything*."

She never saw the blackness coming. . . .

Dru had thought the horse blanket was for Filly. She had never dreamt it was for her. Too late, she realized her mistake when the perfidious Holt tossed the heavy blanket over her head and despite her struggles, whipped a rope around it—and her—trussing her up with a ruthless efficiency that told her this was not the first time he had done such a thing to some innocent, unsuspecting person.

Temporarily disoriented in the stifling blackness and nearly asphyxiated by the smell of horse liniment, she felt Holt pick her up and toss her down in the pile of hay that had almost been their lovers' bed. Then, in a final act of treachery, he lifted her skirt and, despite her efforts to kick away his hand, took her stiletto out of its sheath, for, of course, the minute his back was turned, she meant to cut herself free.

"You can't take my knife, you—" And she said a word she had never thought to hear herself say aloud.

Holt laughed. "Acquit me on that score, my angel. I'm not making off with your pretty toy altogether. I'll leave it driven into the post. I doubt it will take you—clever girl that you are—more than ten minutes to discover it and cut yourself loose. But by that time I'll be well away, past your ability to track me, and you'll have no choice but to come to your senses and deliver my report like the good little apprentice you are."

He was right, of course, on all counts. By the time she had got herself out of the hay pile, hobbled to the post in question, discovered her knife, cut the ropes that bound her, and divested herself of the odoriferous horse blanket, Holt and Filly were gone, man and mare having disappeared without a trace into the labyrinthine streets of Paris.

Holt was still her master in the Game, after all.

With a bitter sigh, Drusilla sheathed her stiletto, brushed the straw out of her hair, picked up her portmanteau, and trudged off to buy her ticket to Brussels.

Chapter Seventeen

On the Eve of Battle

It was the moment Dru had been dreading, the moment when she must learn whatever bubble-brained explanation Christabel had concocted to explain to British society in Belgium where her "secretary" had disappeared to these last ten days.

Christa rustled in, wearing her newest morning dress along with a frown for the benefit of the returning prodigal. "I really do not understand, Drusilla, why you felt it necessary to have your fortune told, of all things. When you did not come back, we had no choice but to leave you. The Thornrose ladies would have gone completely distracted had Charles not absolutely assured us that you would return safely home. I can only hope that Charles gave you a severe setdown for your carelessness."

Worn down by three days spent on a crowded stagecoach worrying about Holt, Drusilla replied dispiritedly that Lord Toddington had made known his concerns—his concern for Holt's welfare and his concern over Marshal Berthier's whereabouts, to be specific—although, of course, Drusilla had no intention of enlightening Christabel as to the specifics of these concerns.

Christa seemed to sense this. "I must say, this is all very odd," she observed, her alabaster brow wrinkling in thought. Lately, she was possessed of the strangest feeling that things were going on all about her that she could not fathom—but, of course, this was an entirely silly notion.

Drusilla, meanwhile, had overcome her weariness enough to ask with some trepidation, "Has there been much talk about my absence?"

Christabel made an airy gesture. "No, and for that you may thank me, for whenever anyone asked about you, I merely said that in the confusion of departure you had been left behind. You *are* a poor relation, after all, and everyone knows how easy it is to overlook a poor relation. The only person who seemed at all curious about where you were was Mr. Eggleston."

"Mr. Eggleston! Is he in Brussels, also?"

Christabel smiled a sweetly diabolical smile. "Not only is Mr. Eggleston in Brussels, but he is residing in this very house."

"What?" gasped Drusilla, appalled.

"Well, he must stay somewhere. All the lodgings in Brussels were taken over by officers, so I offered him one of our spare rooms—and a very good thing I did, too, for I now have the most certain proof that he is madly in love with you." Christabel's tone was nothing short of triumphant. "He has made a sketch of you, which he keeps concealed in his nightcap and which I am certain he takes out upon retiring each night to languish over."

"What?" gasped Drusilla again, freshly appalled. "Why, that is utterly ridiculous. And how would you come to know such a thing in any case?"

"Charles's valet found the drawing when he unpacked Mr. Eggleston's bags and very properly brought it to my attention before returning it to its hiding place. Mind you, it's a perfectly dreadful sketch. Your eyes look ready to cross, your neck is scrawny, and as for your bosom—well! All I can say is that Mr. Eggleston's fevered imagination has endowed your bosom with a handsomeness that it most certainly does not possess in life."

Drusilla shook her head in stunned amazement at the very idea of Mr. Eggleston putting pen to sketch pad on her account—not to mention concealing his artistic rendering in his nightcap. The poor young man must be truly lovesick.

The practical significance of Mr. Eggleston's artistic rendering had not escaped Christabel, either. "Since Mr. Eggleston apparently favors buxom females, I've made an appointment for you with Madame LeSage, the local *corsetière*. She assures me she can design a garment that will provide the twin charms of your bustline with everything nature has neglected to bestow upon them."

Drusilla sank into the nearest chair, uttering many desperate refusals, all of which, she was fearfully certain, would go unheeded. She was home at last, back in Christabel's world, and everything was running along its usual bacon-brained course once more.

On the great stage of Europe, events were also running their course.

The self-described Polite Nations of Europe had declared Bonaparte a renegade and an outlaw. Meanwhile, the Duke of Wellington had left his diplomatic post at the Congress of Vienna and traveled to Brussels to take command of the British and Dutch-Belgian forces in Flanders.

The French Marshal Berthier, the most talented staff officer of his generation, declared his allegiance to Bonaparte and his intention of returning to his old commander's side. But before he could do so, he had the misfortune to fall out a window in the highest turret of his storybook castle in Saxony. It was a mishap he did not survive.

The *Chevaliers de la Foi* had struck again, thought Drusilla with a shiver when she heard of it.

"You will never guess," declared Lady Christabel Toddington to her husband, "what the Thornrose ladies are up to now."

Lord Toddington looked up from his morning newspaper. "I confess, m'dear, I've not the slightest notion." It was a confession that Lord Toddington had had occasion to make several times before during the months he had played host to the Thornrose ladies.

"Well, you will scarcely credit this, Charles. They are talking of organizing a corps of young women of good character to take over the nursing of the soldiers wounded in battle."

Lord Toddington was properly skeptical of this radical notion. "Most nursing duties are already undertaken by camp followers—although, from what I understand, some of those women are as likely to rob you as they are to nurse you."

Christabel nodded wisely. "That is because the camp followers are the only kind of women who can put up with performing such tasks. Really, my dear, can you imagine putting a bandage on a strange man to whom you have not been properly introduced? It will never catch on, this female nursing business."

"Just as you say, m'dear," said Lord Toddington, returning to his newspaper.

Drusilla and Christabel were sitting quite unsuspectingly in the library of the Toddingtons' rented house on the rue Ducale when Grimthwaite brought in a gentleman's card upon his silver salver.

"A Colonel Holt has called upon Miss Drusilla," he announced.

After a moment of stunned silence, Dru picked up the calling card with stiff fingers. She had never before thought of MacRory Holt as a man who would possess a gentleman's calling card, but, of course he must, and there it was, inscribed with his rank and his regiment along with the name of his estate, which was located in a dreadfully Scottish-sounding place called Killiecrankie Crag.

Thankfulness and relief overwhelmed her as she realized what the little pasteboard square meant: *He is alive, after all. He has beaten Lazare, and now I shall see him once more.*

Christabel was all eager curiosity. "But can this be the famous Colonel MacRory Holt? Charles says he is summoned from Scotland for some important new post. But surely it's not Drusilla he is asking for, Grimthwaite?"

"He did ask to see Miss Drusilla most particularly, my lady."

"Well," sniffed Christabel, put on her mettle as mistress of the house by this, "the colonel shall just have to see me as well. Show him in immediately."

Drusilla was jolted out of her bedazzlement with a start. "Christa, there is something you need to know . . . that is, I must explain—"

"Whatever are you babbling about, Drusilla, and why on earth should this Colonel Holt come calling upon you?"

"That is what I'm trying to tell—"

Too late. A tall figure clad in scarlet regimentals appeared in the doorway, and Drusilla, who had never before seen Holt in uniform, marveled at how handsome he was in it . . . and marveled as well at how good he was at hiding his height and handsomeness with his various disguises. Christabel had been staring closely at Holt as well, and she now parted her rosebud lips and let out a shriek that cut through the air like the sound of fingernails on slate.

"It's *him!* The man who stopped our coach . . . the man who kidnapped you . . . the man who called me a *serving maid!*"

"Christabel, calm yourself, my love." Lord Toddington appeared from the adjoining room and took in the situation at a glance. "It's not at all what you think. I shall explain everything to you," he went on in his calming, diplomatist's way. "Colonel, perhaps you and Drusilla would be so kind as to withdraw whilst I have a word with my wife."

Holt bowed and with evident relief escaped from her ladyship's hysterical presence with Drusilla on his arm.

Drusilla's initial happy delirium over seeing Holt alive and in one piece quickly gave way to memory of the fact that the last time she had seen him, he had left her trussed up in a horse blanket. And so she made up her mind that she would be cool, very cool, to him when they were alone in the drawing room.

"I assume," she said, as he seated himself next to her on the settee, "that your presence in uniform means that you are officially here now and not 'in Scotland' anymore."

He grinned. "Well, to be precise, I am—officially, you understand—crossing the channel even as we speak, and I will have arrived in Ostend—officially, that is—by tomorrow, the scent of my native highland heather still about me. However, since my lady peagoose must have alerted all of Brussels to my presence with her screaming, perhaps I should put my arrival forward and officially be here now."

This sally elicited no smile from Drusilla, for she was staring instead at a reddish graze across his right temple, a graze obviously made by a pistol ball that had come close, so dreadfully close, to blowing MacRory Holt's famously clever brains out of his handsome head.

Holt caught the direction of her glance, and the laughter went out of his eyes. "Lazare still lives," he answered her unspoken question, "and now I believe the game between us will go to the final play—on the battlefield."

"Because of your new command?"

He nodded. "The Duke has honored me with the appointment of Chief of the Intelligence Department for the British Army in the field. It's the first time such an appointment has ever been made." A note of pride sounded in his voice as he laid this honor before her, for she was the one woman in all the world who could really understand the dangers he had dared to win this laurel.

Dru melted at once. "Oh, Rory, I am so happy for you," she said softly. "And what must you do to carry out your new commission?"

The wolf light was in his eyes as he told her how he meant to move against the French enemy in what surely would be the most critical mission of his life.

"Tomorrow I travel south to organize a system of agents who will give early, precise warnings of French troop movements. Lazare will, of course, be organizing his own system of confusion agents to plant false rumors and misinformation designed to disguise his master's true intentions. But we'll sort it all out, never fear. Once Bonaparte does commit himself to a line of march, I'll have personal command of the Exploring Officers, who will provide cavalry reconnaissance."

Drusilla knew well enough what this last would mean. Once again, Holt would be a spy in uniform, a lone wolf ranging along the flanks of the French forces, trying to divine their numbers and their armaments, hoping to bring down an unwary courier or a lagging picket in order to extract information from him. Of course, his scarlet uniform would make him a wonderful target for French marksmen, but better to be shot down like a cavalryman in uniform than hanged for a spy out of one. Or at least that was what the Exploring Officers maintained.

Drusilla summoned up a smile for Holt's benefit, despite the myriad dangers that this commission must surely hold for him. "I'm sure His Grace has never made a wiser appointment."

A strange, strained silence fell between them then, during which Holt seemed uncharacteristically abstracted, almost fidgety, and certainly not his usual imperturbable self.

Finally Drusilla asked, "Have you come, then, to ask me to undertake some mission—"

"No!" He cut her off with a sharpness that was almost harsh and got to his feet to stand looking down at her. After another lengthy hesitation, he clasped his hands behind his back as if he were at attention and about to make a report to a superior officer. In the time that it took him to speak his next few sentences, his words lifted Drusilla up to the heights of happiness and then plummeted her into the depths of despair.

"You must be aware that I have the deepest possible regard for you. I therefore have the honor to ask you to become my wife. I am by no means wealthy, but I believe my estate in Scotland to be adequate for your support. I shall return home as often as possible, and I hope that you will come to regard my home as yours while I am away. . . ."

He trailed off then, uncertain as to how his suit was being received, and when Drusilla only stared up at him in unnerving, accusing silence, he finally snapped, "Good God, woman, I've just proposed marriage to you! It's customary to say *something*."

And so she did. "Why," she asked him, giving him a very

straight look, "do you not wish to take me with you to your postings? Are you ashamed of me?"

So that was it, he thought in relief. "Good God, no, my angel. But can't you see how dangerous it will be? And it will only grow more so as the years pass. Look at Lady Toddington, the victim of a plot on her husband's account. And I will be on the front lines far more than Charles Toddington ever was. No, I must have you safe in Scotland, surrounded by my own kinsmen."

"But what would I do with myself whilst you are gone?"

"Why, as to that . . ." In truth, Holt had very little notion of what the wives of Scots gentry did do to occupy their time. "I suppose you shall do whatever it is that women do . . . supervise the servants, trim the roses, weave tartans by the fire."

But sitting at her loom, endlessly awaiting her man's return like some Caledonian Penelope, had no allure for Drusilla. "But why cannot the two of us continue as we did before, only as man and wife?"

Holt's expression darkened to hear her even suggest such a thing. "Do you think I could subject my own wife to the dangers of the Great Game and still call myself a man? I'd have to be the biggest scoundrel unhung to put you at risk in that way. Surely you understand that you cannot be the colonel's apprentice and the colonel's lady, too. It must be the colonel's lady now, or nothing."

Trust MacRory Holt, thought Drusilla bitterly, to make a marriage proposal sound like an ultimatum.

"And," he went on, his tone almost angry, "I can assure you that this colonel does not intend to have his lady wearing a dagger under her skirt, showing her ankles at masquerades, or kissing French doormen."

Though these dictates struck Drusilla as being wretchedly

unfair, she did not challenge him on this score but only on the most important one. "Tell me, Rory, in the fourteen years that you have been in the British army, how many times were you allowed home on leave? And for how long?"

"Four times, and the longest I was home was for three months." He answered her question truthfully and unflinchingly, even though he was beginning to suspect that his answer might mean the death of all his hopes.

After a long moment, Drusilla got rather shakily to her feet and confirmed his suspicion. "I . . . cannot conceive that I could be happily married under such circumstances. I watched my mother grieve bitterly when my father left to soldier in foreign parts. I am convinced that no hardship of following the drum could have been worse for her than the fate of having been left behind."

"You refuse me, then?" he asked, incredulous.

"Not you, Rory," she whispered, "never you. What I refuse is a lonely existence in which I would have your name and your estate but nothing of your life, only endless years of worry about your safety across the sea."

"Unfortunately, my angel"— his voice was taut—"this is all I can honorably offer you."

"Then it is not enough." Her voice was low but clear. "And so I must refuse your kind offer, sir."

"By God, you will not!" he snapped, for it had never occurred to him that she would refuse him, not after those clinging kisses she had given him, not after she had lain down in the stable straw in his embrace.

His hands closed hard upon her shoulders, and he dealt her more kisses, as he had dreamt of doing all the time they had been apart. Finally his hungering mouth parted from hers, and he held her at arm's length to look into her face. Certain of his victory, and said huskily, "Never fear, my

215

angel, I'll not send you off to Scotland before we have our wedding night, nor as many long nights after that as I can contrive before I return to the Game."

He let her go, and she met his eyes steadily, though with a glitter of tears on her long lashes. "So you offer me a few nights of wedded bliss to be measured against years of loneliness. Is that it?"

And in that moment he knew he had lost her, that all his hot-hearted lovemaking and talk of bridal nights had been for naught. Wretched enough to be spurned, he thought bitterly, worse to be spurned after such a panting display of how much he desired her. He'd done everything to properly win her over except get down on one knee and recite Byron to her. And still she refused him.

The silence reverberated between them like a knell.

At length, once more in command of himself, he said coldly, "Very well. If my lands and my name in honorable marriage are not enough, then I see no alternative except to bid you farewell."

He turned and walked across the room, hoping against hope that she would call after him, as she was hoping against hope that he would turn back to her.

But he did not, and she did not, and soon there was a closed door between them.

It was difficult to say who was more shattered by Colonel Holt's call, Drusilla or Christabel. Characteristically, Christabel was far more vocal about her devastated nerves than Drusilla was about her broken heart.

"I shall never—never!—get over the shock of this to my dying day," she proclaimed from her sitting-room couch, upon which she had been palely convalescing from said shock. "That that dreadful brigand should turn out to be a

British officer in disguise, that he should be so taken with you, Drusilla, that he should reappear out of the blue seven months later and have the gall to ask you to marry him and remove you to some crag in Scotland—well, it passes all reason. You had much better accept Mr. Eggleston, who will only take you as far as Wiltshire."

Having expended so much time and effort in backing Mr. Eggleston, Christabel had no intention of switching her allegiance to Colonel Holt at this late date, especially when his sudden appearance on the scene had reduced Drusilla to such a fit of mopery that she was of no earthly use to anyone.

"I do wish, Drusilla, that you would pinch your cheeks and then put yourself in the way of Mr. Eggleston when he comes out of Charles's study. He sounded very serious when he asked Charles for a moment of his time. I wonder what the two of them can be discussing. . . ."

Lord Toddington regarded the young man who sat opposite him with some bemusement. "Let me understand you, sir. You wish me to help you purchase a commission in one of the cavalry units stationed in Flanders."

"Yes, my lord, in whatever regiment this could be achieved—it is of no moment which one. I'll be proud to serve in any English unit so long as I may have a hand in giving the Frenchies a good thrashing."

"Your patriotism does you great credit, Mr. Eggleston, and, God knows, now is the time for all good Englishmen to stand against the Corsican. But I fear I have no authority to procure military commissions."

"And yet," persisted Mr. Eggleston, "you've influence with those who do."

Lord Toddington cautiously allowed that he might, adding, "But have you considered that, as a cavalry officer, you will be required to provide your own mount? And not just any average nag, either. Let me advise you, sir, that decent horseflesh is in devilish short supply in Brussels at the moment. Everyone says there's not a spare mount to be had anywhere, for either love or money."

Mr. Eggleston smiled. "I believe I have the advantage of you there, my lord. I've had my eye on a prime bit of horseflesh for some time."

"You surprise me, sir. I'd have sworn that every prime bit of horseflesh in this city was already bespoken."

"True, but the horse I have in mind is such a high-spirited brute of a stallion that no one has been willing to mount the four-footed devil up 'til now."

"Well," said Lord Toddington doubtfully, "if you can procure the mount—and manage to ride him—then we will discuss the matter further."

Mr. Eggleston smiled with the inborn confidence of the galloping squire. "I'm a bruising rider, if I do say so myself, and I fancy it won't take me long to bring the beast to heel."

Mr. Eggleston's confidence was misplaced, however. It was the beast who brought him to heel.

"Mr. Eggleston!" gasped Drusilla and Christabel in unison. "What have you done to yourself?"

"I believe it would be more to the point, ladies," said Mr. Eggleston through set teeth, "to inquire what that brute of a horse has done to me."

Mr. Eggleston was at this moment being helped along by two footmen, his leg having been heavily bandaged from toe to knee, rather in the manner of an Egyptian mummy. His grimace of pain became even more pronounced when he saw that the ladies were joined in the hallway by the Chevalier de Saint-Armand, that French gentleman having fled Paris out of fear of the Emperor's return—or so he said. Drusilla was still of the opinion that the man could not be trusted.

The chevalier oozed spurious sympathy over Mr. Eggleston's mishap. "Ah, the misfortunes of war, monsieur. Many are called, but few are chosen, eh?"

Mr. Eggleston's reply to this could not be ascertained, for he and his gargantuanly bandaged leg had been borne round the curve of the staircase by the two footmen.

It was left to Drusilla to inquire pointedly of the chevalier, "And what of you, Chevalier? Do you by chance hear the call to military service in this hour of crisis?"

"Not I, mademoiselle," replied the chevalier in his customary tone of light banter. "Not even the echo of a distant trumpet do I hear. My duty in this crisis"—and he smiled beguilingly into Christabel's eyes—"shall be to console the beautiful ladies of Brussels, who are sure to be most sadly neglected while their men prepare to make war."

Brussels was a very social city, aswarm with all manner of fashionable folk. From every corner of Europe they had descended upon the Belgian capital in the belief that in this time of crisis, the safest place to be on the entire European continent was right behind the Duke of Wellington.

The British upper crust was well represented in Brussels as that city waltzed gaily on the brink of war. There were Pagets and Percivals and Mountnourisses; there were Darymples, Stuarts, Grevilles, and Lennoxes; there were Wedderborn-Websters and Wellesley-Poles, to name but a few. On hand as well to record the follies, philanderings, and gallivantings of the British colony in Brussels was that indefatigable diarist and arch-gossip, Thomas Creevey.

And much gossip there was for Mr. Creevey to record.

There were the mad antics of Lady Caroline Lamb, Lord

Byron's former inamorata, who had lost nothing of the febrile charm that had so attracted the poet several years before.

There were the whispers about Lady Frances Webster, pale and languishing and just twenty-one, who reportedly was the Duke of Wellington's new *chere amie* now that the Duchess of Wellington had been sent back to England to tend to her knitting.

And there was the Duchess of Richmond—who desired to give a grand ball on the night of June 15.

"Duke," said the Duchess of Richmond to the Duke of Wellington, "I do not wish to pry into your secrets, but I wish to give a ball, and all I ask is, may I give my ball? If you say, 'Duchess, don't give your ball,' it is quite sufficient. I ask no reason."

"Duchess," said the Duke of Wellington to the Duchess of Richmond, "you may give your ball in the greatest safety, without fear of interruption."

Chapter Eighteen

In Which Lord Byron Has
the First and Last Word

There was a sound of revelry by night,
And Belgium's capital had gather'd then
Her Beauty and her Chivalry, and bright
The lamps shone o'er fair women and brave men;
A thousand hearts beat happily and when
Music arose, with its voluptuous swell,
Soft eyes look'd love to eyes which spake again,
And all went merry as a marriage bell . . .

> Lord Byron
> "On the Field of Waterloo"
> *Childe Harold's Pilgrimage*, Canto III

To the Duchess of Richmond's ball went Miss Drusilla Sedgewick, clad in a dress of sylvan green that made her hazel eyes look quite as green as those of a certain absent officer of daring reputation.

To the ball on the arm of her diplomatist husband went Lady Christabel Toddington, dressed in a low-cut gown of celestial blue, the diaphanous tarlatan netting about her neckline a delightfully unsuccessful counterfeit of modesty.

To the ball the Misses Faith, Hope, and Charity Thornrose did not go, all three being engaged in rolling bandages for the battle that must surely come, for already rumors were flying round Brussels that the armies of France were massing at the frontier, and surely the fateful hour was close at hand.

The Duchess of Richmond's ball was held in the grand mansion that the Duke of Richmond had rented for the season on the rue de la Blanchisserie. The ballroom was situated in its own separate wing of the house, and every care had been taken to ensure that the affair was the most brilliant of the season.

Hundreds of candles burned in gilded wall sconces and in magnificent chandeliers. Banked masses of flowers exuded summery perfumes and showed elegantly against the green-trellised wallpaper that patterned the ballroom walls. Rich curtains hung about the entrances and alcoves, while the marble pillars that supported the ceiling were wrapped with velvet ribbons and gold leaf.

In the days leading up to the much-anticipated event, the fashionable ladies of Brussels had dithered exceedingly over what to wear. But Lady Toddington, with her impeccable sense of fashion and occasion, declined to dither over *her* costume.

"It won't make a particle of difference what any of us of wear," she declared roundly. "There will be so many officers in showy uniforms that our gowns will be quite cast into the shade. There will be so many medals and decorations displayed upon the gentlemen that mere female jewelry will not be noticed. I fear it would profit us more to parade about stark-naked than to wear a new gown."

Of course, Christabel did not go to the ball naked, and, of course, she did have a new gown, which it must be noted was very *décolleté*, and most of the males she encountered did, indeed, note it. Standing beside her at the refreshment table,

Drusilla observed that when Christabel leaned over to select some dainty to nibble upon, the men standing round the table listed forward as well.

Amongst those teetering admiringly toward a better view of Christabel's charms was the ubiquitous Chevalier de Saint- Armand, whose insinuating address had earned him an invitation to tonight's affair. Once again, Drusilla marveled at the *entrée* that the chevalier enjoyed, and she vowed inwardly that she would unmask this man for whatever he was.

The chevalier was in high spirits for a man in exile. "I am promised by His Majesty a lucrative position in the government when—"

"Assuming His Majesty ever again has a government," Drusilla could not help pointing out dryly.

The chevalier was not deflated. "And I am promised my estate back by royal land grant."

"Assuming His Majesty ever again has a kingdom to make royal land grants from," Drusilla could not refrain from adding acidly.

The chevalier regarded her with surprise. "But how gloomy you are tonight, Mlle. Sedgewick. Do you doubt the final outcome? But how can you, when you look at the gallant officers gathered here?"

Drusilla had looked—in vain hope had she looked—but the only gallant officer she wished to see was not here, as she had known in her heart he could not be.

She had not meant to come to the ball at all, for she had felt it her duty to aid the Thornrose ladies in their bandage-rolling, or, in the alternative, to read aloud to poor Mr. Eggleston, who still could barely hobble about. In the end, however, she went to the ball in the hope of hearing word of Holt from one of the staff officers who would surely be attending.

Lord Toddington had claimed to know nothing of his former star agent's activities. "Colonel Holt reports directly to Wellington now," he had told her. "I am as much in the dark as anyone."

"Drusilla! For heavens sake!" Christabel's imperative voice broke into her thoughts. "You had better dance, or you shall be taken for a potted plant in that green dress of yours." (Christabel had not favored Drusilla's green dress, as she felt it did not complement her celestial blue one.) "I can see," said Christa, "that you are too indolent to find yourself a suitable partner, and so," she concluded threateningly, "the chevalier and I will just have to provide one for you."

This threat was soon realized in the person of the fearsomely Teutonic Baron Buddenburg Homburg-Philippsthal, a military aide to the Duke of Brunswick. The baron had a quizzing glass, a chest covered with a corselet of medals, and a pair of gleaming boots that he clicked together in military fashion even as he danced Drusilla through a quadrille. At the end of her terpsichorean exercise with the baron, Dru left the dance floor feeling as though she had just been quick-marched several times round a parade ground.

She fetched up next in the company of three titled gentlemen, who, in an earlier era, might have served as inspiration for Walter Scott's famous poem, "The Barons of England Who Fight for the Crown." Either barons themselves or heirs to their fathers' baronies, they were happy to enlighten a pretty young lady about things military.

There was Captain Lord Nicholas, "Old Nick," Ryder, that handsome black-haired giant of the Heavy Cavalry, who expounded at length upon the Heavies' decision to file down their famous hatchet-tipped swords to points for this crucial battle.

There was Captain the Honorable George Ferrers, a

fair-haired dandy whose sartorial *élan* was in no way diminished by his having lost an eye at Badajoz. Tonight, he wore a black silk eye patch with his regimental crest embroidered upon it, and he was most wittily enlightening about the different uniforms to be seen in the crowded ballroom.

And then there was Ensign Lord John Cecil, fresh from the playing fields of Eton, who really did not know enough about anything to be enlightening, except that he was very certain that one English ensign was worth ten of his Froggie counterparts. The sands of Lord Cecil's young life were fast running out, only he did not know it, and he thought himself dashed lucky to win Miss Sedgewick out to the dance floor over the opportunings of two such idolized officers as Ryder and Ferrers.

And in the coming battle, vowed young Lord Cecil, *I shall be as heroic as they.*

These, then, the barons of England who fought for the crown.

The ballroom was by now a veritable Babel of Continental tongues and accents, an *attroupement* of commanding officers from across the face the Europe. Watching the gorgeously uniformed officers dancing with their wives, Drusilla felt a stab of envy.

MacRory Holt's lady would never be able to walk with him at any glittering affair and hear his famous victories spoken of admiringly. Holt's heroics must almost always be secret, his biggest victories hidden in the shadows. There could be no peacetime respite for him either, for the Great Game went on as fiercely in peace as it did in war. And if he died in the secret service of his country, there would be no medals or eulogies to console his widow.

There was a high price to be paid by the lady who would

love MacRory Holt. *But then,* she reminded herself bitterly, *you turned down your chance to be his lady, didn't you?*

Every circumstance of that evening seemed designed to remind her of Holt, even the entertainment.

The Duchess of Richmond had prevailed upon the Forty-second Highlanders, who were billeted in Brussels, to allow their regimental bagpipers to play for the amusement of her guests. Into the ballroom they marched in kilts and tartans, the strange, wildly sweet music of their pipes filling the ballroom with martial airs that the Scots called *pibrochs.* There were sword dancers, too, a relic of Scotland's Celtic past, and the pipers played fiercely as the Highlanders performed their ancient war dance.

Drusilla wondered if Holt had ever watched the sword dance at a clan gathering and if the music of the bagpipes could be heard at twilight atop Killiecrankie Crag. They were thoughts that brought tears of foolish regret to her eyes.

At midnight the Duke of Wellington arrived with a number of his staff officers, and shortly thereafter the great man sat down to supper with the palely beautiful Lady Frances Webster at his right and the rosily beautiful Lady Georgianna Lennox at his left.

His appearance elicited a sigh of relief from Christabel. "If the Duke is here tonight," she said to Drusilla, "then surely the war must not be so close after all."

It had only recently sunk into Christabel's mind that Brussels might not be the haven she had thought it to be. The city was unfortified and located only fifty miles from the French border, and might not the Corsican Ogre gobble up Brussels as he had gobbled up so many other cities in the past?

Gathering up her celestial blue train, Christabel said, "We

may as well go in to supper so we can watch the Duke flirt with that ninny Frances Webster."

But throughout dinner it was noticed that there was a good deal of whispering and tense looks being exchanged among staff officers, and then the Prince of Orange came in with several dispatches for the Duke. Already many of the officers were leaving, including Drusilla's three barons, off to their respective regiments to fight as gallantly on the morrow as they had flirted and danced tonight.

She was standing somewhat abstractedly at the punch table when Lord Toddington's undersecretary came to ask her if she would be so good as to wait upon his lordship in His Grace's study.

As she walked the length of the ballroom, Drusilla could not know that MacRory Holt had recently been sent across the border in France with instructions from Wellington to send back one message and one message only: precisely when and whither did Bonaparte march.

She could not know that such was Wellington's faith in his trusty Colonel Holt that the entire Allied army would not be moved an inch without word from him.

She could not know that now, incredibly, there was indisputable evidence that the French army was on the march, yet no word had come from Holt. . . .

The small room that served as the Duke of Richmond's study was occupied not only by Lord Toddington but also by the Dukes of Wellington and Richmond and several of Wellington's staff officers. A map was spread out on the desk, and the military officers were gathered round it.

The conversation fell off as Drusilla walked into the room, and all eyes went to this slender young woman who was reputed to have received some mark of partiality from the famous Colonel Holt. And now, as she stood gracefully cool as a green willow amidst all the officers in their gold-encrusted scarlet, there was not a man there who did not think of MacRory Holt when he saw her.

Lord Toddington, ever the polished diplomatist, brought her forward and presented her, but it was obvious that Wellington was impatient with civilities. The Duke immediately and bluntly fired out a question in a voice that could make half his army quail. "Miss Sedgewick, have you heard from Holt these last few days?"

Drusilla answered him back fast as fire in Holt's defense. "No, Your Grace, I've heard nothing, nor would I expect to. He would never jeopardize his mission to send a message to me."

Wellington was silent for a moment, looking down his famous beaked nose at her. Then he turned toward his men, and his clenched fist came down on the map. "Bonaparte has humbugged me, by God! He has stolen a twenty-four-hour march on me."

"And Holt has failed to send us word of it," said one of the scarlet-uniformed staff officers.

This remark Drusilla could not let stand. Before England's greatest living commander, she could not let this stand.

"Not while he lives would Colonel Holt *fail* Your Grace," she said, her voice as clear and carrying and strong as she could make it, despite the agonizing fear that was blossoming in her breast.

And as she turned to leave the room, not an officer there believed that MacRory Holt still lived.

Returned to the ballroom by the undersecretary, Drusilla's brave facade slowly crumbled. She knew too much about how the Great Game was played not to realize the implications of what she had just learned.

Could it be that Henri Lazare's confusion agents had confused even the great MacRory Holt? That Holt was dead did not bear thinking about. But if he was not dead, then he had failed at this most supremely important mission of his life, when the very fate of all Europe hung in the balance.

Death or failure for MacRory Holt. She knew very well which he would prefer.

All round her, word was sweeping the ballroom that the fateful hour was indeed at hand. Those few officers who had not yet departed were leaving now in haste, and the sense of onrushing events had fallen heavily over the gathering, though the musicians played on, though the waltzes still spilled out the tall ballroom windows into the warm summer night.

Like one in a walking dream, Drusilla let herself be taken away from the Duchess of Richmond's ballroom and driven through the streets of Brussels, where the forces of war were gathering.

> And there was mounting in hot haste; the steed,
> The mustering squadron and the clattering car,
> Went pouring forward with impetuous speed,
> And swiftly forming in the ranks of war;
> And the deep thunder, peal on peal afar;
> And near, the beat of the alarming drum
> Roused up the soldier, 'ere the morning star;
> While thronged the citizens with terror dumb,
> Or whispering with white lips—"The foe! they come,
>   they come!"
>
> > Lord Byron
> > "On the Field of Waterloo"
> > *Childe Harold's Pilgrimage*, Canto III

Chapter Nineteen

In Which the Battle Is Fought
and the Masks Come Off

The Thornrose ladies had for some time been engaged in forming their own little brigade of nursing volunteers. Several weeks before, they had descended in full trio upon Dr. Brugsman, the Belgian physician in charge of military hospitals, to volunteer their services. To their amazement, their services were brusquely declined by Dr. Brugsman on the grounds that it was not proper for women to nurse men outside their domestic circle.

"Piffle!"

"Poppycock!"

"Balderdash!"

"*Quelle bêtise!*" translated Dru helpfully.

Dr. Brugsman, it may be said, had not hitherto experienced anything remotely resembling the Thornrose sisters, and in the end, he somehow found himself giving the ladies a task.

Tents, he informed them, were to be erected throughout the city in case the wounded overflowed the hospitals. The ladies could have charge of one of the tents, assuming, he admonished them sternly, that sufficient numbers of wounded were brought back to the city from the battlefield. And on no account, he further admonished the ladies, were they to divert any of the hospital-bound casualties to their tent.

"Foolish man!" huffed Miss Faith after their interview.

"Not in the least farsighted," agreed Miss Hope.

"Doesn't he realize," observed Miss Charity, "that there will soon be more than enough wounded to go around?"

On the afternoon of the day after the Duchess of Richmond's ball, distant cannonading was suddenly to be heard. The Bruxellois ran out of their houses to stare at the reverberating horizon. Such was the force of the noise that horses shied in the streets at the sound of it. Hour after hour the distant booming filled the sky, and so Drusilla thought she had better go and comfort the other girl Holt had left behind.

Filbertine had been lodged in a nearby livery stable, replaced in Holt's affections by a string of deep-chested, corn-fed stallions that could carry him swiftly over difficult terrain.

And perhaps one of those swift stallions had already carried him to his death, thought Dru miserably as she fed Filly the apples she had brought in her pockets.

Filly, the veteran of many a bombardment on the Peninsula, did not seem noticeably upset by the cannons' distant roar. She did seem put out, however, by all the human tears being shed upon her muzzle.

Late in the night, the body of the Duke of Brunswick was brought into Brussels on a funeral hearse, a sad harbinger of the wounded who would soon flood into the city, casualties of the fighting at Ligny. On the morning of June 17, the cannons had ceased, but the ominous news did not. The Highlanders who had piped and danced at the Duchess of Richmond's ball were all dead, killed to a man by the French *cuirassiers.*

Drusilla took it as a black omen for her own Scotsman, but

231

she had not many hours to brood over it, for the wagons bearing the wounded were now rolling up to the gates of Brussels, and by the next morning there was a scene in the city streets that no human tongue could tell.

Wagonload after wagonload of maimed, bleeding, dying men were being conveyed to the city hospitals. The walking wounded were coming in as well, to collapse, exhausted, in the streets. Every open space was filled with stretchers, or crude litters made out of whatever was handy, or even piles of straw upon which the wounded lay groaning and the dead lay stiffening.

It seemed unbelievable that only a few days before it was reckoned there would be no need for volunteer nurses. Now, in the name of suffering humanity, the entire city volunteered. The Bruxellois opened their houses to take in the soldiers who had fallen upon their doorsteps; the chemists and apothecaries gave away the entire contents of their shops; Sisters of Mercy emerged from their convent armed with dippers and barrels of clean rainwater; English ladies, highborn and low, ventured into the streets to give what aid they could to their fallen countrymen.

The Thornrose ladies, better prepared than most, had marshaled their own little group of volunteers. These consisted of the Mrs. Martinson and Miss Lyme, the wife and sister-in-law respectively of Chaplain Martinson; Mrs. Baines and Mrs. Niddery, the wives of army surgeons serving in the field; as well as Drusilla—and Lady Christabel Toddington.

To say that Christabel actually nursed the wounded would have been an exaggeration. She did what she did best, which was simply to be the highly finished piece of nature she was. She was the picture-perfect image of English womanhood on whose behalf these soldiers fought—had fought these last twenty years—to keep the English home shores safe from the French.

Many a poor soldier slipped away to his death that bloody day in June convinced that an English angel had descended from heaven to guide him from this foreign battlefield to a better place.

As for Christabel, she would remain to the end of her years a fabulous flibbertigibbet with candy-floss brains, though with a deep-dyed secret from now on . . . for after this day of Waterloo, the golden locks of hair at her temples grew out white as snow.

These, then, the women of England, who came with ministering hands to tend to the bloody issue of war.

On the morning of the nineteenth, Lord Toddington returned from his consultations (battles may come and go, but consultations go on forever) to tell his wife that he was bound for Ghent to consult with King Louis on behalf of the Foreign Office.

He had brought with him the news that, although the outcome was still not entirely clear, it seemed the Allies had won a great victory, indeed, though the losses on both sides were shocking. Amongst their own little group of intimates were already many sad casualties: Colonel Canning, Sir Alexander Gordon, and Lord William Hay were all dead, Colonel de Lancey was wounded unto death, and Fitzroy Somerset, serving as Wellington's military secretary, had lost an arm.

For Drusilla, Lord Toddington had better news. "I've word of Holt. He's alive and has been acting as an aide-de-camp to Wellington these past few days."

Drusilla suddenly found that her legs would not support her, and she had to sit down on one of the Sisters of Mercy's overturned rain barrels. But then, out of her great relief came another haunting thought, which she voiced to Lord Toddington. "His failure to discover Bonaparte's advance must torture him beyond anything."

Lord Toddington shook his head. "Not so much as you might think, for he did send Wellington timely word of the precise French troop movements an entire day in advance. Unfortunately, the message came to the hand of General Dornberg, who discounted it because he had received so many conflicting and false reports."

"Lazare's confusion agents," hissed Drusilla.

"So it would seem," agreed Lord Toddington. "Holt was not fooled, but Dornberg was. When Holt realized what had happened, he rode like a fiend to Quatre Bras to report personally to the Duke. But by then the battle was joined, and so Holt was assigned to Wellington's staff for the duration." He looked down at her pale face and put a kindly hand on her shoulder. "My dear, you must go home and rest. You look exhausted."

Drusilla smiled faintly. "I am to go home, as it happens, but only to obtain another crock of the cherry-water that Cook has been making. Our patients seem quite fond of the taste, though what actual medicinal powers it may have, I've no notion."

Lord Toddington took her hand and bowed over it. "Then I bid you farewell, my dear, as I am off to Ghent. You will do me a great favor to look after Christabel in my absence, though I must say"—his eyes strayed fondly to where his wife sat, in fair-haired magnificence, scraping lint for bandages—"she has been simply splendid, hasn't she?"

"Yes," said Drusilla without irony, "she has been."

The distance between the Thornrose tent hospital and the Toddington house on the rue Ducale had to be walked. The streets were so crowded with ambulance wagons, carts bearing away the dead, and crowds of distraught relatives searching for loved ones among the wounded that no progress could be made other than on foot.

Entering the house, Dru suffered a moment of mild surprise that Grimthwaite was not there to greet her, and then, hard upon the heels of that mild surprise, she suffered a nearly mortal shock when a pistol shot rang out at the top of the stairs, and a figure tumbled heavily down the risers.

It was the Chevalier de Saint-Armand, with a patch of blood spreading over the right shoulder of his coat.

Once upon a time, Dru might have been frozen with horror at such a sight, but she had seen so many maimed men these past few days that she was past being appalled by any sort of wound. Instantly she knelt by chevalier and took her handkerchief out of her sleeve to staunch the bleeding, further padding the wound with the chevalier's own handkerchief, bracing his hand atop the wadded linen to hold it in place.

She was certain that the shot had missed his lung and that he would live if the bleeding could be controlled.

During her frantic ministrations, the chevalier had opened his dark eyes and said one word. "Treason," he muttered in French before losing consciousness again.

Drusilla was now aware of a pair of booted feet descending the stairs above her. Her gaze flew upward, and she saw a face—a face she knew, yet a stranger's face. This hard-eyed stranger was Farnshaw Eggleston, and he came down the steps toward her, pistol in hand.

She got slowly to her feet, guessing instinctively that the cards in the Great Game had just been reshuffled much to her disadvantage.

"You have killed the chevalier," she whispered in the desperate hope that he might take her word for it and not reload his pistol and finish the Frenchman off. "In God's name, why?"

Mr. Eggleston spared the unfortunate Frenchman not a glance. "Let us just say that I have struck a blow for abolition. The chevalier, you see, was in the pay of the slaveholders and under the command of the Comte d'Artois, who has always sided with the *colons*. I am certain that while the chevalier whispered sweet nothings into her ladyship's ear, he overheard many revealing conversations between the Thornrose ladies and their abolitionist allies."

Drusilla's mind whirled sickeningly to think how she had been deceived.

"And what is your part in this, sir?"

Mr. Eggleston smiled at her coldly. "And well you might ask, you who connive with MacRory Holt."

So there it was. The Farnshaw Eggleston mask was off, the countrified manner gone from his speech—and the bandage was off his foot as well, she noticed peripherally.

"What kind of Englishman are you," she demanded, "to sell yourself to Henri Lazare?"

"Why, no Englishman at all," he replied in excellent, perfectly accented French. "I am French, both dam and sire, though raised in England and having the good fortune to resemble my Austrian grandmother, who traveled to France in the train of Marie Antoinette."

Drusilla shook her head, not sure if any of this could be believed. "If your grandmother was of the old French court, then how is it you are a Bonapartist?"

Mr. Eggleston's smile thinned. "You may be a poor relation, my dear Drusilla, but you still have the arrogance of a baron's granddaughter. Marie Antoinette brought with her laundresses as well as her ladies of the court."

"I see. And by what name"—she was playing for time now, and where were the servants, for God's sake?—"ought I to be calling you now, since Mr. Eggleston obviously will not do."

"*Égalité* will do for the moment. Jean-Claude Égalité."

"Why, how very republican, monsieur. Is that the name your parents gave you?"

"I think you know better than that, my dear Drusilla. But since I intend to deliver you into the keeping of the man who gave me this name, you may put the question to him. Now if you would be so good as to put these on"—a pair of iron manacles clattered down the stairs toward her—"we have a considerable journey before us."

"Why should Lazare wish to make me a prisoner?" she asked as much out of puzzlement as out of apprehension. "I am of no consequence."

"You underestimate yourself. Surely Colonel Holt will not leave his dauntless English tea rose in the hands of his old enemy."

So that was it. Drusilla stiffened her spine. "I have no intention of going anywhere with you."

"You forget I have a pistol."

"Which I assume you smuggled in, along with your manacles, concealed in the ridiculous bandage on your leg."

Égalité shrugged. "What would you have me do, with her ladyship's servants regularly searching my belongings?"

"However," Dru pointed out crisply, "since you have failed to reload your pistol after shooting the chevalier, I do not think I have anything to fear from your weapon, and by the time you reload it, I will have summoned the servants."

Jean-Claude Égalité came down another step. "As usual, you are quick on the uptake, Drusilla, but not quite so quick as you fancy yourself." He flicked back his coat, withdrew another pistol from his belt, and pointed it directly at her breast.

"It was a pair of pistols that I smuggled in inside my ridiculous bandage, and three pairs of manacles as well. The manacles now adorn several of the servants, who have all been locked in the wine cellar."

"I don't believe it," she said, though suddenly her courage seemed to be draining away through the toes of her shoes. "I don't believe you could overcome half a dozen servants by yourself."

"And what makes you think, pray, that I did so by myself?"

Warned by some deep instinct, she turned and looked into a shadowed doorway behind her. Four men stepped out of it, four men whom she had first seen that day in the Picardy forest, then, again, backstage at the Théâtre du Palais Royal.

One of them stepped toward her and growled in a voice of triumphant menace, "This time, *milady,* you do not escape us."

"Well, Charles," said Lady Toddington brightly to her husband upon his return from Ghent, "you will never guess what has happened in your absence."

"I'm sure I could not guess, m'dear, so you will just have to tell me."

And so she did, for, of course, it had not taken her very long to puzzle out the significance of the strange and mysterious events that had occurred within her household, to wit:

The chevalier found shot and unconscious on the stairs.

The servants overpowered by a gang of strange men.

Mr. Eggleston missing, with all his baggage.

Drusilla missing, with none of hers.

It was perfectly obvious, Christabel informed her husband, that Mr. Eggleston's leg having mended sufficiently, he and Drusilla had eloped, Drusilla, as they well knew, being perfectly capable of departing with no baggage whatsoever.

Shortly after the eloping couple had decamped, Christabel further informed her bemused husband, a gang of looters had invaded the house and bound up the servants; indeed, there were reports of deserting soldiers robbing other dwellings. But before they could make away with any valuables, the Chevalier de Saint-Armand had the misfortune to call, and, catching them in the act, was himself shot by these selfsame looting deserters (or was that deserting looters?), who then took to their heels.

Listening to his wife's recitation, Lord Toddington was never better served by his diplomatist's sangfroid. "Well, m'dear," he said when she had finished, "we must hope that the chevalier soon recovers enough to tell us precisely what happened. In the meantime, I must send a message to Colonel Holt regarding Drusilla."

"Colonel Holt is in Brussels?" Christabel did not sound overjoyed.

"He rides in with the Duke this afternoon, and I am obligated to inform him of this, since his affections were so much engaged by Drusilla."

"Oh, pooh!" said Christabel dismissively. "If his affections were truly engaged, he would never wish to maroon her on some drafty crag in Scotland where there is no society and nothing to do but card wool and dine on sheep bladders."

"I believe you mean sheep stomachs, m'dear, and your feelings about *haggis* notwithstanding, I am still convinced that we must inform Colonel Holt as soon as possible."

"Eloped! I don't believe it," snapped Holt.

He had survived the battle unscathed, though the lines of fatigue were harshly etched on his face, for serving as an aide-de-camp to the Duke of Wellington at the battle of Waterloo had been a dangerous and exhausting assignment.

Having called as requested at the Toddington residence, he was mindful now of Lady Toddington's inconvenient presence in the drawing room and so said obliquely to her husband, "I think a different game is afoot here."

Lord Toddington took his meaning. "My thoughts as well, Colonel."

Holt paced the length of the room with scarcely curbed fury—and vain regret. "I never should have accepted her rejection of my proposal so tamely. I should have forced her consent to a drumhead wedding, and then, once she was my wife, I should have packed her safely off to Killiecrankie Crag whether she wanted to go or not."

"Well," sniffed Christabel, "if that's your notion of a wedding trip, it's no wonder Mr. Eggleston beat you out in Drusilla's affections."

Holt swiveled toward her with his cold green gaze, but Christabel was unfazed, having been the recipient of far colder gazes from the jealous dragonesses at Almack's.

What Holt might have said in his own defense was never to be known, for at that moment Grimthwaite appeared, looking as close to being in a tizzy as his stately countenance would allow. "My lord, if you would be so good as to step into the hall. An unusual matter of some moment has arisen."

Lord Toddington departed but soon came back, carrying in his hand a blood-spattered sheet of writing paper, which he handed to Holt, saying, "This was in the chevalier's pocket and only just now discovered. It is written on my wife's stationery, but it is not her writing." (Christabel had dreadful penmanship and worse spelling, although, of course, his lordship did not say that.) "In any case," Lord Toddington continued, "I saw her at the hospital-tent at the very time of this supposed assignation."

Christabel, who had been enduring Colonel Holt's grim

company from a settee by the window, suddenly pricked up her ears. "Charles, what are you talking about? What is this about my stationery?"

She appropriated the bloodstained note from Holt and proceeded to read it aloud, her voice gradually rising in incredulous outrage as she did so.

My dearest Guy,
All are away from the house this day. I yearn for your caress.
Come to me at once.

C.

"Why . . . why . . ." Christabel was nearly speechless with indignation. "Of all the infernal cheek! I never wrote this, nor would I ever, and in any case, I certainly know there is no *a* in *yearn*."

"So," said Holt, his eyes narrowing in thought, "now we see how Saint-Armand came to be shot on your staircase. He was lured here by a forged *billet doux*. The question is, by whom and for what purpose?"

"It must have been Eggleston," hazarded Lord Toddington. "Who else would have the opportunity?" He shook his head in bafflement. "But what could be his game—and what the devil has he done with Drusilla?"

The answer to that question, as if borne to them by the three Fates, came an instant later when the Thornrose ladies entered the room in the wake of Grimthwaite's stately tread.

"We have received a message addressed to Colonel Holt," announced Miss Faith.

"A street urchin brought it to our tent, saying it concerned Drusilla, but the child ran away before we could question him," elaborated Miss Hope.

"We cannot pretend," concluded Miss Charity, "that the

letter's trappings inspire us to confidence that it contains good news."

The "trappings" that adorned the scrolled piece of paper were red ribbons and a single red rose. As Holt slid out his knife and cut the ribbons, everyone silently recalled the ribbons and red roses that the *émigrée* ladies wore in honor of their guillotined loved ones. As Holt unrolled the letter, everyone could not help thinking that it looked uncannily like a Decree of Execution.

Nothing loath, Christabel peered over Holt's shoulder and proclaimed, "Why, it's just gibberish!"

"It's in one of my personal ciphers from the Peninsula," said Holt to Lord Toddington. "It is Lazare's way of taunting me, letting me know how clever he is. If you give me a moment, I can decipher it in my head."

"But who is this Lazare person?" demanded Miss Faith on behalf of the Thornrose sisters. "And what has this to do with our Drusilla?"

"Yes, Charles," demanded Christabel, "what is going on here?"

Lord Toddington held up a silencing hand. "Ladies, there is a great deal to be explained, and I promise you that in due time it *will* be explained to you."

Holt looked up then, his face grey for an instant beneath his tan. It was the only outward sign he showed of his inward fear and fury and chagrin. "Eggleston has taken her, all right, and at Lazare's command. If I want her back, I must come to Paris for her—at the Montmartre Abattoir."

The Thornrose ladies gasped in horrified unison while Lord Toddington exclaimed, "Good God! The man's more of a monster than even I imagined."

"What's an *abattoir?*" asked Christabel.

"So," said Holt slowly, "it seems that all along this

Eggleston was a confidential intelligencer planted by Lazare, and no one knew."

The Thornrose ladies found this theory difficult to swallow.

"He seemed like such a down-to-earth young man."

"And so enamored of Drusilla."

"He had even done a sketch of her."

Holt's eyes narrowed. "Did you actually see him sketch her—or anything else for that matter?"

Three heads shook in unison, and this clinched the matter as far as Holt was concerned. "Eggleston never made that sketch. He got it from Henri Lazare. It has always been Lazare's way to send his agents drawings of persons he wants captured or assassinated. He had several of me circulated during the war. Eggleston must have received one of Drusilla, along with orders to bring her to Lazare if he found her."

Now Lord Toddington shook his head. "You must realize that this is nothing but a trap." He gestured to the coded letter. "It is Lazare's invitation to the famous MacRory Holt to come and die and be damned."

"I know it," said Holt cooly.

"And there is something else to consider," Lord Toddington continued, looking grave. "It could be weeks before Paris falls to the Allies, if ever. Who knows what will happen now? And after the horrific losses the French have taken, the Parisians will be killing-mad against the English. If you are discovered for a British officer, they will hang you from the nearest lamppost."

"I know that, too," said Holt.

"So what do you mean to do?"

"Take a nap, pay some calls, gather together a few useful sundries, and procure a traveling carriage to take me to Paris."

"But should you not go at once by horse?" protested Miss Faith. "What will happen to our poor Drusilla in the meantime?"

"Nothing very drastic, I shouldn't imagine. I'm the one they want. They'll not dispose of the lure until I arrive."

"But . . . but Drusilla is a prisoner in an *abattoir!*" pointed out Miss Hope.

"Drusilla will endure it," said Holt with a shrug.

"Well," harrumphed Miss Charity, "you are in no hurry to become a knight errant, are you, sir?"

"Drusilla knows better than to expect it of me, I'm sure," said Holt with a faint smile. Turning to Lord Toddington, he said, "And now, my lord, if I could impose upon you for the use of a spare bedroom, I'll retire."

"Er, yes, Grimthwaite will take you up," said his lordship, marveling inwardly at the ice water in Holt's veins. Had Christabel been in Excelsior's clutches, he knew he could not have remained so collected.

As Holt left the room, Christabel turned to her husband and asked plaintively, "But, Charles, what *is* an *abbattoir?*"

Chapter Twenty

The Final Play

The Montmartre Abattoir was located on the right bank of the Seine near the Rochechouart Gate. Its construction had been ordered by the Emperor himself. The noted architect Poitevin had drawn up the plans. The first stone had been laid in solemn ceremony by the Interior Minister, Count Cretet.

Drusilla did not care. To her, a slaughterhouse was still a slaughterhouse, even if it was a fancy French one known as "The Palace of the Butcher's Art."

Although the construction of this sprawling complex of cages, chutes, scalding rooms, rendering kettles, and pulley-driven meat hooks was nearly complete, no work had gone forward here for nearly a year. Like many other civic projects begun during the reign of Bonaparte, it had been ordered abandoned by the Bourbons.

Finished or no, the slaughterhouse was a perfect prison for Drusilla and a perfect deathtrap for MacRory Holt.

And Henri Lazare, Excelsior of the Great Game, was the perfect slaughterman.

By the twenty-third of June, the Emperor Napoleon had withdrawn to Paris in defeat. Driving into the city on his heels—though of course the Emperor did not know this—was MacRory Holt, a man who over the years had done more than most to bring about Bonaparte's final downfall.

But Holt's mind, as he drove through a Paris grief-stricken with defeat, was not on the Emperor, closeted now in the Tuileries with his desperate advisors. Holt's mind was on the Emperor's ferret, Henri Lazare.

And across the River Seine in the Montmartre Abattoir, Lazare waited for MacRory Holt to come to him. Their two masters had contended on the field of battle, and the star of Holt's master had risen higher. But Lazare meant to dim that star a little, bloody it a bit, before his own master's star went into its final eclipse. And so Henri Lazare lay in wait beside the she-wolf's cage in the Montmartre Abattoir.

Other entrapments Excelsior had devised for Holt as well—at the Ministry of the Interior and at the business chambers of Monsieur Poitevin and Associates, Architects. Should Holt attempt to obtain the plans of the *abattoir* from either of these places, soldiers would be lying in wait for him.

But Holt had anticipated this gambit and instead stopped to tour every slaughtering facility between Brussels and Paris, engaging the men who worked there in converse about how their establishment compared with the famous *abattoir* being built in Paris.

Butchers liked to talk about their art as much as did any tradesman, and by the time Holt rode into Paris, he had a fair idea of the layout of the Montmartre Abattoir, as well as a strong notion as to where within the sprawling one-story complex Drusilla might be confined.

Your gambit fails, Excelsior, thought MacRory Holt as he went to earth in his Left Bank lair, *and I'll have her back, by God, before too many nights have passed.*

Drusilla had not been badly treated—if you discounted being locked up in a kidney-handling stall. She knew it was a kidney-handling stall by the helpful picture of a cow and its kidney that was painted on the wooden signpost that stood outside the stall to serve as a guide to those in the meat trade who could not read.

It was enough, she thought with gallows humor, to put her off steak-and-kidney pie for life, assuming (more gallows humor here) that she and Holt were able to get out of this ghastly trap alive.

She did not let herself call him Rory in her mind, for she felt she had not the right to do so. She had sent him away on the eve of battle with a broken heart, and now she felt that, in justice, she could have no claim upon that heart . . . though that did not stop her from imagining him comforting her as she lay huddled in her stall during the long, lonely nights of her captivity.

He would come here, of course, for he would no more ignore Henri Lazare's challenge than he could stop breathing. He would come here for sheer love of the Game, and perhaps he would come because he loved her a little still. . . .

And if the two of them did win through to safety, she vowed to herself that she would happily take up residence atop his drafty Scots crag and weave plaids until she was cross-eyed and patiently await his quadrennial homecomings and not be jealous of the adventures he would have and the women who would look at him with wanting in their eyes . . . if only he did not die on her account.

On the fourth afternoon of her imprisonment, when the bright summer sun flooded in to light up the slaughtering cubicles and meat-hook bars, Henri Lazare came to the stall where she had been locked. As she got to her feet to face him, she realized that Lazare had found his ideal setting in this place of death and falling blades, this place whose very name shivered the blood.

She said nothing as he entered the stall to gaze at her silently with his flat, watching eyes, staring at her with a lust that had nothing to do with masculine desire; rather, it was the desire of a hunter for his prey, of the collector for an interesting specimen.

He was not much above her height, and so his eyes were level with hers and hard to escape. It was a point of honor with her to match him stare for stare, to commit his features to memory, for it was always wise to memorize the face of your enemy when it was presented to you without disguise. Holt had taught her that.

At last Henri Lazare said to her, "I wanted to look at you in full daylight. I had not seen you so before."

"As your sketch clearly showed," she said.

"True," he acknowledged. "Yet it sufficed. You are here, and Holt comes after you."

"How can you know that for sure?" she asked, teetering on the edge of hope and fear. She had great faith in Holt, but she also had great fear of Henri Lazare.

"Oh, Holt will come," said Lazare with horrific certainty. "He is baited and hooked already and needs only to be reeled in and gaffed."

"And you think to accomplish that by yourself?" she asked him contemptuously, hoping that he would be foolish enough to try it.

But, of course, he was not. "There are twenty men about this place eager to put an end to Holt, for they have all lost a brother or a father in the war against the British. I chose them for just that reason . . . for the same reason, I apprehend, that Holt chose you, the daughter of Giles Sedgewick, killed by the French at La Coruña."

Drusilla flinched in spite of herself that "Excelsior" should have this knowledge of her life, obtained no doubt from "Égalité," who had it no doubt from Christabel. Still, she tried to do what a canny player in the Game would do; she tried to find out all she could about the trap in which she was the bait. "I suppose all these men have been shown a sketch of Colonel Holt."

"Indeed, and a better sketch I have of him than of you, for I had many a day to study him when I interrogated him on the Peninsula."

"Where you failed to break him, as you will fail to entrap him now," said Drusilla, praying with all her heart that this boast would come true.

"I failed to break Holt," said Henri Lazare, "because that benighted fool, General Marmont, insisted on treating him as an officer and a gentleman instead of the spy he was. I assure you, no such niceties will prevail in the Montmartre Abattoir, nor among the twenty men outside."

Though her heart shuddered in her breast, Drusilla forced herself to keep on bandying words with Henri Lazare. "And will Monsieur Égalité be one of those twenty men?"

"Hardly." Lazare gave a dismissive shrug, as if she had asked a stupid question. "Why put a lad of Égalité's talent among the thugs who wait for Holt? Holt will most certainly dispatch some of them—I know that full well. But he will not dispatch them all, nor, in the end, will he escape me, for which circumstance I offer you my thanks."

A feeling of despair was beginning to enter Drusilla's soul, and surely Henri Lazare with his anatomizer's mind intended for her courage to be whittled down by his verbal cut and thrusts. And now it seemed that he meant to administer the *coup de grâce*.

"That is why I have come to look at you by daylight, Mademoiselle Sedgewick. I wanted to see what it was about you that could turn a cool-headed man like Holt into a hot-loined fool. I must confess," he said after another endless moment of contemplating her as if she were some strange cipher, "that your allure escapes me. In fact, I find it quite unfathomable. That MacRory Holt will come here and die for such as you is tragic. Even I, his great enemy, say it is a waste."

He turned and left her standing there, his words twisting in her heart like a knife heated in fire. Ever so deftly "Excelsior" had made her feel unworthy of Holt, unworthy of rescue. Ever so deftly he had made her fear that both she and Holt were being outplayed by a cleverer hand.

Though she did not know it, Holt was nearby and watching her place of imprisonment, waiting for the moment to spring.

He was armed with all the tricks and weapons of his trade, riding upon Filbertine, the steadiest of horses, who never started at anything, including the report of the long-barreled horse pistol strapped to her saddle.

On his person, Holt carried his usual arsenal and more: a knife up his sleeve, another in his boot, pocket pistols in each side of his coat and in the secret leather pouch. A light cavalry sword was sheathed on one side of his belt, a provost's truncheon hung from a loop on the other side.

In his knapsack, he carried five of the black powder devices that had recently proved so spectacularly incendiary, if also spectacularly unreliable, since they could not be accurately directed. Still, there was no denying their destructive potential: They had set Copenhagen afire, they had turned aside a cavalry charge at Leipzig, they had glared red over Fort McHenry in the battle of Baltimore. They were called the devil's artillery, otherwise known as rockets, and Holt had requisitioned five of them in the three pound size, the smallest available.

Lastly, Holt carried inside the breast of his shirt a shepherd's sling and a pouch of ammunition—no mere stones but forged metal balls. A modern David, was Holt, against a twenty-headed Goliath.

He did not know, of course, the exact number of men arrayed against him but guessed it must be near two dozen. For all the *mano a mano* language of the challenge that had been issued to him, he knew Lazare had no intention of meeting him in single combat on the field of honor.

What Lazare did intend was an ambuscade, planned and laid out in advance to catch MacRory Holt when he came for his woman.

His woman. The thought had several times taken Holt unawares.

Through the veils of memory he saw Dru as he had seen her that first time on the Picardy road, where her hazel eyes had met his courageously, and her spirit had leapt to the challenge of his.

He saw her clear-featured profile as she stood among the Gypsies, her straight nose, the long, lovely line of her throat, her mouth softly parting as she turned to him and smiled.

He saw her shining chestnut curls tumbled against the yellow straw in the stable where he would have dearly loved to tumble her. . . .

He would get her back or die trying—that he knew. But once he had her back, what the devil would he do with her? That he did not know.

On the first full-mooned night, Holt made his move. He was as he always was at the beginning of a mission: alert, exhilarated, confident of his abilities and his strategies, taut as a bowstring ready to snap an arrow toward his target. Tonight, he was all this and more, for never before had he had such a personal stake in the Great Game.

251

Sentries were posted outside the slaughterhouse walls. Holt had already decided which wall and which man to down first, but he cursed inwardly when the initial metal ball he slung went wide. But the beauty of a slingshot was that, unlike a pistol shot, a miss made no great noise and caused no great alarm to the potential victim.

The sentry merely heard a small *thunk* behind him. Mildly curious, he turned, the back of his head making a most inviting target. Holt hit him squarely this time, crumpling him into a heap. Whether he lived or died would depend on the thickness of his skull.

Holt loped past the still form and, his bulky knapsack notwithstanding, hoisted himself over the wall and into the narrow roofless maze through which cattle were driven for counting. The angling moonlight threw the counting maze into a trough of shadows, through which he moved unseen toward the sentry posted atop one of the barriers.

Reaching up, he grabbed the sentry's ankle, yanked him into the trough, and clouted him insensible with his truncheon before the man let out a warning yell.

Holt ranged onward, his goal, the roof.

And a wonderful roof it was, compared to some of the exposed and precipitously sloping housetops he had negotiated in his career. This roof was flat and punctuated by the dozens of concealing chimneys rising up from the sixty-four scalding rooms and ten lard-rendering rooms below.

He slung off his knapsack and went to work.

Drusilla awoke with a start from an uneasy sleep. Shouts and running feet sounded all round her. The door to her stall swung open, and a lantern was thrust before her eyes. Lazare's face was behind the lantern, ghastly white in the flickering light.

"My felicitations to you, Mlle. Sedgewick," he said. "It seems you've won the heart of our lone wolf after all."

To the men behind him he said, "Put her in manacles and bring her along with us."

The wolf was loose in the slaughterhouse. His pursuers mustered in the large central courtyard to begin their search for him among the innumerable cubicles, stalls, and sheds. Holt knew he must work fast. He must catch as many of Excelsior's men down in the courtyard as he could, get in as many rounds as possible before the French fish swam out of the barrel and, most importantly, before they searched the roof.

He took out the five small rockets that Captain Edward Whinyates of the Royal Horse Artillery Rocket Troop had especially altered to his specifications. He laid the rockets side by side on the parapet wall, a yard between each for safety's sake, and then unwound their slow-burning fuses, the longest of which extended close to twelve feet.

Battlefield rockets were launched from iron tripods and guided by sticks twenty foot long, but there was no need of those devices here since the distance was so short. Lighting the fuses was trickier, since Holt had no gunner's portfire at his disposal but must depend on tinderbox and candle to do the work.

But the gods of fire and brimstone were watching over him tonight as he put his candle to the first fuse with a muttered invocation of, "Confusion to our enemies!"

There was a sharp report and a hellish shrieking as the first sped off the parapet to arch over the courtyard and then zigzag downward like a chain of lightning to blast a smoking hole in the flagstones below.

The sound of the explosion rattled through the huge

building, and against the flaring red light Holt saw the silhouettes of men's bodies being thrown back. After that, he had no more time to watch, only time to light the remaining fuses and depart down the nearest chimney, leaving behind four flames burning slowly toward the black-powder-filled rockets.

The chimneys of the Montmartre Abattoir were built in the modern style, with helpful hand- and footholds for the sweeps—helpful to MacRory Holt as well. Clambering down the chimney, he found himself landing, somewhat disconcertingly, in one of the gigantic lard-rendering kettles.

But not so bad a retreat, after all, he decided when the next rocket went off, and the walls seemed ready to tumble down.

Drusilla was feeling quite dreadfully constrained, perhaps due to the fact that before departing, her guards had, at Lazare's orders, hooked her manacle chain over one of the rope-and-pulley-driven meat hooks that ran from the loading bay out into the courtyard. Never had she been so glad to be such a Long Meg, for her feet could just touch the planked floor of the loading platform, and she was surreptitiously but industriously attempting to jerk her chain off the hook when the first explosion sounded.

If she was mortified to be hanging about in such an unnerving semblance of a side of beef, she could at least take some consolation from the fact that her captors were now in an equally perturbed state.

A man ran up to the loading bay, shouting, "They are shelling us, Inspector Lazare! The English are shelling us!"

"Don't be a fool." Lazare's voice was icily controlled despite the pandemonium. "It's a trick."

But the second explosion must have convinced everyone—including Drusilla—that if it was a trick, it was a stupendous one. Frantically, she jiggled the chain, and then her eyes went to the pulley device, and a plan began to take shape in her mind.

"Holt disappoints me with such bludgeoning tactics," observed Lazare. "They will avail him nothing."

Just before the third explosion lit the courtyard, Dru glimpsed a red, burning comet zooming upward before it blasted to earth immediately outside the loading bay.

"Casualties!" shouted a police sergeant, leaping onto the platform to stand before Henri Lazare and his pendent prisoner. "We have casualties, sir! What are your orders?"

"Never mind the casualties." Lazare was forced to raise his voice at last, and still it sounded thin and shrill against the tumult. "The whole city will be down upon us now."

He turned to Drusilla, and for the first time she saw emotion in the reptilian eyes of Henri Lazare, and that emotion was the cold fury of a man who prides himself on his wits and who has been outwitted. It was the fury of a snake that has missed its strike.

"And now," said Excelsior, and Drusilla knew he was speaking her death sentence, "I believe it's time to take the pretty pawn out of the game altogether."

"Lazare!" came a shout, and a tall figure with a pistol in each hand materialized out of the smoking inferno of the courtyard.

Although Lazare was no fighting man, his reflexes were admirable, his instincts unerring. He took one quick step, just one, and it was the police sergeant, still babbling of casualties, who took Holt's bullet, even as Lazare moved to bring his blade down upon Drusilla's neck.

But Drusilla escaped him. Like a bird winging away from a striking snake, she pushed herself off the platform and fluttered away on the pulley device that the noted architect

Poitevin had designed to carry dressed sides of beef out to the market carts.

Only, at the moment, there was no market cart to receive her. Even the cleverest plans have a flaw or two, she thought as she dangled at the end of the pulley rope, safe for the moment but dancing on air as much as any hanged man.

Outside, the fourth rocket flared and struck, and she felt herself shaken like an aspen leaf on a limb.

In the aftershock, which set chunks of the ceiling falling, Holt came at a run to put an arm round her knees to lift her free. And then they both saw how close to death she had come, for Lazare's knife, which he had thrown after her, was caught in the folds of her skirt.

"I suppose you'll be wanting a promotion to journeyman after this," observed Holt with his usual imperturbability as he slipped his pistol out of its hidden pouch and thrust it into her manacled hands. Then, with a crisp order of "Guard my back," he moved forward toward Excelsior, and she moved with him, watching the entry from the courtyard, where a fire had taken hold amongst the straw scattered about the flagstones.

Lazare had not been idle. After the explosion, he had rolled over the wounded policeman and wrenched the pistol out of the man's belt, and now he and Holt stood facing each other, pistols mutually pointed.

In the old days Holt would have thought, *Shoot him and be damned!*

But that was before. Before he knew what he had learned in the last few seconds, when he saw Dru balanced on the knife-edge of death: that all his hatred of Lazare would be as nothing against the pain of losing her. In this pivotal instant, did he dare to risk his one remaining shot on killing Lazare?

Lazare, too, was husbanding his one shot, inwardly debating the risks. Even if he brought Holt down with it, that would still leave him defenseless before the girl and her pistol, and he did not want to be defenseless before any woman—particularly MacRory Holt's woman—when he had just killed her man.

The fifth rocket brought an end to the standoff, slamming into the roof above them, sending a ceiling beam crashing onto the platform between them and forcing both combatants to abandon their duelists' stance.

"Come on!" shouted Holt, and together he and Dru ran out into the courtyard, which looked like a battlefield now, with smoking shell holes, fallen wounded, and straw and clothes burning. In the distance they could hear the clanging of the fire brigade; soon the secret of the Montmartre Abattoir would be a secret no more.

As they threaded their way amongst the fires and the fallen men, Dru tried not to look down at the wounded, but Holt was looking at them closely, intent on scavenging a pistol. Finding one, he motioned her into a scalding room. After taking the precaution of reloading his own pistol so his armaments were again at full strength, he picked up the scavenged weapon.

"Raise your hands, my angel," he told her, "and don't flinch."

She raised her manacled hands above her head. He caught the chain across the mouth of the pistol and shot the links, the noise muffled inside the stone walls. The wrist irons would have to wait, he told her, until he could attend to them with his "locksmith" tools.

The fire brigade wagons with their hand pumps and huge water barrels were at the gate now, along with a crowd of neighbors looking to extinguish the mysterious conflagration in the *abattoir* before it threatened their own nearby dwellings. It was these reinforcements Holt had counted on when he hatched his plan of attack.

Once the crowd had surged inside, MacRory Holt and Drusilla Sedgewick passed amongst them with the ease of practiced skulkers and made good their escape from Henri Lazare's slaughterhouse.

They did not speak until they came to the hidden niche in the city wall where Holt had left Filly, not tied but with her reins slipped over the saddle pommel, ready for his swift mounting if it came to that. Filly knew what this meant and was waiting for them, alert, head up. She shied a little, however, protesting that her humans had that burning smell that horses instinctively mistrusted.

Holt took an instant to soothe her and then turned to Drusilla, taking in both her strained face and the iron manacles on her wrists. He knew then that, for better or worse, his own invincible completeness within himself would never again be enough for him. No use, he thought, to fight against it anymore. He must take this strange and wonderful prize that the Great Game had sent his way—and take along with it the risk of losing her, as he almost had tonight.

"Oh, God," he said to her, "come here."

He drew her to him, smoothed back her tangled chestnut curls, and took her pale face between his hands. He kissed her deeply and lingeringly, the iron nerve and fighting strength that had sustained them both this night gradually giving way to a glorious feeling of relief and rejoicing. For long minutes they stood together, joying in a closeness for which there were no words.

But these minutes were not theirs to spend, for the city of Paris and the country of France were still in the hands of their mortal enemies and would be for untold weeks to come. For who knew if Napoleon's defeat at Waterloo was his final downfall? Who knew if he would again be toppled from his Imperial throne? In the meantime, the hunt would be on in earnest for the pair of them. "Excelsior" and "Égalité" would see to that.

"They'll be after us now," said Holt, "and every policeman in Paris as well."

"Where shall we go?" she asked him.

"To my lair, of course." He smiled down at her. "Your lair, too, now. I'll carry you over the threshold if you like."

She smiled up at him, her hand in his. "Let's go home then, shall we?"

Chapter Twenty-one

An Epistolary Epilogue in Which Loose Ends Are Tied Up and Further Adventures in the Great Game Promised

From the Rt. Hon. Lord Toddington to the Foreign Office
Private & Secret
Item: We alert you to a certain Chevalier Guy de Saint-Armand, lately revealed to be in the pay of the colons *and the Comte d'Artois. . . .*

Lord Toddington paused in his writing, his subtle spy master's mind busy behind his frank diplomatist's features. What to do about that perfidious Bourbon prince, the Comte d'Artois? Even as Britain spent her blood and treasure to keep the Bourbons on the throne, her scorpion-ally, Comte d'Artois was scheming to thwart Britain's anti-slavery policies. And such a scheme! To insinuate the Chevalier Saint-Armand into the Toddington circle of acquaintances so that he could spy upon the Thornrose ladies and their abolitionist colleagues, so that he could enmesh Christabel in a web of adultery and force her to reveal her husband's secrets.

But if the Comte d'Artois could spin webs, so could Charles Toddington.

Saint-Armand (who really was chevalier, after all) was healed of his wound, but did not know that his true allegiance was revealed, a development from which much advantage could be derived, and would be as soon as possible. Lord Toddington smiled subtly to himself and resumed writing.

Item: We alert you to a young fellow of French extraction who can pass for a Wiltshireman born and who has recently assumed the names of Farnshaw Eggleston and Jean-Claude Égalité. . . .

A clever and dangerous man for one so young, Lord Toddington mused; surely this Jean-Claude "Égalité" was Henri Lazare's whelp in spirit if not in body.

And what of Henri Lazare, the Excelsior of the Great Game?

Item: We alert you to the fact that many of Bonaparte's confidential agents are being recruited into the Russian Bureau of Secret Intelligence. That Henri Lazare, code name Excelsior, will sell his services to the Tsar is considered likely, in Col. H.'s opinion. . . .

MacRory Holt.

Again, Lord Toddington's pen poised above his dispatch as he considered the fate that had befallen his most daring operative. Could a man who set so much store by one young, adventurous, hazel-eyed woman remain the cool and cunning master of the Great Game that he had once been? Only time would tell.

In any case, the die was cast, and the board had been played. The Great Game went on.

Item: We alert you to disturbing rumors concerning the activities of Tsarist agents in Austria. We therefore deem it advisable to send Col. H. and his bride on a wedding trip to Vienna. . . .

Historical Note

The term "the Great Game" is most commonly associated with the struggle that began in the 1830s between British and Russian agents for control of the vast territories north of India. However, since it was the dissolution of the Napoleonic Empire that set the stage for this struggle, and since the term so perfectly conveys the war of wits engaged in by intelligence agents, I felt justified in using the designation here.

The pro-royalist underground groups, the *Chouans* and the *Chevaliers de la Foi,* operated much as I have described, including the *Chevaliers'* penchant for dispatching their enemies by defenestration.

Nicholas-François Appert (1750?–1841) was a real personage, known today as the "Father of Canning." Though there is no doubt that the British military was concerned that Appert's advances might benefit the French war machine, attributing damage done to his commercial cannery—the world's first—to British sabotage is my own invention.

A Rocket Troop under the command of Captain Edward Whinyates did participate in the battle of Waterloo.

As for my hero, MacRory Holt, many readers will no doubt realize that I have appropriated to him the honors and heroics of the remarkable Colonel Colquhoun Grant, the first official chief of British Military Intelligence and the man who was widely known during the Peninsular War as Wellington's eyes and ears.

Grant married several years after Waterloo, and his wife, Margaret, followed him to his later postings in the Far East. But her health broke down in the tropical climate, and she was forced to sail home to Scotland.

In one of the strange ironies of history, Margaret Grant died just as the ship on which she had taken passage came in sight of St. Helena. She was buried in the island cemetery, a short distance from the grave of the exiled Napoleon Bonaparte, who had perished there several years before, poisoned, some modern scholars now believe, by secret agents of the Comte d'Artois.

Readers may be assured, however, that no such fate befell our Drusilla.

G.B.